Y0-DBW-691

WILDE AT THE WALDORF

WILDE AT THE WALDORF

FIRST IN THE SAMANTHA WILDE SERIES

J.G. MATHENY

To Carman—
I love you already—
because you are Liz's
dad! Here's hoping you
enjoy my book that to you
write and my wish
for wonderful adventures
and your mysteries!
Best Wishes,
Judy
J G Matheny
9-3-2015

Published by August Words Publishing

AUGUST WORDS PUBLISHING

august words.org
WRITE WELL. DO GOOD.

www.augustwords.org

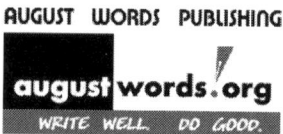

Copyright © 2015 by J.G. Matheny

Thank you for buying an authorized edition of this book and for complying with copyright laws by not reproducing, scanning, or distributing any part of it in any form, except for short passages for educational purposes, without express permission. In doing so you actively sustain the copyrights of writers, which fuels creativity, encourages diverse voices, promotes free speech, and creates a vibrant culture. Your support of working writers allows August WordsPublishing to continue to publish books for readers just like you, but it also allows support of literary and literacy charities which is the heart of augustwords.org.

ISBN: 978-1-942018-02-5

Publisher's Note: This is a work of fiction and entirely an intentional product of the author's imagination in the pursuit of telling an original tale to reach a higher truth. As such, any names, characters, places, and incidents are fabricated or are used fictitiously, and any resemblance to actual persons (living or dead), businesses, companies, events, or locales is entirely coincidental and surely unintentional.

CHAPTER ONE

Manhasset, Long Island

Champagne dripped from the plastic goblet onto her fingers. Samantha bent cautiously to lick it away, leaning against the teak balustrade. The heady aroma of sea air mixed with the descending twilight quieted the butterflies waging war in her stomach.

An arm encircled her waist. She felt smooth skin against her neck. A wet tongue lapped her flesh like a dog licking summer sweat. A hand crept down her back, its palm resting at the base of her tailbone, its fingers gently massaging their way toward her butt.

"Jeeses, Dan, *stop that*! He's not even looking yet."

"I need practice getting into my character, baby," he breathed.

"Don't give me that! You're not some method actor. You're an undercover *cop*," Samantha hissed in his ear, and then swatted his arm. He backed away, laughing.

"Aw, baby, you take all the fun out. Why can't you just relax and enjoy it? Remember how I used to drive you crazy?" he asked. A wide smile exploded across his tanned, handsome face.

Samantha thought for a moment. She and Dan Anguilo hadn't dated for nearly two years. Even during their relationship his undercover roles became too distracting for intimacy.

"*No.* We've been friends too long for you to drive me crazy, at least *sexually*. We don't need to practice. We need to get started. I was too nervous to eat from the buffet when we got on board and now this champagne is going straight to my head. We left dock almost two hours ago. I thought this thing was supposed to go quick."

"Shush! Don't talk so loud." Dan looked up. Judging from the reactions of those around him on the yacht, no one had heard.

"Sorry. This assignment should have come with an instruction manual," Samantha whispered.

Dan lowered his voice.

"It's okay. We just keep our eyes open for the *Baron*. He'll introduce me to Alex. Since Alex thinks I'm a player and the *Baron's* pal, he'll cozy up and I'll be *inside*. Piece of cake. Then your job is done."

"But what's taking so long?" Samantha asked. Dan shrugged.

"Can't find the *Baron*. Maybe something happened to him. Nobody knows. I can't contact my guys doing surveillance so we stay in the dark. If he doesn't show up soon I'll have to take matters into my own hands and initiate with Alex on my own. But keep an eye out. The Baron's a skinny, suave little guy about fifty. Got a European accent – French or somethin'. Sounds fake."

Samantha laughed. "Oh, Dan, to you anything sophisticated sounds *fake*. I'm sure he's simply an elegant gentleman."

Dan pouted. He hated being second-guessed.

"After tonight the *Baron's* gonna encounter health problems and tell everybody he's retiring. I'll be on the inside, and he'll get whisked away into the fed's witness protection program. They'll parade him out to testify at trial. If he's not on board, then maybe something's happened and the plan might be off. Anyway, just act like you're crazy about me, look beautiful and keep your mouth shut. When Alex and I get down to business you can break away and do some dancin' upstairs."

A herd of feet thumped in time to the music on the bridge deck above their heads. *Swinging and swaying to the Disco Tunes of D.J. Jim* as the program read. D.J. Jim's tunes were pretty hot, and the group was turning rowdy.

Samantha looked up. Alexander Post stood a distance across the deck, his eyes burning into her dress. She disliked him immediately.

"He's watching us *now*," she breathed. Dan took the cue and spun her around in a dance move that ended with a huge dip. Samantha's long blonde hair got caught under Dan's polished shoe, and her breasts nearly burst from the black Lycra strapless dress. She clung to him.

Alex Post was eating it up. As Dan returned her to her feet, the clingy dress rose higher up her thigh. Post's gaze nearly burned a hole in her lace stockings. Dan laughed.

"You're doin' great. Don't look so pissed. You're the perfect undercover bimbo," he whispered.

"I'm a teacher for god's sake. Why do I have to behave like this?"

"Relax baby. If they knew you were smart, the bad guys would clam up around you. You dazzle them and they let down their guard. It's that simple. Alex launders money for the cartel but he's really just an accountant. The less smart you act around him the better. Now do me a favor and run along for a while. I'm gonna initiate," Dan said in dismissal.

Feeling both comforted and enraged, Samantha returned the dimwitted smile to her lips, and let go of Dan's shoulders. She looked up and caught Post's eye. Deliberately she straightened her dress, smoothing the black mesh down over her hips, and tugged gently on her black stockings. Slowly she slinked toward the stairway, swaying with the big boat's gentle yaw.

Samantha dropped the trashy act at the top step to navigate down the narrow steps. She caught her breath as she entered a private sitting room. Someone speculated Post had paid six million dollars for the yacht, and customized it to the tune of another million.

"I believe it now," she said aloud. This lower deck was obviously private space. No money had been spared on the rich, plush carpet, and the Brazilian leather sofa and chair arranged to form a sitting alcove. Bookcases built into the rich teak paneling housed a digital stereo system and bar. Little brass lamps softly lit miniature ship paintings framed in gilt. The ceiling was low, and the only windows were tiny portholes, but the room gave an illusion of luxury and space.

"Hey baby, know where you're going?"

The man's voice startled her. Samantha turned to see a short, muscled man emerge from a narrow hallway. He had black wavy hair and an olive pock-marked complexion. He wore khaki slacks, a navy polo shirt and enough gold jewelry to sink the boat.

"Yes, thank you, I think I know the general direction," Samantha responded. He probably thinks I'm drunk, she thought. Oh, well, so much the better.

Samantha followed the wall signs to the ship's powder room. Once inside, she tossed cool water on her wrists, and surveyed her reflection in the mirror. Deep green eyes stared back, made enormous by a set of false eyelashes and eye shadow the color of a Mexican sunset. The freckles that had adorned her cheeks and nose were obliterated under too much sun beige foundation.

And too much *hair*. She liked wearing an upsweep held in place by a large tortoise shell clip, or simply allowing her hair to hang straight. *Not like tonight*, sprayed and teased like some music diva.

Samantha grabbed her hair and pulled it severely back. Intelligent alert eyes stared back. *This* was Samantha Wilde's all too familiar face, with the intense intellect that had earned an honors degree in Elementary Education and a masters just one year later. Samantha stared for a moment, and then released her hair. She had to admit being *Sammy* for tonight was fun.

She had to strip herself of all vestiges of her true identity to become *Sammy*. They lay in a stuff sack locked inside a surveillance car's trunk parked behind the Marriott off the Grand Central Parkway. Along with her jeans, T-shirt, and comfortable shoes. Feeling apprehension and excitement, she'd donned the undercover garb, a tight black cocktail dress that corralled and propelled Mother Nature's minor endowments upward into two round masses poking out the bodice, stiletto heels, and a saucy attitude.

Samantha gave the bathroom mirror one last big smile, put Sammy's vague expression back in place, and drew in a deep breath summoning courage up through her lungs.

"It's show time!"

She expelled the air and flung open the bathroom door.

A voice floating down the corridor from the direction of the Brazilian couches had a heavy Brooklyn accent, the kind that pushed sound through the nose. Samantha pulled the opened door closed except for a tiny crack, and stopped to listen.

"I don't give a *fuck* what Post says. We shouldn't have left without Vincent. Fuck an A."

The man's accent made *fuck* sound more like *fork*.

"Yah, Julio. Vincent's gonna be mighty pissed, don' ya think?"

That voice was a high-pitched whine. It laughed nervously.

"I ain't worried about pissing Vincent off. He'll be out of the picture soon. It's that prick Post. He thinks he's runnin' the show. He's gotten too *fuckin'* arrogant if you ask me. You can bet your ass I'll fill Papa in on Post's bullshit."

"When do we make our move?" The whiny voice asked.

"Soon. Soon. *Fork an A.*"

The men laughed.

"Maybe we'll blow up the boat," the whiny voice said.

"Nah we won't. Just scare the fuckin' shit outta Post! He'd sell his fuckin' mother to save this boat. Wait until he hears the big booms!"

"So this was Vincent's idea?"

"Yah," Julio said.

They both laughed together for a moment, as Samantha adjusted her weight against the bathroom door and strained to catch every word.

"Hey, Julio, who's that guy with Post tonight? I ain't ever seen him before. The one with the blonde?"

"*Fork*, I don' know. A bodyguard maybe," Julio replied.

"Hey, if Post needs a bodyguard, maybe he's making some moves on his own?"

"That'd be a big *forkin' mistake,*" Julio answered coldly.

The sinister edge made Samantha's skin crawl. She opened the door wider to get a good view of the two men, but the light caught their attention and they turned toward her.

"Hey baby, everythin' come out okay?" the voice belonging to Julio called.

Samantha recognized the heavy gold jewelry, and the pock marked face now smiling broadly in her direction.

"Fork you," Samantha breathed, but *Sammy* smiled mindlessly, and sashayed down the corridor past the two men. Julio let out a mild wolf whistle, but his whiny voiced companion eyed her suspiciously. She tried not to look at him too as she headed for the narrow stairway, but their eyes met and held briefly. Big round marbles the color of tiger's eye were set deep inside thick black lashes and heavy eyebrows. He had a swarthy look, but his face was too large and intense for his slender body. His gaze was both sensual and evil.

Better stay clear of these guys, Samantha thought as she pulled herself up the steps by the railing, feeling their eyes burning into her backside.

———

Kowloon, Hong Kong

Colorfully lit lanterns sparkled through amber, turning the elegant 25-year old Hennessy alternately bright green and yellow as the party sampan passed below the balcony railing. Suspending his crystal snifter out over the water, he traced the sampan's progress along Victoria Harbor.

Once the sampan was out of sight, he raised the snifter toward the lights of Hong Kong Island and toasted their nearness. He was terminally jet-lagged and the brandy represented a final effort to avert sleep. Once the glass was empty, he would rest.

In the suspended moments of mental acuity earned only through extreme exhaustion, his mind raced. There were still so many details to conclude. He looked at his Rolex watch. Eighteen hours and it would be complete.

Such a brilliant plan. Such marvelous execution. And now, only eighteen hours to freedom. He congratulated himself again, tipping the last ounces of cognac down his throat. Carefully, he drew himself from the railing, and turned. Kowloon's elegant China Regent suite invited him from the balcony. Grasping the finely carved cane firmly, he hobbled carefully toward his bed.

CHAPTER TWO

"Green four to Green One."

"Green One, go."

"Hey Jimmy, we're back. Chris just brought back the first batch of snaps. I don't know. Maybe you should take a close look at some of these photos. There's a possible here that *could* be him. But I don't wanna make the call alone."

"Pull your car around behind mine, and I'll take a look. I'd know the *Baron* anywhere. I'll pick him out. By the way, who's got point?"

"Hey boss - It's me, Green six. I've got point. We're takin' license plates. The boat's down the bay somewhere, past Sands Point. We ain't gonna lose it. It's a pretty big yacht. Ha ha."

The F.B.I. surveillance van pulled alongside the gray Chevy Caprice. Green four handed a proof page of miniature black and white photos through the passenger side window.

"This one's a look-a-like," Green Four indicated. Supervisory Special Agent Steven Flores, known in surveillance circles as Green One, studied the shot. From the Caprice's glove box, he extracted a flashlight and magnifying glass.

"It's close," he announced. "Stuart will have my ass if we're wrong. I don't see how we could have missed him."

"So you think it's him?" Green Four was hopeful. To fail to identify the *Baron* getting on board Alex Post's yacht would be a major fuck-up. And so far it looked like they'd fucked up.

"I'd say it's a *possible*. Who's this?" Agent Flores pointed to a photo of a tall, dark-haired figure walking confidently up the dock.

"That's Double D, aka Dapper Dan. He's the police department's undercover."

"And her?"

Green Four smiled. "We called her Double B."

"What's that for? Or should I ask?"

"B.B. *Blonde Bimbo*. Nobody knows her real name, so we had to make something up. She's a friend of Double D. Not one of us. He said he needed somebody he knew so he could get into his character better. Asshole thinks he's Robert DeNiro, for Chris sakes."

Green One took a final look at the photos and handed them back through the window.

"So, I tell the AUSA we've got a *positive* on the *Baron*?"

"It's your call Boss. I think it looks like him."

"So *him* it is," Agent Flores laughed, and picked up the radio car microphone. "Green One to Command Post. Never mind our prior alert. Looks like we got a positive. Call Stuart and tell him the *Baron's* on board."

———

Putting on Sammy's strut, Samantha crossed the deck to where Dan stood with his arm draped over Alex Post's shoulder. He seemed to be making important progress. Post was listening intently. So this guy is Mr. Big, thought Samantha, and studied him more closely. He didn't look at all like any criminals she'd met before with Dan. He looks like the neighbor who does my taxes, she thought. He looks like the little kid that always follows after the big boys, wanting to play their games. Maybe that was what he was doing now. Julio and his friend were going to eat him alive.

Samantha ran her fingers up Dan's suntanned arm. He looked up, annoyed. Whoops! Screwed up again, she thought.

But Dan's look softened when Alex Post stopped talking, his milky blue eyes taking her in, gawking shamelessly at her chest smashed into the tight little dress.

"May I present *Sammy*, my date?" Dan said.

Post looked eager. He was dressed in a crisp white broadcloth shirt and an expensive crested navy blazer. His brown hair was receding dangerously, with thin wisps brushed sideways across his forehead in a futile attempt to disguise the encroaching baldness. He was maybe forty years old. He *looked* like an accountant.

Taking her *Sammy* cue, Samantha moved up close to him, wrapping her arm around his waist. She stood an even six foot in her four-inch heels and seemed to tower over the man. Alex Post's body was thin and lanky, but an inner tube of fat encircled his middle.

"I can't believe you own this *gorgeous,* big boat," Samantha gushed and nearly gagged on her words. But Post looked pleased.

"It's a yacht, actually. I've always had this great love for the sea," said Post.

Samantha smiled provocatively. She furrowed her brow pretending extreme interest.

Post nervously swept his hand through what was left of his hair. His eyes drifted from her face to her chest and she felt naked. Dan didn't seem to notice. He just smiled encouragingly until he caught sight of the two men emerging from below deck. Post saw them too and suddenly looked alarmed. So everybody already knows each other, Samantha thought. Julio passed Post slowly, a malevolent smirk on his pockmarked face.

Post dropped his death grip on her waist, and he and Dan now looked out toward the water. Maybe it's time I take a walk, Samantha thought. Quietly she eased herself away from them, and wandered toward the main cabin.

D.J. Jim and his hot tunes wafted from the deck above. Suddenly hungry, Samantha wandered down toward the galley kitchen hoping to find a left over canapé or a couple of crackers. But it was empty, the caterer long ago packed up. Just a few silver trays with food-smeared paper doilies. She sighed and refilled her glass from a lone champagne bottle left on the counter.

Samantha wandered to the pale blue leather sofa in the alcove adjoining the kitchen. Muted amber light glowed from cone-shaped lamps mounted along the wall. Kneeling on the soft leather, she peered through onionskin window shades to the deck below. It was small and deserted except for two wooden benches pushed up against the railing.

Laying her head back against the soft cushions, she mentally plotted the final hours of her undercover role. Once the boat docked back at Manhasset, she and Dan would drive to some Denny's Restaurant for a debriefing. The choice of Denny's seemed low budget if this was such an important assignment. Why not a plush hotel suite where they could order coffee and muffins from room service? A Grand Slam breakfast didn't sound appealing.

Who would debrief her and what they'd want to know was a mystery. Dan hadn't filled her in. Perhaps he didn't think she'd have much to contribute, Samantha thought. She hadn't enough information to even *know* if she'd seen or heard anything important.

Julio, his steely-eyed friend, and their conversation below deck was probably significant. Julio and his friend could be drug dealers, if Alex Post was really in the money laundering business.

Muffled footsteps and something heavy being dragged along the deck outside roused Samantha from her musings. Peering below the shade, she saw Julio and his friend hefting something large and dark from one of the wooden benches. From the second bench they dragged another bundle, this one a long khaki green duffle bag. Slowly they dragged the bundles toward the bow and out of Samantha's sight.

A cabin boy wearing white slacks and a Wedgwood blue button down shirt entered through an adjacent door and strode past the sitting room, oblivious to Samantha's presence. He disappeared into the galley kitchen and emerged moments later carrying a tray filled with cookies and little pastries.

Samantha dropped the shade. How had she missed the *cookies*? The possibility that nourishment was just around the corner lit her hunger like a torch, and she nearly ran into the dimly lit galley. White bakery boxes splayed open on the stainless steel counter, but all were empty. Her heart sank. Crossing to the large stainless steel refrigerator, she tugged hard at the wide handle, the suction releasing the door in a quick motion that almost sent her backwards off her heels. It swung hard and thumped against something human.

"Whoa," said a deep voice.

Samantha sheepishly peeked over the door into two of the deepest blue eyes she'd ever seen. The eyes looked back in surprise.

"I was looking for cookies," she stammered.

"I was looking for my brother," the voice replied, his eyes locked on hers.

"I don't know him. I don't know anyone on the yacht. Well, almost no one. I, ah, I know a few people. But probably not your brother. I'm sure of it. Unless he's a cabin boy, and if so, I just saw him exit that way."

Samantha realized she was babbling. She stopped and pointed toward the main deck.

"That's definitely not my brother. But thanks for your help."

The blue eyes released her and disappeared down the narrow cabin steps. Who was that *man*, Samantha wondered, struggling to regain her composure.

BANG.

The concussion jolted her forward. It reverberated through her stomach. It lingered in the night air. She ran toward the stairway.

Bang. Bang. Pop. Pop. Pop.

Alarmed voices yelled from the bridge deck. Footsteps clattered in a confused shuffle as the partiers converged to the railing, craning their necks.

OOHH. AAHH.

Aha. *Fireworks*, Samantha laughed.Bouncing up the stairs to the deck, Samantha saw glittering little bits of crystal color filling the sky immediately above the boat. They shot from canisters aimed off the bow, stoked repeatedly by Julio and his friend from the large khaki duffle bag on the deck. Each time one ignited, the bow glowed in light.

"So *that* was what was in the bench," Samantha thought. For a moment she'd actually thought Julio and his friend were lugging a body. But wait, she thought. Where is the *other* bag?

"What the *hell* are they doing?"

Alex Post appeared from nowhere, rushing past her toward the bow. Dan was close on his heels.

"Get over there and stop them. Do they want to blow us up?" Alex yelled to no one in particular.

Not wanting to join the melee, Samantha cut back to the other side of the yacht, hoping to approach the action unnoticed from the other side.

She jogged carefully in her heels down the deck and past the two wooden benches she'd seen from behind the onionskin shade.

Something in the corner caught her attention. She stopped and bent to retrieve a small, glittering piece of metal. She turned it over and over in her hand.

Now, *this* is mysterious, Samantha thought. A .22 caliber shell casing right next to the storage benches. Samantha wasn't a gun nut, but her dad had taught her to shoot since age twelve and she recognized ammunition. She dropped the shell casing into the top of her dress and felt it roll uncomfortably until finding a hollow home between her breasts. Then she walked forward toward the fireworks and what appeared to be the start of a major argument between Alex Post, Dan, Julio and his friend, and that handsome man with the blue eyes she'd just seen in the kitchen.

"What sa matter? Ya scared a few sparks will hurt your boat?" Julio laughed his sinister laugh. He upended a box of sparklers onto the teak deck, and tossed a lighted match on top. Within a moment one ignited the next, until the pile became alive, hissing and tossing shards of color onto the deck.

"Whee! These sure are pretty. *Fuck an A.*"

Julio and his friend laughed while Post tried stomping the sparks out like a winemaker stomping grapes. His awkward hops made Julio laugh louder, and reach for another sparkler box. But his arm never made it that far, being grabbed in mid-motion and twisted backward. Julio's body writhed in agony. His free arm instinctively reached toward the cleft in his back. But that arm was immobilized also and he stood momentarily defenseless.

"Who th' fuck is this?" Julio yelled, twisting violently. His captor stood nearly a head above him, and was every bit a match for Julio's wiry strength. Julio glared malevolently at Post.

"Let him go," Alex Post said, kicking the charred sparklers into the water. Beads of perspiration had formed along his lip and he was out of breath. "The party's over."

"Don't give me that shit, Alex. This asshole has been intimidating you, and scaring the living hell out of your guests. I'm sure as hell not going to..."

"*Ethan*, just let him go. I'll take care of it. Later." With a twist of the wrist intended to inflict just one final moment of pain, the man from the kitchen released his hold on Julio. The smaller, wiry man reeled on him, sweeping his leg around in a karate kick directed toward the taller man's neck. With a swift step backwards, the taller man raised his muscled arm to deflect the kick, and send Julio backward onto the deck. He fell with a loud *thud*.

"Yeah, right, big brother. *You* take care of it later. Just don't turn your back on this asshole."

Ethan Post glared at Julio, and then at his brother.

"You got some strange friends, Alex," he said as he strode past them back toward the main cabin.

Dan signaled to Samantha, and she cautiously left the safety of the railing to cross the deck toward him.

"That was pretty exciting," she whispered, but too loudly. Alex Post glared at her, and brushed his hair. If you keep doing that, it's really going to fall out, Samantha wanted to tell him. Dan wrapped his arms around her from behind and pulled her up close.

"I think I have something to show you," Samantha whispered, much lower this time.

"Not now. It's not just the fireworks that have Alex all screwed up. That guy that was just here? He's his brother. Showed up without warning tonight. There's bad blood. He's some kind of Navy pilot. An instructor at Annapolis. Been snoopin' around it seems, and Alex is all shook up. He could screw things up for *us*, also. And the *Baron's* not on board. He didn't show up, an' Alex is fuckin' paranoid about why. I'm tryin' to put it all together," Dan said.

Alex Post picked up the large cardboard box with the remaining fireworks, and tossed it over the side. A deckhand standing nearby, attracted to the commotion, stepped forward to protest. But he, too, was cowed by Alex's glare.

"Do you think the brother's involved?" Samantha whispered, hoping to sound nonchalant.

Dan shrugged. "After that display, I'd say *not*. But I don't know if he's got any idea how dangerous Alex's crowd is. He keeps wringing their arms like that, an' he'll find *himself* six feet under."

CHAPTER THREE

The late August moon glimmered off the still water as the yacht inched toward the dock. Quietly, a deckhand tossed cushioned tubes over the side, and guided the large boat against the tall pilings. Jumping onto the dock, he grabbed two long white ropes and expertly wrapped them around iron anchors. The gangplank lowered, its rubber wheels rolling back and forth.

"They're startin' to come off guys. Look alive."

"Green Four is up and ready. You want some pictures on the way off, too?"

"Yeah, Bobby. Take some more shots."

"Ho-kay. Whadaya think guys? After four hours and lots of champagne, I'll bet some of those guests will take a header coming down that rockin' plank. Anybody in?"

"Put me down for five. All female."

"I'll take three, Bobby. But I bet one will be a blue-blazer stud tripping over his topsiders."

"Okay guys. Just do your job. Let's keep these airways open for official messages *only*, okay?" Supervisory Agent Flores said.

———

Samantha watched the couple in front of her carefully navigate the gangplank. The woman wore a bright floral print strapless dress with a huge bow across the front, and yellow heels. A wave rocked the boat just as she readied her last step, and she had to throw her leg far forward and hop to the deck. It was a graceful move under the circumstances. Her partner grasped both sides of the cable banister and jumped the entire distance.

They must be pretty sober, Samantha thought. Deliberately, she removed her stilettos and padded confidently down the plank and onto the deck.

———

"Smile, sweetheart," Green Four breathed, as he depressed the Nikon's plunger. The shutter clicked from its tripod perch, letting in optimum light. He reached across the seat into the surveillance van's glove box for the night-viewing binoculars. Climbing into the back, he directed their focus out the rear window and scoured the yacht's decks. He picked up the radio microphone.

"I just gotta great one of Miss Double B. But I'm lookin' for her partner now and can't find him. There's a guy in the pilothouse with some binocs of his own. Tall guy. Polo shirt. Short dark hair. Pretty clean cut."

"You think he's spotted us?" Green six asked.

"No, don' think so. Looks like he's checkin' out our little Blonde Bimbo. She's mighty cute, ya' know?"

"Yeah Bobby, don' surprise me you'd turn this assignment into a girl watch. You're a closet voyeur."

"Closet, hell!" Green Four laughed. "I'm out front and damn proud of it!"

———

Samantha waited nearly half an hour in the limo at the marina before Dan finally joined her. It was pleasant as she sat back and relaxed. She stretched out on the black leather seat and nearly fell asleep.

"Where are we headed next?" she asked drowsily when Dan finally jumped in beside her.

The limo pulled away from the marina and wound along the shore drive to the highway. Dan said nothing.

"Are we headed to Denny's?" she asked. He nodded.

Samantha closed her eyes.

She awoke as the sleek stretch limousine exited the Grand Central Parkway in the direction of LaGuardia Airport. The limo swung to a stop in the horseshoe entrance to the Marriott Hotel. Dan got out and walked around the car, opening Samantha's door.

"Follow me," he said in response to her confused look. He looked tired and tense.

He led her into the hotel reception area, through the lobby, and out a rear door. Parked outside in a fire zone was a nondescript navy Chevrolet van with its engine running. The side panel opened as they approached, and Dan climbed in, pulling Samantha in after him. The short dress and high heels made the maneuver very difficult.

The van pulled away just as the door slid shut behind her, and made a wide circle around the hotel, exiting in the opposite direction from where they'd come.

"Denny's?" she asked hopefully.

"Next stop," Dan replied.

They were alone in the van's gutted interior separated from the driver and passenger by a heavy, opaque black curtain joined with Velcro along the center seam. The small side and rear windows were smoked dark gray.

She and Dan sat on carpeted wooden benches built along the sides. There were two chrome camera briefcases stacked in one corner, and a stationary camera tripod bolted to the floor, and aimed out the rear window. It was dark and smelled of stale cigarettes. Two small lights bathed the interior in an eerie rose glow.

Dan leaned forward, poking his head through the Velcro-seam. The driver and a passenger spoke to him quietly. The police radio squelched.

Dan sat back. It was difficult to see his face clearly in the subtle light, but his expression was subdued.

"Something fucked up. The *Baron's* out of pocket. Ya know, *gone*. The surveillance guys thought they had a look-alike but I just ID'd *that* guy as the captain. So the *Baron* didn't make the boat and he hasn't shown up yet at checkpoint."

"Denny's is checkpoint?" Samantha ventured. Dan nodded.

"What does that mean?" she asked, trying to match his concern.

Dan shrugged. "Who knows? But it's not good."

They lapsed into silence, interrupted occasionally by muffled conversations from the front seat.

The van slowed and pulled into a large parking lot. Samantha took comfort in the yellow Denny's sign. She could use a good cup of coffee. But the van bypassed the restaurant to the parking lot's outer corner, pulling alongside a similar dark- colored van with blackened windows. The side panels of both vans opened facing each other, and Dan jumped out and into the adjoining vehicle. He didn't look back at Samantha. The driver and passenger followed suit.

"This is *stupid*," Samantha thought after a few minutes. There was nothing to do, and the van was becoming claustrophobic. She took her shoes off and stood up, hitting her head on the ceiling. Bending over, she took a step forward and grasped the sliding door for balance in order to peer outside.

A tall black man took that exact moment to peer inside her van. They almost collided. He wore a black *Yankees* cap, a black t-shirt and black leather jacket.

He stared up into her surprised face and extended a blue to-go cup. "Coffee?"

"You're a saint," Samantha replied.

She recovered her composure and stepped from the van. The concrete was cold and hard on her stocking feet. The tight mesh dress rode up. She pushed it down self-consciously and reached for the coffee cup.

"Were you hiding?" the man asked. His bright white teeth contrasted sharply with his ebony skin and deep brown eyes.

Hiding was a good term.

"Waiting to be debriefed," she said. He seemed satisfied with her answer and drifted away, but not before flashing her a mischievous smile.

"I'm glad someone's enjoying himself," she thought. Fifteen minutes dragged by as she sipped her coffee.

"Maybe nobody wants to talk to me at all," she thought. It certainly didn't appear anyone had any plans for her. She wanted desperately to change into the blue jeans and T-shirt she'd brought. The air was cool and the black dress left her feeling chilled and exposed. But the bag carrying her street clothes was in the trunk of someone's car.

Two men hovered between the vans, and four or five others gathered around a group of parked cars off to the right. They were all dressed in jeans, t-shirts, and lightweight navy windbreakers. They seemed not to notice her.

Dan was still crowded into the adjoining van with five other men, his back toward her. A small man with slumped shoulders and hair like Albert Einstein's sat in the group's center and appeared to issue instructions. Two others listened intently from the front seat.

The short man with the wild hair suddenly pushed his way from the van and brushed past her, bumping her arm as he passed but offering no acknowledgment. Coffee jolted from her cup and she jumped back just in time to avoid it splashing on her dress.

Wearing a blue suit coat over faded jeans, he strode to the gathered cars. Just as in the van, everyone around him listened intently.

He left them and headed back toward the van. Samantha moved in the nick of time, avoiding yet another collision.

He stopped short, and then spun around.

"Were you wired?" he barked.

"Excuse me?" Samantha said, looking back over her shoulder, unsure to whom he was speaking.

"I *asked* you if you were *wired*. It's a simple question," the man said impatiently. Then his eyes raked over her, taking in every aspect of her appearance.

"Oh, yeah. Of course *not*," he said dismissively. He climbed back into the van.

Samantha watched him helplessly, wondering if she'd done something wrong.

"He means the dress," said a voice from behind her.

She turned. It was the coffee man.

"What?" Samantha asked.

"The *dress*. There's no place to put it. Not that I'm complaining."

Samantha looked confused.

"Too tight, ya know? Hey, help me out here, sweetheart. Ya can't be that naive or they wouldn't have used you tonight."

"A *wire*. Like a listening device? He thought I was wearing a *wire*." Samantha was happy she'd finally put it together. "Nobody told me to wear one. I don't think I was supposed to wear one."

She suddenly felt embarrassed, and conspicuous in the tight black dress. Her coffee man offered his jacket and she gladly wrapped it around her shoulders. He extended his hand.

"The name's Bobby Washington. *Detective* Bobby Washington, NYPD. Green Four in surveillance speak."

"I'm Samantha Wilde. Tonight they've been calling me Sammy," she said and shook his hand enthusiastically.

Bobby laughed. "I like that name."

"Thanks." Samantha smiled and sipped her coffee.

Another car pulled up silently. The woman in the bright floral dress and her date emerged. Samantha remembered them from the yacht, and watched them in surprise.

"*She* wore the wire," Bobby said, nodding toward the pair. "They're FBI. We work together on the bigger cases."

"This is a big case?" Samantha asked.

"Looks like it, sweetheart. You see those guys over there? They're my partners. We're a special surveillance team for the New York Organized Crime Task Force. So that's why we're here. Why are you?" Bobby asked.

"I'm not a cop or anything. Dan Anguilo - he's the undercover detective over there- asked me to help out tonight. I've done a few of these things before with him. But nothing on this scale. I'm really just a junior high school teacher," Samantha offered.

Bobby laughed. "We were all wondering what you were. I guess this all happened so quick, you were probably the best they could do under the circumstances."

"I've done this before," Samantha pressed, feeling a little offended. "Dan and I have known each other for almost four years. We dated at the beginning but now we're just friends. He's always worked undercover. Every now and then he took me to picnics or movies or little dinner parties as his date."

"Did the department know about this?" Bobby asked skeptically.

"Uh-huh. I know how it sounds, but it started innocently enough. He'd show my picture to the bad guys when they tried to set him up with their sister, or cousin. That way he wouldn't have to make excuses that might draw attention to him," she said. "And every now and then he needed to produce me."

"I guess bad guys do normal things, too, eh?" Bobby smiled.

"He was undercover as a garbage hauler once. We went to a lot of potlucks," Samantha explained.

"I can see it. But you haven't answered my question. Did the department know?"

"Well, I guess it's okay for me to explain. In order to be Dan's date, the department opened me as a *confidential informant*. They did a background investigation to make sure I was trustworthy first. Then after each social event, I'd sit down with Dan and tell him what I'd observed or found out. It was fun. I have a file at headquarters. You can check it out," she concluded.

Bobby whistled, "Well, you sure *look* better than a lot of lady cops they could've fixed Dan up with."

Samantha adjusted the leather jacket more tightly around her.

"That's not much of a compliment, Detective Washington. I'd gotten the idea people might be interested in what I've seen or heard tonight, but I suppose this damned dress makes me look more like a bimbo than a thinking human being. I assure you this is just a role. My normal attire is jeans. You'll pass that on to any of your partners who were wondering about me tonight?"

"Hey, baby, I didn't mean to embarrass you. Really. Me and the guys, well, we get a little bored sittin' out in the cars. Nothing *personal*. But I'll tell 'em we talked and you're *okay*. So, where ya' teach? Manhattan? Upper West Side?"

"The *extreme* upper west side. Washington Heights," Samantha replied.

"Hey, you *are* okay, baby. That's a tough neighborhood. I gotta hand it to you."

Samantha smiled.

"Make it up to me, detective. Find out who's supposed to debrief me so I can go home?"

"Hey baby, I'll do it myself if these jack asses take any longer," Bobby said with a wink.

The wild haired man *again* climbed out of the van, and *again* hurried past her. He gave instructions to several of the men in the parking lot. Slowly they entered their vehicles and drove off.

"Who is he?" Samantha asked.

"Stuart Birkwell. The task force attorney."

"Excuse me," ventured Samantha as the man almost ran her down for the fourth time. He whirled on her impatiently, his eyes hurriedly scanning her face, showing no hint of recognition or welcome. Samantha gulped.

"I'm supposed to meet with someone. Perhaps it is you. To be debriefed about tonight?"

Still no recognition. The dark eyes regarded her coldly.

"I have some information you might need. I was working with Detective Dan Anguilo?"

Samantha's voice trailed off.

"Somebody please take her home," he called to no one in particular and climbed back into the van. His voice was loud enough that several members of the surveillance team looked up and stared.

Clutching Bobby's jacket around her, Samantha gathered up her shoes from the van, and struck out in anger across the parking lot toward the yellow and orange Denny's sign in the distance. Bobby ran to keep up.

"I'm getting coffee and calling a cab," she cried, hearing his footsteps coming up behind. He grabbed her arm and spun her around. They stopped just short of the restaurant entrance, both awash in the eerie yellowish green glow of Denny's neon sign.

"Hey, come on baby, chill out. Stuart Birkwell is an *asshole*. We all know he's an asshole, but you're new here so you didn't know. Now you do. Don't be so sensitive." He looked at Samantha, imploring her to smile.

"He's a bastard," she said.

"*That* he is. Don't worry about it."

Bobby's voice was soft and soothing, like a caress. His wide, white smile cut his face in half.

"My clothes are back there someplace, in one of those cars," she said more calmly. Without another word, Bobby turned and jogged back toward the vans and the parked cars. A few minutes later he returned carrying Samantha's backpack.

"*Now* let's get some coffee," he said, putting an arm around her shoulder and guiding her into the restaurant.

Denny's wasn't crowded at that late hour, so they chose a large end booth. In the light, she looked at Detective Washington aka Green Four closely for the first time. His perfect white teeth and deep brown eyes were set in a dark handsome, almost ageless face, but gray hair curled at his temples. His shoulders, chest and forearms were densely muscled, evidencing decades of bodybuilding.

Samantha excused herself after a gulp of coffee to change clothes. The bathroom stalls were wide, and by now her anger had subsided. Her cheeks still burned hot though, and tension pounded against her skull.

Samantha threw the backpack on the floor and dropped Bobby's jacket beside it. She hiked the black dress up to her waist and maneuvered to bring it above her arms and off over her head. She wadded it up in the jacket.

Pulling her white T-shirt on, she shimmied into her jeans, and slipped on white Sketchers. She brushed the bigness from her hair, and fastened it back with a spangled *scrunchie*.

Gathering up the jacket and remnants of her black costume, she rejoined Bobby. Her coffee had been reheated. A small spiral notebook was open next to his coffee mug. He lounged back against the plastic cushions.

"*I'm* going to debrief you," he said, smiling at her.

"You don't have to bother," Samantha started, but he interrupted, suddenly serious.

"Something happened tonight. I don't know what but I think it could be pretty serious. Something fucked up. Stuart Birkwell *is* a jerk, but he usually has a pretty good reason. Who knows? Maybe you saw something important."

"So you're not trying to humor me?"

"Nah, baby. You can relax. Besides, I think you helped us real nice tonight. You're a schoolteacher for chis sakes. An *educator*. You didn't have to do this for us. I want to hear what you have to say."

Samantha smiled.

"So let's get started. Those guys on deck…"

"Julio and his creepy friend?"

"Yeah, those guys. Tell me about 'em," Bobby instructed.

She described the bundles they unloaded from the bench, and the unexpected fireworks.

"The first one was the loudest. It sounded almost like a gunshot. But it was really fireworks."

She felt obliged to tell him about Alex's brother, too.

"I get the impression there's friction between them. Dan says he's a Navy pilot. Maybe he thinks his brother is up to something and he doesn't approve."

Bobby studied her carefully for a moment.

"Oh, he doesn't, does he?" he said in a velvety voice, a smile easing out his serious expression.

"No, I don't think so," Samantha continued in her most professional tone.

Bobby sat back against the cushion, watching her.

"So what's this Navy *stud* look like? Come on baby, you can tell Bobby. Hey, we're friends, ain't we?"

Samantha squirmed against the plastic cushion. Then laughed.

"It's that *obvious*?" she asked.

"Hey, I'm a cop, baby. I'm trained for this stuff. Besides, you're too easy to read. No match for a boy from the Bronx. A classy lady like you couldn't possibly be interested in our Double D. So I figure, sure, a Navy pilot. Now that's more your style."

Samantha sighed.

"Okay, so he's *really* good looking. Can I continue with my story?"

"Yeah, but tell me first why you think he's not involved."

"He damn near broke Julio's arm. I could tell Alex was afraid of Julio, but his brother wasn't."

She recounted the fireworks scene and then suddenly stopped. She rummaged through the backpack for her dress. She took it out and shook it. Nothing. Where had it gone?

Bobby grabbed his jacket to give her more room to look. He noticed a shiny object nestled in a fold.

"Is this what you're looking for?" he asked, holding it up between his thumb and forefinger. Samantha nodded.

"A .22 caliber. Not much damage from a distance, but up close it can be lethal."

He rotated the casing slowly in his fingers. Samantha looked at him expectantly. Bobby exhaled a thoughtful whistle.

"You said the first fireworks sounded like a gunshot?"

Samantha nodded. "I don't think it was, though. At least not a shot fired by Julio or his friend."

"And you said they dragged two bags from the benches?"

Samantha nodded. "But I only saw one on deck – the one that held the fireworks."

Bobbie cupped the shell in his fist, and then deposited it into his jeans pocket.

"I think you may have helped us out real nice tonight, baby. Real nice."

"Well, *you* take my information back there. Tell your pal Stuart what I found and tell him to go to hell. I'm calling a cab," Samantha announced.

The taxi arrived a few minutes later and Samantha climbed in while Bobby held the door.

"You're a nice lady. I think you did a hell of a job tonight. It was a pleasure working with you."

"Thanks. You made me feel important."

"You *are* important, baby. Besides, ya got great legs," Bobby said and closed the taxi door.

CHAPTER FOUR

Samantha positioned her cup under the tall chrome coffee maker, and pushed the little black toggle. Nothing. She felt momentary panic. Grasping the side handles, she leaned the pot forward, simultaneously depressing the toggle again. This time the black liquid dribbled forth, filling the polystyrene vessel to three-quarters.

The coffee was a little furry. Samantha scowled. Bottom of the pot coffee. Chewy coffee. She swirled it around like a wine taster, the grounds clinging to the cup's little white dimples. Her lipstick residue rimmed the lip.

"If I'm so damned important to this mission, the least they could have done was make enough coffee," she thought. But what the hell. She shrugged and took a drink of the thick liquid.

She walked back to her seat on the bleachers, her boot heels clicking and ringing noisily from the concrete floor off the Quonset hut's aluminum and steel walls. She no longer cared if she attracted attention.

Her early morning teacher's conference had gone badly. Tisha Adams, the principal, had tried to talk her into more after school programs. Samantha had declined. Then came the call that halted everything. AUSA Stuart Birkwell needed to speak with her immediately.

As she sat down on the bleachers and pushed her hair away from her face, she wondered why Stuart felt her presence here so necessary. The place was packed with detectives and federal agents dressed in blue jeans and T-shirts, wearing guns and carrying backpacks and large leather shoulder bags with protruding radio equipment. Once again, Samantha felt inappropriately dressed.

She'd been told to report to the NYPD training center at Rodmen's Neck by eleven. There was going to be a big meeting. She'd assumed eleven was when the meeting started, but she was wrong. Everybody else had been there since nine. But she wasn't *cleared* for the two hours of information that preceded her arrival. She didn't have a *need to know* that information.

Rodmen's Neck occupied a remote stretch of land between New York's Eastchester Bay and the Long Island Sound. It wasn't a secret place. It was on the map, and Samantha had found adequate signs to direct her from the Bronx Pelham Parkway after crossing the Throg's Neck Bridge.

It was the place the NYPD used for firearms training. She'd only had moderate trouble getting in. The man at the security gate wanted to see her badge. She told him she didn't have one.

"You're supposed to have my name on a list," she'd told him.

"And you're supposed to have a badge, lady," he'd told her.

He made a few calls, and finally raised the barrier gate. He directed her past rows of identical aluminum structures to the last hut on the left. The parking lot was full.

Merely opening the door rattled the hut's rafters and attracted too much attention. She'd scanned the bleachers for a familiar face, finally resting on Bobby Washington's. He smiled. An unidentified man in a blue polyester suit was giving a lecture from the open area in front of the bleachers.

Someone grabbed her by the elbow. Turning, she realized it was Stuart Birkwell.

"Get some coffee. Thanks for taking the time to come. We really appreciate it," he said and smiled awkwardly.

"You're still an asshole," Samantha thought.

"I'm up next," he said.

"For the benefit of those here who don't know who I am or just why we're here..." Stuart began a few minutes later.

Samantha was the only one present who fit that profile, so everyone turned to look at her.

"I'm Stuart Birkwell, Assistant United States Attorney with the District of New York, assigned to the Organized Crime Division. This investigation began a couple weeks ago when Vincent Vuillard, code name The *Baron*, came forward. He informed us he'd constructed an intricate money laundering operation for the De Yambi drug cartel, a Columbian organization we have known for quite some time."

Stuart cleared his throat as if addressing a jury.

"You have all just been briefed on who the subjects involved in that drug cartel are."

Sure, everyone but me, thought Samantha.

"The *Baron* believed his situation was getting out of control. He was being pressured to push increasing amounts of money through his network and he felt it was only time before his operation would be detected by the banks being used. He also feared for his life."

That last comment brought knowledgeable nods from the gallery.

"You all didn't have the opportunity to meet the *Baron*. Those of us who did, who questioned him for a week straight, recognized him to be a weak link, an expendable part of the drug organization. He was a gentleman. He loved good brandy and a fine cigar."

"And other guys, too," somebody piped up from the bleachers.

Stuart paused a moment to allow The *Baron*'s image to be absorbed.

"The *Baron* knew he was a weak link. That's why he came to us."

Stuart began to pace back and forth before his armed audience, telling the story.

"The *Baron* was Austrian born. He received his bank training in Switzerland where he became intimately familiar with international money movement. I will skip the details of how he became entangled with the drug cartel, but suffice to say, his expertise was noticed and rewarded. For the past five years he's lived in a suite of rooms at the Waldorf Astoria Hotel. He kept all the books for the laundering operation in a series of safe deposit boxes in Switzerland and New York. Recently, he retrieved those books and gave them to us."

"Wow."

"Holy shit."

Stuart's last words garnered surprised comments from his gallery. This was *new* information for everybody, and he obviously reveled in the response.

"The *Baron* knew that when his operation was discovered, and he believed that would be very soon, his more violent business associates would find him expendable. He wanted our protection, and an opportunity to disappear back to Europe with his life and a new identity. Last week, The *Baron* agreed to introduce an undercover from the NYPD into that operation."

Stuart was talking about Dan. She looked around for him. It made sense that he wasn't there. She glanced around at the others, hoping they all had a need to know this information. This was dangerous stuff. She found she had new respect for the gate keeper and his security measures.

"The *Baron* had identified Alexander Post as the De Yambi Drug Cartel's chief US money launderer. He was The *Baron's* protégé, another weak link. If we could compromise Post, we might turn him into working for us," Stuart explained.

"Both The *Baron* and Alex Post are the brains in the operation."

Stuart's voice droned on. On a bi-weekly basis, the *Baron* had been directing a small portion of the Colombian cartel funds to an account in Switzerland as payment to international consultants who designed the phony companies through which the funds traveled before they emerged back into the mainstream, all laundered and clean. The *Baron* was supposed to introduce Dan as one of these *consultants*.

Samantha pretty much knew the rest. Dan had been invited to the yacht party. The *Baron* had insisted he bring an escort to disguise the business nature of his presence. Dan couldn't find an appropriate woman among the female detectives available, so on short notice he'd asked Samantha. And Samantha was available because she hadn't had a date in god knew how long and didn't have any plans for Saturday night.

It's interesting how life works out sometimes, she thought. How a rotten social life can lead a usually normal person into the middle of a drug cartel.

Now Stuart was getting to the good part. The part where Samantha had saved the day. The part that he, Dan and Bobby had explained to her during their unexpected visit to her apartment last night. She wondered if Stuart would give her credit, in front of all these people.

"Now we all expected The *Baron* to be on the boat Saturday night. The plan was to debrief him after the party, then fly him out to an undisclosed location where he would stay in protective custody until our investigation was concluded."

Stuart stopped pacing and looked meaningfully at the audience.

"The *Baron* never showed up," he said, punctuating those five words.

"An undercover operative on board the yacht observed two men lugging something large from a storage bench. That same operative later retrieved a spent .22 caliber shell from next to that storage bench," Stuart continued, slowly for emphasis.

"This was immediately *after* the same two men had set off an unexpected fireworks display."

"Yay me," Samantha said to herself. The *undercover operative*. She obviously wasn't going to be vindicated in this crowd. They'd only know her as the bimbo in the black dress hanging around for no purpose Saturday night. And the bitch with the noisy heels today.

Stuart continued.

"We watched with excruciating difficulty Saturday night, or more accurately Sunday morning as two DeYambi members scrubbed down the yacht and the chrome railings until they glistened. All remains of a possible crime scene were removed. One surveillance agent re-boarded and, posing as a disoriented partier who had inadvertently left something on board, had a look around. He found something really important - a bloody pillow stuffed in a large duffle bag that had been wadded into the same wooden bench from which the two men had dragged the fireworks bag. The pillow had a hole in it the size of a .22 caliber shell."

The man in the cheap blue suit approached awkwardly from Stuart's peripheral vision, trying to get his attention without interrupting. Stuart stopped, beckoning the man over. They whispered in conference for a moment, and then the man retreated.

Stuart again cleared his throat, signaling the advent of important information. Samantha leaned forward in her seat.

"Sergeant Lenihan has informed me that the lab just completed their analysis of blood found on the pillow."

He stopped, and surveyed his audience to make sure they were paying attention. All eyes were on Stuart.

"As a point of background, we'd concocted a cover story so the *Baron* could extricate himself from the organization without raising suspicion. He was going to complain of health problems, high blood pressure. To make his story good, he'd even gone to a doctor just this past Wednesday to have some blood tests. We were able to retrieve that blood and compare it with the samples on the pillow."

Samantha was dying from the suspense. Stuart was deliberately drawing this out.

"Well," he said, drawing in his breath, "I guess it's a match. Ladies and gentleman, I believe we have a murder on our hands."

CHAPTER FIVE

Tuesday morning it was raining. The streets of Manhattan's upper west side were littered with deep, round oily puddles. Cars hissed by on the wet pavement. Samantha longed to stay in bed.

She remembered when she was little, and how she loved to lie and watch the raindrops land against the windowpane, and slide in little rivulets down the slippery glass. She could almost smell the dewy grass from a summer shower.

It was a comforting memory. The country was beautiful when it rained. Manhattan wasn't.

Struggling out of bed, she retrieved a pair of running shorts from the wadded mess of her dresser drawer and grabbed her favorite baggy sweatshirt, pulling it down over her head. The trusted Nikes were missing from the closet.

Looking around in a groggy search, she found them under the couch but the running socks had holes in the heel. She padded back to the dresser for another pair. Bright pink ones were all that were left.

Laundry today, she thought. Just another item on the day's agenda. After releasing the two dead bolts and the chain lock, Samantha let herself out into the humid, musty smelling hall. The worn marble stairs were dirty with footprints. She trudged downward trying to summon courage to go out in the rain. It was seven am.

Her legs felt wooden as she headed south through the heavy mist. After about a mile she turned back, retracing the route. Traffic was heavier now. The rain actually made the run more pleasant, the water drowning the automobile exhaust fumes which could almost choke her on hotter, drier days.

She slowed to a walk a block from her building, cooling down. The Korean tailor was as usual just opening his shop. He waved at her as she passed.

Once inside her building, she pawed through a pile of newspapers, retrieving her _New York Times_. Inside the apartment, she showered and dressed in jeans and a V-neck T-shirt, headed to the subway that would take her to Sixth Avenue and 20th Street for some plant shopping. An hour and forty-five minutes later Samantha returned, laden with a bag of potting soil. Flipping on the answering machine, she was surprised to hear Dan's voice.

"Hi. Uh. Hello, Samantha?" Dan's voice was hesitant. He never liked these machines.

"I need you to meet me today. About five o'clock at the lobby lounge in the Waldorf Astoria. You know the one."

She and Dan had met there once when they'd just started dating. It was very romantic, but too pricey for their budgets. They'd never gone back.

"Call me when you get in." Dan paused as if he wanted to say something else, but decided against it.

Picking up the phone, she punched in Dan's cell number. He picked up almost instantly.

"You got my message? So, is five o'clock all right?" he asked. Taking her silence as an affirmation, he continued. "I'll meet you in the Peacock Alley lounge. I'll be at one of the front tables nearest the lobby. It's an open area, but we can still talk privately. I'll fill you in then. What are you wearing?"

"What do you care? You shouldn't have trouble recognizing me," she replied.

"Seriously, what are you wearing? I need you to look like Sammy as much as possible."

"Okay. Right now I'm in jeans and a T-shirt."

"_Change!_" Dan ordered.

Samantha's wardrobe couldn't sustain another Sammy Wilde night. Sammy needed a black mini and Samantha didn't own one. Her wardrobe was saturated with khaki and denim. Sammy needed Dolce and Gabbana.

Samantha had Gap. She compromised with a navy silk halter dress with a slit up the side. The last time she'd worn it was to her best friend's wedding in June. This would be a treat, Samantha thought, allowing herself to get excited. The idea of being part of the Task Force investigation was becoming more appealing by the moment.

She twisted her hair to an upsweep and secured it with a gold clip. She looked more like a *Town and Country* cover girl than trashy Sammy Wilde, but Dan wouldn't care as long as she didn't show up in jeans.

It was almost five o'clock when she exited the apartment, and raised her arm demandingly. A bright yellow taxi with a severely dented fender rolled to a stop almost immediately. Samantha jumped in, and they sped downtown, timing the stoplights perfectly. The afternoon sun cast wide columns of light across the Manhattan buildings. Their journey slowed as the taxi wove through Central Park. Traffic intensified as they struggled through the final four blocks to reach 50th Street, and the Waldorf Astoria Hotel. Samantha exited the cab at the Park Avenue entrance. Catching her reflection in the brass frame of the huge revolving door, she realized the humidity had already done a number on her Sammy-do.

She ducked into the big ladies room. An attendant in a white uniform greeted her. Samantha entered one of the private stalls, and poked the hairs back into place. A hair spray can set out for patrons cemented the look. A bottle of perfume stood nearby. Samantha took a whiff. Satisfied that it didn't smell like something her grandmother would wear, she sprayed two short puffs under each ear.

Exiting the stall, Samantha dropped a dollar into the attendant's tip tray. She reconsidered and then fished an additional fifty cents from her purse.

Dan sat on an upholstered divan just inside the long cherry wood planters separating the Waldorf Astoria lobby from the Peacock Alley restaurant. The planters were filled with tall ferns that created a natural buffer between the busy lobby and the more serene lounge. A man in a black tuxedo played a show tune from the grand piano in the middle of the floor, while waiters in white dinner jackets served drinks. Enormous vases filled with fronds of fresh flowers rested on marble pedestals, and murals of white peacocks rose from the floor to ceiling. The lighting was subdued.

Samantha sighed. This was one of her favorite places in New York City.

She strode to the entry and looked around. The maître d' approached her just as her eyes fell on Dan. He waved. She excused herself past the maître d' and joined him at the little table. Hesitating, she considered whether to sit next to him on the divan, or face him in a chair.

Dan's hand tapped the cushion beside his thigh. Samantha took the cue, and sat down next to him. She scooched close but made sure there was at least six inches between them.

"You smell great," he said, smiling in greeting. "What are you wearing?"

"God only knows," she replied.

Dan's hair was different. It was combed back from the hairline in a European style, accentuating his eyes and his broad jaw line. His suit was an elegant Italian cut, an expensive silk weave in a soft gray-green color. A dark silk tie hung against his shirt.

He watched her with amused eyes as she took in his appearance. He looked incredibly sexy. He also smelled incredibly sexy. Samantha wished she had a drink. She grabbed his wine glass and took a gulp. It did the trick.

"A new look for you? You might want to take this role on permanently. You look great," she said.

"Can you believe the department sprung for this? At least I think they have. They haven't gotten the bill yet. We can get down to business in a minute, but let's have a few drinks first. Thank god they're pickin' up the tab tonight. These drinks cost a fortune. Can you believe it?" he asked, wide eyed.

Samantha laughed. The spell was broken. For a minute she'd almost lusted after him.

"So, what's on the agenda for tonight? Why are we here? Are we going to search the *Baron*'s apartment?" Samantha raised a teasing eyebrow.

"As a matter of fact, yes," Dan said. "The *Baron* gave us an apartment key before he disappeared. We're going up to have a look around. Just you and me."

"I was being facetious. Why us? Why *me*? Isn't that a better job for the police? I mean, for the *uniformed* police? Isn't it a crime scene or something like that?"

"Well, that's the sticky part," Dan said, suddenly lowering his voice. Samantha leaned closer to hear his words.

"We technically have his consent to go in because he gave us a key. Stuart can't risk the investigation by sending cops into the apartment right now. It might be a *tip off* to people that we don't even know about yet; that we're on to the *Baron* and his operation. I was here last week with the *Baron*, so I can go in without attracting attention. And so can you, because you're my *girlfriend*."

Dan patted her hand, and sat back against the cushion. A waiter placed a glass of red wine in front of her. Samantha took a long sip and then grabbed a handful of almonds from the nut bowl.

"Do you think we're being watched now?" she asked.

"I don't think so. This is all as a precaution." He noticed her worried expression.

"Samantha, honey, I know you've never done anything like this before. If I'd known how it was going to work out, I never would have asked you to that boat party. But we're onto something really important. As soon as we can learn more about that Julio guy and his friend, and I get a bet-ter feel for Alex Post and learn somethin' about the *Baron*'s murder, we'll break you free. But we need you right now. *I* need you. You're not having much fun, are you?" He stopped and put his arm around her shoulder.

"You know, Dan, I think I really want to be part of this investigation. These last three days have been unexpectedly exciting. I don't know if I want to be broken free just yet. But *murder*? Now that's *not* fun. It scares me. Just a little. "

"Oh, Samantha, there's nothing to be afraid of just now. This isn't the dangerous part. Besides, I'm right here with you."

"No, that's not it. I'm not afraid of the *danger*. Its two weeks until classes begin for the new school year and instead of focusing on my new curriculum, I'm playing Charlie's Angels. And I'm *liking* it. What will hap-pen to my *real* life when this is over? I keep thinking about the *Baron* and how he put his life on the line. I envision this dapper little man getting his brains blown out by an evil drug dealer with a face like Julio. I think about all the drugs that have to be sold to produce *so* much money that it has to be laundered through scores of banks. I think of the kids in my class who know more about drugs and weapons than U.S. geography. I've never had to deal with any of this directly before. But now, after just three short days, I'm *involved* with it." Samantha paused. Dan looked uncomfortable.

"It's not something you can't walk away from, Samantha."

"That's just the point. I don't think I want to walk away. I want to see this through. What really frightens me is that I'll get swept up in the intrigue, and I won't care about teaching anymore, or all these goals I've been working toward. I see my life changing, but this is just another assignment to you. Our risks are different, yours and mine."

They sat in silence. Dan's arm still hung loosely around her shoulder. He nursed his wine.

"Ya know, that's what happened to me," Dan said after a moment. "I started doing these under-cover operations, and they were so *great* that nothing else mattered. *You* didn't matter."

He looked at her. Samantha just nodded. She'd known. They'd never communicated, but she'd always known.

"Sometimes I just want it to stop. I want to walk away and go back to a normal life. I want to have kids. Buy a little house. Maybe even teach at the police academy. But at the same time, I don't know how I could give this up," Dan's glance took in the expensive surroundings, his suit, the wine. He sighed.

"You're a wise woman, Samantha. You can see it coming. You can control it if you see it coming. I never could see it. I got swallowed up," he said, his hand resting her head on his shoulder. His fingers threaded through her hair.

They sat that like that for a moment; then he abruptly straightened and kissed her forehead.

"You'll be all right. Just take it a day at a time. Who knows? You might even decide to hang up the eraser and become a cop. You could do worse." Dan signaled for the check.

"Come on, Sammy Wilde. We have a job to do."

CHAPTER SIX

There's something unnatural about a dead man's home. An eerie stillness blankets rooms recently occupied. Chair cushions hold indentations made by a body that won't be returning. Clothes hanging in closets still bear the odor of the living person.

Samantha felt like a voyeur wandering through the quiet apartment. She imagined the Baron giving them the tour of his place, showing them first the expansive foyer with the Italian marble tile floor. Then guiding them through the living room, pointing out the Manhattan skyline from the giant picture window.

She'd never even seen a picture of him, but in her mind the *Baron* was already a three dimensional character. She imagined him sitting at the Queen Anne desk in the living room, reviewing bank statements and recording the flow of money through his network.

The rich, mauve carpet in the living room fit her perception of his decorating taste, although what control he could have exercised over the color scheme in a Waldorf apartment was arguable. The room's expensive, yet sparse furnishings were elegantly arranged. Impressionist oil paintings hung from the eggshell colored walls.

Despite the decor fitting her expectations, Samantha saw little evidence of the *Baron's* personal effects. Everything was very ordered, like a sitting room where children weren't allowed. There were no family pictures. The books arranged on the bookcases along one wall looked to have been put there only for decoration.

She glanced at a few of the titles, an eclectic mix of classics, Russian literature and decaying political volumes. Perhaps the *Baron* was a vintage book collector? Or more realistically, this was the Waldorf's collection he'd inherited with the apartment.

The apartment had been thoroughly cleaned. Trails of raised nap suggested the rug had just been vacuumed. Surely the maid had noticed the *Baron's* disappearance, she thought. Although these were private apartments, she knew the hotel provided daily maid and valet service. Or perhaps it was commonplace for tenants to appear and disappear in the apartment towers without notice.

Dan brushed past her as he moved from the bedroom to the dining room. He opened a hall closet. A Burberry raincoat hung alone on the clothing rod. There was an umbrella propped in the corner, and a lone pair of rubber galoshes.

"He could have used those today," Samantha mused. On the shelf above sat an extra pillow and a yellow blanket. Standard hotel closet fare.

They continued to explore the apartment in silence. Samantha crossed over to the desk. It faced the room on an angle, behind it the large picture window that looked down thirty-seven stories onto the gilded dome of St. Bartholomew's Church.

Samantha searched the desk cubbyholes. She found a roll of stamps and a Monte Blanc pen case. A leather portfolio was neatly placed in one of the side drawers. She opened it. It held a fresh yellow legal pad, but nothing else.

"Did this guy even live here? I don't see anything a normal person would accumulate," she called to Dan.

She pulled open the bottom desk drawer. It was the largest drawer, and appeared to be about a foot deep. It took a few tugs before it finally flew open under her effort and fell with a thud on the carpet.

"Hello," Samantha said.

The drawer was filled to the top with a disorganized mess of envelopes, notes, pens, maps and scattered papers. Samantha began to paw through the contents. Dan heard her efforts and joined her.

"Find something?"

"Dunno. Looks like a catch-all drawer. A place you put things that don't belong anywhere but you don't want to throw out."

"Maybe the maid just shoveled that stuff in there when she cleaned," Dan suggested.

Samantha grabbed a handful of the letters and off-sized notes and held them up.

"Do you want me to look through them?"

He shrugged.

"Sure. Why not? I'll call down to room service and order us some coffee."

Dan sought out the internal hotel phone. He found it on the wall, near the foyer, and pressed the number five for room service.

"Mr. Vuillard," said a friendly male voice. "It is nice to have you back. What can we do for you this evening?"

Dan hesitated, calling up his character role. He responded in a forced, affable voice.

"No, this isn't Mr. Vuillard. He hasn't returned just yet. This is Mr. Giacometti. Dan Giacometti." Dan rolled the syllables of his undercover name slowly over his tongue for emphasis. "I should be on Mr. Vuillard's guest list."

"Ahhh, yes. Mr. Giacometti. We have you right here. Welcome, sir. May we serve you dinner tonight?"

"No, just coffee...." he began, and then reconsidered.

"Well, perhaps dinner is *really* what we want. What are my choices?" Covering the mouthpiece with his hand, he gestured toward her.

"We want dinner, right?" Dan whispered.

Samantha laughed. "Sure, why not? What can I have?"

"The special is salmon in a mustard dill sauce," Dan whispered, repeating the words coming to him over the phone. "And.... a vegetable medley. What's in a medley?"

"No, I'm sorry. I was just checking the menu with my dinner companion. I *know* what's in a medley, heh-heh. We'll take *two*. Yes, that will be fine."

"Do we want wine?" he whispered.

"Hey, it's up to you Dan. This is your show," Samantha said and walked away shaking her head.

"What do you suggest? Yes. A bottle. That will be fine. Two glasses. Oh, and you should probably bring coffee, too."

He hung up the phone, and strutted into the living room to find Samantha cross-legged on the floor, the contents of the drawer arranged around her. With elaborate motion, Dan removed his suit coat, and laid it on the sofa. He removed the tie and folded it into a pocket. With one hand, he unloosened the top buttons of his shirt. He rolled his shirt cuffs up twice in a jaunty style, and crossed over to the bar.

Pouring himself a hefty portion of scotch, he next sought out the stereo system. He began to rifle though a small collection of compact discs.

"He's only got classical *shit*. Oops, sorry Samantha. My language has gone to hell, huh?"

"Jeeses, Dan, he's Austrian. He probably likes that classical *shit*. Put on some Wagner."

Dan found a Wagner CD, and inserted it. With robotic response, the disc disappeared noiselessly into the stereo. Moments later the room was filled with the bold orchestral sound.

Samantha looked up briefly, taking in the beautiful music. Dan was now seated cross-legged on the sofa, like a king smugly surveying his domain. He winked at her.

"Isn't this great!"

Samantha cringed.

"No, Dan. What this is, is *weird*. How can you so blithely forget the *Baron* and his probable murder and enjoy yourself like this. It seems so callous."

"Hell, I am a *cop*. I'm *supposed* to be callous. Ya know I've seen so many ugly things happen out there. I'm not as sensitive as a regular guy."

"I think that's just a convenient excuse."

Dan shrugged.

Samantha continued her search through the drawer. Most of the letters weren't letters, just empty envelopes with dated postmarks. The *Baron's* junk had been accumulating for years. She focused on a couple hand-scribbled notes.

"Here's something interesting."

She stood and took the piece of yellow-lined paper to Dan.

"It looks like he was doing a crossword puzzle or something. It looks pretty worn."

On the top of the paper was scribbled in pencil the letters *HK*. Underneath were listed eight rhyming words, four marked by little asterisks for emphasis. *Wong, Long, Nung, Chung.*

"What do you think?" Samantha asked. Dan studied the paper, mystified.

"Was this attached to anything? Any other piece of paper?"

Samantha shook her head.

"Beats me. Could be just doodling. Who knows. What else have ya found in there?"

"Nothing that seems important. There are phone bills, some miscellaneous receipts, and some bank statements. I separated out the statements in case you need them. But this paper is really the only thing that's unusual. I can't figure it out."

"Let me look at the receipts."

Samantha brought them over to the sofa. They scrutinized them together. Most were clothing receipts. The Burberry raincoat receipt dated last year, and another for the compact disc player.

"Here's one dated just last Wednesday," Samantha pointed. It was a cash receipt for $27.96 from a pharmacy down the street. A computer-generated tally listed only internal inventory codes.

"Can't tell from this what he bought," Dan said and tossed the paper back to her. "Maybe aspirin. I think what you're doing is probably gonna turn out to be a waste of time. I don't know what I expected to find here tonight. Maybe evidence that somebody else had been in here, searching the place. Maybe the people who had knocked the *Baron* off. But, with this damn maid service, they could have completely torn the place apart. And we wouldn't be able to tell now because everything is so damned *clean.*"

He swept his hand over the surface of an end table for emphasis, and held up his palm. It *was* clean.

The doorbell rang. Dan answered it while Samantha returned her bundle to the desk. She carefully separated out the receipts, placing the one from the pharmacy on top. She then folded the yellow note with the *HK* rhymes, and placed it and the receipts in her purse.

A waiter was wheeling a loaded cart into the dining room. He set the dining room table with china and silverware, and placed a wine bucket at the corner. He positioned a bud vase with a single red rose at the table's center. He then lit the candelabra. Dan watched him awkwardly, feeling that maybe he should help.

With great flourish, the waiter removed the cork from the bottle of Chardonnay, and passed it to Dan for his inspection. Dan sniffed it, and shrugged. The waiter poured a small splash of wine in a crystal goblet, and handed it to Dan. Dan stared at it for a moment, and then absently took a sip.

"That'll be fine," he said, wishing the waiter would disappear. He felt intimidated. None of his past under-covers had been this high-rent. He didn't know the wine tasting routine.

The waiter wrapped the wine bottle in a white napkin muffler, and placed it in the wine bucket.

Dan fumbled in his pocket, and withdrew a ten-dollar bill, shoving it in the waiter's direction.

"I think that's all we'll need." Taking his cue, the waiter pocketed the money and withdrew from the apartment.

Samantha hadn't been paying attention to Dan or the waiter. She'd gone into the bathroom, and become absorbed in studying the huge Jacuzzi tub encased in porcelain tile. The tub took up almost half the bathroom's area. A wide tile shelf surrounded it.

She sat on the shelf next to the tub, and began to stroke the tiles. They were smooth and cool to the touch. She imagined herself walking naked over the cool tile, and immersing herself into a hot bath. She could see her image reflected in the mirrored walls as she climbed into the water, envisioning little candles lined up along the tub, blinking soft light against the marble.

Her mind drifted. Billows of steam wafted into the room as she slid herself beneath the hot water. Suddenly, Ethan Post entered the steamy room. She hadn't been thinking of him, but now he was *there*, dressed in a black tuxedo. The crisp, white points of his starched shirt framed his sculpted jaw. His tanned face turned his eyes electric blue under soft brown lashes. They flashed at her, seeing her for the first time, yet somehow knowing she would be there, intending to find her there.

Slowly he released the strings of his black silk tie, and tossed it upon the floor. Taking one, then another step toward her, he unbuttoned the diamond studs confining his muscular chest behind the white cotton. With a practiced, fluid motion, he shrugged the tuxedo jacket and shirt from his shoulders.

Then he was sitting almost naked next to her on the tile. Smooth skin stretched taught across his chest and stomach. As he moved his arm to reach into the tub, his pectoral muscles flexed and relaxed in a mesmerizing dance. His abdomen rippled as he leaned forward toward her, his blue eyes enveloping her body, boring into her *soul*.

The fantasy was out of control. Samantha shook her head hard, recapturing reality, and ran, almost gasping from the bathroom. I need more dates, she thought as she returned to the safety of the living room.

In her absence, Dan had switched off the lights, and dimmed the chandelier in the dining room to a mere faint glow, leaving the room bathed in candlelight. Glancing at Samantha, he began to pour the Chardonnay, the light from the candles reflecting off the crisp, clear liquid. Sounds of Wagner wafted through the room.

"What the hell are you *doing*?" Samantha asked, still flushed from her unexpected fantasy.

"Just shut up and humor me."

Dan held out her chair. She sat down at the table rather stiffly.

"Here's to you. And me," Dan said, lifting his wine glass and downing its contents. Leaning over, he grasped her face in one hand and kissed her hard on the mouth. It was meant to be a good, strong kiss, but instead it felt more like a collision. She couldn't help herself. She laughed.

Dan scowled and quickly poured himself another glass of wine, finishing it off in one gulp. Samantha could tell he was angry. She shrugged her shoulders helplessly, suppressing a smile.

"Hey, you took me by surprise. I wasn't laughing at you. It's just not in your character to be this romantic. And I'm hardly the appropriate person, anyway. I didn't mean to hurt your feelings. Really I didn't."

"Your fish is getting cold," he said.

Dan managed to empty the wine bottle as the meal stretched on in silence. It was all too familiar. He finished his salmon, and was toying with his fork.

"Maybe we should leave now," he said, but made no move to get up. Samantha threw her napkin down.

"Come on Dan. You know we're working. We're not on a date."

"Hey, maybe I got carried away, okay? I thought maybe you were having as much fun as I was. I don't know what's wrong with you, Samantha. It's okay to throw yourself at me when we're playing *Dan and Sammy*. But when it's just me, you can't stand me touching you."

"Dan, get a grip! We broke up over two years ago."

"But after Saturday night and rubbin' up against me on the yacht all night, what the hell am I supposed to think?"

"You think I was coming on to *you*?" Samantha yelled, horrified.

He pushed his chair violently away from the table.

Samantha jumped up, too. This had gone too far. He's really mixed up, she thought, following him into the living room. She grabbed hold of one shoulder, and spun him around with all her strength.

"Dan, it was a *role*! It was a role *you* gave me. You coached me on how to behave. I was doing my *job*."

"Your job? You're a school teacher, for god's sake. That's your only real *job*. You're just helpin' me out, Samantha. You're not a professional, so stop tryin' to act like one! You're just a girlfriend. *My* girlfriend."

He stopped. Samantha's mouth hung open in a look of absolute shock. He began to run his hand through his hair.

"Jesus Christ. Samantha, I'm sorry. I don't know where I get these ideas sometimes."

If he hadn't looked so confused, she would have slugged him. Instead she put her arms around him and hugged his body close.

"Dan, we've been through a lot together, but we're *friends* now. That's all. I think all your years of undercover work have taken a toll on you."

He seemed to think about this for a moment, then abruptly pushed her away, regaining his composure.

"So, what do you think? Are we outta here?"

"I suppose so," she said. All these emotions expended, she thought, and it was only quarter after nine.

Dan excused himself to use the bathroom. Samantha walked to the hall mirror to adjust her makeup when the doorbell rang. Hesitantly she opened the door. A middle aged Spanish woman in a maid's uniform stood outside.

"Senor Vuillard has returned? I will prepare his bed." She moved forward to enter the apartment.

"No, " Samantha replied, placing her body to prevent the maid's advance. "Senor...ah.. Mr. Vuillard has not returned. He is, ah.. Still out of the country. I had promised him I would stop by the apartment every now and then to make sure everything is all right."

The maid accepted her explanation without comment.

"When will you expect him back?" the maid inquired.

"It's hard to say. Do you come here every night?"

"Yes, senorita. Every evening at fifteen past nine. I turn down his bed. The valet then brings him tea at thirty past nine. That is his schedule."

"He certainly has a beautiful apartment," Samantha ventured. "My boyfriend and Mr. Vuillard are business partners. This is my first visit to his home. He's got some wonderful antiques. I just love the way he has it decorated."

The maid smiled graciously.

"In all fairness, senorita, I work for the Waldorf Astoria Hotel and I must therefore tell you that you are mistaken. Senor Vuillard is a well-traveled gentleman of great personal taste, however all the furniture and decor you so admire were provided for him by the Waldorf Astoria."

She took great pride in making that statement, Samantha thought.

"So nothing in here is the Baron's...ah.. Mr. Vuillard's?" Samantha asked, catching herself.

"Ah, but yes, there was one item Senor Vuillard loved dearly. It was an exquisite grandfather clock of hand carved mahogany. Um, excuse me, please senorita?" she asked as she leaned into the apartment and pointed to the end of the foyer.

"It would stand there," she pointed to an area by the wall. "We were all instructed not to touch the instrument. It kept wonderfully exact time."

"But where is it now?"

"Senor Vuillard had it removed perhaps three weeks ago. He advised me it was to be cleaned, and the chimes repaired. I thought it unnecessary because it kept such exquisite time, but Senor Vuillard, he loved it so. Perhaps it was like a child to him."

The maid smiled at Samantha.

"Perhaps you can tell me..ah...."

"Maria, senorita. My name is Maria."

"Perhaps you can tell me, Maria, has Senor Vuillard had any visitors since this past weekend?"

"Oh, no, senorita. You are the first. I have not heard anyone mention any other guests for Senor Vuillard."

Samantha was mystified at Maria's certainty, but then recalled stories she had heard about the internal grapevine at high end hotels like this. Between the cleaning staff, the valet and kitchen, there were few secrets. A couple of thugs searching his room would definitely have been noticed.

"It was wonderful speaking with you, Senorita. I hope that you will visit Mr. Vuillard again. And I look forward to his soon return."

Maria bowed slightly, and proceeded down the hall. Samantha watched her go, and then closed the apartment door. She walked to the foyer wall where the clock had once stood.

Dan emerged from the hallway.

"Who was that?"

Samantha didn't reply right away. She kept staring at the wall.

She said, "It's really strange. At least I *think* it's strange. The Baron doesn't own anything in this apartment, besides that compact disc player and a raincoat. I was just speaking with the maid. The only thing he owned and really cared about was a grandfather clock and he had that moved out of here three weeks ago. That was maybe before he even approached Stuart and the task force. Don't you think that's strange?" Samantha asked.

Dan thought about it a minute.

"Well, not really. Maybe he expected the police would ultimately be the ones to move his furniture after he went into witness protection and he didn't trust us to do a good job. And that's not really *strange*. That's just really *smart*."

Samantha shrugged and turned out the light. Dan locked the apartment door and together they walked to the elevator. The tension between them had subsided. The old Dan had returned.

CHAPTER SEVEN

The dark blue Ford LTD slowed at the entry gate, the early morning sun reflecting off the gray smoked windshield. Its two occupants removed small leather folders from their suit coat pockets and presented them to the guard on duty. The guard carefully surveyed each set of credentials. He looked into the car through the driver's window, and matched the faces on each identification card with the car's occupants.

"Special Agent McKenzie," he said to the passenger. FBI Agent Walter McKenzie nodded in introduction.

"Special Agent Maxwell," the guard now addressed the young driver. FBI Agent Steve Maxwell nodded.

"We have an appointment with Admiral Roger Massey," Maxwell informed the guard.

"That will be just a moment, gentlemen," the guard stated. He returned moments later.

"Please proceed through this gate, and follow the signs to Academy Administration Headquarters. There is adequate visitor parking. You'll have no problem finding Superintendent Massey's office."

The guard smiled and saluted. The Ford LTD drove quietly through the entry gate and onto the grounds of the US Naval Academy.

Both men waited silently in the Admiral's anteroom. They declined the coffee offered by the Admiral's secretary. She'd desisted in her efforts to make them feel comfortable, allowing them to wait in their solemn silence.

Margaret Rice had worked as Admiral Massey's secretary for over ten years. And seven more for his predecessor. Except for the occasional errant cadet, people who came to the Admiral's office were generally pleased to be there. These two gentlemen this morning were different. Margaret was concerned, and worried.

Roger Massey was an affable career military man of about fifty-five years old. Although a strict disciplinarian with his troops, he'd developed a reputation for fairness and judicial judgment during his years in command. His promotion to the academy had allowed him to expand his gentler side, and he'd relished the role.

Margaret eyed the two men waiting to see the Admiral with suspicion, but went about her typing. Moments later the door to Admiral Massey's office opened. A uniformed cadet exited, waved to Margaret and departed.

"Admiral Massey will see you now."

Special Agents McKenzie and Maxwell nodded to her as they walked past and into the Admiral's office.

"Walter, how are you? The last time I saw you, you'd just missed a birdie putt on the twelfth hole at Lakeview! But judging from this early hour, and the look on your faces, you're not here to talk golf. Please, have a seat. Tell me what this is all about."

Roger Massey looked concerned. FBI business on the academy grounds was not a usual occurrence. He eyed the uniform coat jacket hung over his leather desk chair. He wished now he'd put it on. His shirtsleeves seemed too casual for this meeting.

"Admiral, we're here on a highly sensitive matter," McKenzie began with an uneasy smile. "We wanted to alert you to the situation, and to solicit your cooperation in this ongoing confidential investigation."

Massey shifted his weight in his chair. His smile appeared strained.

"As always, we will be totally cooperative. I appreciate you coming to me directly like this. I will keep whatever we discuss in the strictest confidence."

McKenzie relaxed. They understood each other.

"What we need right now, Admiral, is any available information on Commander Ethan Post. It is our understanding that he has recently been assigned here to the academy, and will be teaching a course beginning next month," Agent McKenzie explained.

Admiral Massey was distressed. Ethan Post. Why Ethan Post? Post seemed the least likely person he knew to prompt a secret FBI meeting. He ran his hand through his wavy gray hair and cleared his throat.

"Yes, Commander Post joined our faculty just this month. He's a highly decorated naval officer and pilot. I knew his father personally. Is there a problem with Commander Post?"

There was an edge to his voice.

"Admiral, we have no information that would implicate Commander Post personally in any wrongdoing," Maxwell replied. He wanted to reassure the Admiral, but knew he couldn't say too much.

Massey pressed a button on his telephone and rang for Margaret. When he heard her voice, he requested Ethan Post's personnel file. Moments later Margaret opened the office door, and delivered the file to the Admiral. He handed the file to the agents.

"He's not living at the academy?"

"No, it isn't necessary. His family has a large home here in Annapolis. His father served prominently in Vietnam. He retired as a Naval Captain. He died four years ago. I believe the oldest son, Alexander Post *Junior*, lives somewhere outside New York City."

Agents McKenzie and Maxwell exchanged looks.

"This has something to do with the *brother*, then?" Admiral Massey noted their reactions. He was somewhat relieved. The Admiral knew little about the elder son.

"We have reason to believe Alexander Post is involved in a criminal enterprise. He's the target of an investigation by our New York office. We can't discount at this time any involvement his brother may have in this operation. But let me emphasize, nor do we have information that would implicate Ethan Post at this time," McKenzie said.

Roger Massey stood up and crossed to the picture window looking out over the cadet parade grounds. He absently studied the red and purple flowers growing beneath the flagpole outside. After a moment, he turned back to his visitors.

"So what do you want to do?"

"We'll be placing Ethan Post under regular surveillance until we're sufficiently satisfied he's not involved," said Maxwell. "If you can provide us his regular schedule here at the academy, it won't be necessary to impede his activities here. It is not our desire to interfere with the operations of this academy."

"And we greatly *appreciate* that," Massey replied in a strained voice. Sitting at the edge of his huge desk, he addressed the agents in a controlled voice, trying hard to mask his growing agitation.

"I am extremely concerned that a fine Naval Officer may find his reputation tarnished as a result of this. Does Commander Post have any idea that his brother may be involved in, what did you call it, a criminal enterprise? He's been stationed at international bases for the past fifteen years. He didn't even return to Annapolis until three weeks ago."

The agents shifted uncomfortably in their chairs.

"Once again, Admiral, we have no reason to believe Commander Post is aware of his brother's activities," McKenzie stated.

"Then why don't you interview Ethan Post, and enlist his help in your investigation?" the Admiral asked pointedly.

McKenzie laughed uncomfortably. "We can't do that at this time, Admiral. We must first be satisfied of his innocence. Then we must determine if he could be trusted with the knowledge of our investigation. It's not our practice to place that burden on an individual who might have greater allegiance to his family."

The admiral shifted his weight in his chair, and chose his words carefully.

"Commander Post is a *career* Naval Officer. His father was a *career* Naval Officer. Between them, they have both demonstrated unquestionable loyalty to the U.S. Government. I have absolute faith in Commander Post's integrity and allegiance."

Roger Massey stood up from his desk, signaling the interview's end.

"I am happy to cooperate with your investigation. However I suggest you quickly exonerate Commander Post. Your surveillance and investigation of him is, in my estimation, a waste of your time and the taxpayer's money."

Agents McKenzie and Maxwell gathered their papers together. They'd expected this meeting with Admiral Massey to be somewhat uncomfortable, but they hadn't expected to be virtually thrown out of his office. Maxwell held Ethan's file for a moment, unsure whether to return it to the Admiral, or collect it in his briefcase with his other papers.

"You'll find Commander Post's Academy schedule in that file, as well as his home address. Please copy what you need from the file and return it to Margaret before you leave. There is a small private reception room next to this office you may use to review the file. If you don't mind, gentlemen, I have another appointment."

The Admiral walked to his office door, giving Agents Maxwell and McKenzie no choice but to follow. They shook the Admiral's hand formally and retreated.

"So what do we do now?" the younger agent asked.

"I'm going to phone the Command Post in New York. They're givin' the gas to this case. We can throw it in *their* laps," McKenzie said.

"So, ya think the Admiral will ever play golf with you again?"

"Hell no," McKenzie snorted.

———

Bobby Washington sat in a rear booth at the *Volga Cafe*, sipping coffee from a large mug, the *Daily News* spread out before him on the table. He hadn't noticed Samantha when she entered the restaurant, so engrossed was he in the newspaper's crossword puzzle. The cafe was crowded with its usual morning clientele, an eclectic mix of writers and out of work actors who prowled this lower Manhattan neighborhood. It had a reputation for good food that was plentiful and cheap.

Samantha threaded her way past the lines at the pastry counter and into the main eating area. She was wearing a white T-shirt with hand painted pink flowers on the front and blue jeans. Her hair was tied back in a loose ponytail. Arriving at Bobby's table, she tossed her heavy leather satchel on the red Formica tabletop and wrestled his attention from the crossword. Bobby looked up and smiled his broad smile.

"What took you so long? Hell, baby, I called you half an hour ago. What did you do, fly here?"

"I was up already. I told you that. And you said the magic word. *Coffee.* I'm out. I'd rather have you buy than go to the supermarket."

She took a chair facing him.

"A lady after my own heart."

Bobby folded the newspaper away. A waitress came over and placed a hot cup of coffee in front of Samantha.

"The *Volga*'s got the best coffee in town. And you've got to try their French toast. It's my favorite. Besides, it's only three bucks."

Bobby smacked his lips.

"Okay, I'm sold."

The café's comfortable atmosphere invited lounging, so Samantha stretched out, resting her feet on the bench.

"You're not working today?" she asked.

"As a matter of fact I'm working right now. Right this very *minute*," Bobby stated. "We get contracted out to work a whole lot of different investigations. Today and tomorrow we were scheduled to surveil this one dude who lives just around the corner. We got here at seven am and he was already gone. They picked his voice up about an hour ago on a wiretap out of Los Angeles."

"So he's in L.A.?

"Yeah, and we're *here*. And nobody has any two-day work for us. Everybody wants us for weeks at a time, an' we can't do that, 'cuz me and my surveillance team have gotta cover a big shindig this weekend."

"So you're just drinking coffee on the government's dime?"

"Tastes best that way, don't you think?" Bobby winked at her.

Samantha nodded, and toasted him with her mug. Then frowned.

"You've got another party to spy on, eh? I thought you'd be working the *Baron*'s case? They're putting you on something else?"

Bobby raised an eyebrow. "You haven't heard?"

"Heard what?"

"Gosh, baby, I thought you were just bein' paranoid the other night, when you said they were treating you like shit. But they're really keeping you in the dark! You don't *know*? You and Dan have got a big social date at Alex Post's mansion at Manhasset this weekend. We've been setting' it up for the past thirty-six hours."

"But I was with Dan last night, and he didn't mention a word."

Bobby shrugged.

"Probably forgot. Anyway sweetheart, I'll take responsibility for you going forward. I'll be the torch that lights your way. Jeeses, hey, you could have had plans, right?"

Samantha laughed. "Yeah, sure."

"I think I know somethin' *else* you haven't heard."

Samantha leaned forward, but the waitress took just that moment to assault their table. Bobby ordered French toast for them both, and then waited until the waitress disappeared behind the pastry counter.

"You know that Navy stud pilot you couldn't help but tell me about the other night? The one that got you so hot?"

"*Yes*, Bobby. I *know* the one. His name is Ethan Post and I was passing on important information, which is why I brought him up in the first place."

"Heh, heh, I love it when you get defensive. But that's not the point. Seems we've put your lover boy stud under surveillance. *Full time*."

Samantha nearly dropped her mug.

"But Bobby, *why*? That doesn't make any *sense*."

"Welcome to the world of the trained investigator, Princess. Not everything is designed to make sense. At least not to the layman, whom I will point out as delicately as possible, you still are. Actually, it's a natural step in the investigation. I figured this would happen."

"So *what's* happened? What did they do?"

"It seems two feds paid a visit to the Naval Academy early this morning. They should be set up, watching his residence right about now." Bobby tapped his watch.

"But Bobby, if the *Baron's* been murdered, I'd be looking into *his* business, not Ethan Post's. Why do that? It doesn't sound like a natural next step to me. Besides, I don't think he's involved."

"Yeah, well I don't think you're alone. I guess the Admiral damn near threw the agents out on their asses."

"I know I'm a novice at this investigation game and I don't want you to think I'm questioning the professionals. It's just that I think they're wasting their time."

Samantha stopped and took a drink of coffee. Bobby flipped his coffee spoon in her direction.

"Relax, princess. As I told you, you're not alone. Nobody really thinks your stud is involved. They just have to make sure he isn't. Then maybe they can put him to work for us. Remember, they think Alex Post is a weak link. His brother might help us flip him."

"You mean Ethan could influence Alex to work for *us*?"

"Influence. Yeah, that's a better word. Ethan's the little fish that gets us to Alex, a bigger fish. Alex gets us to bigger fish still. Et-cetera, et-cetera, et-cetera."

Their French toast arrived and both concentrated on eating for a few moments. A waitress refilled their mugs.

"So, what else don't I know about? You can trust me Bobby. I'll never reveal my source of information."

Bobby thought for a minute.

"I know that you and Dan are staying at Alex Post's house in Manhasset. Houseguests, you are."

"Jeeses, they don't waste much time taking over my *life*," Samantha said.

"Well, tell me to stop if you don't want to hear these things. I just thought maybe it would be nicer coming from me instead of your pal Dan. Somebody has to take responsibility for you. Stuart can't, and Dan's useless for anyone but himself."

Samantha thought about that for comment. It reminded her of thoughts she'd had last night.

"Bobby, how long have you known Dan?"

"Dan and I were in uniform together. I'd been on the job about six years when Dan got out of the police academy. I got my gold shield and joined the Detective Bureau maybe two years later. I guess I didn't see him again until a year ago. I was asked to join the Organized Crime task force, and he was being used as an undercover. Now don't get me wrong when I said he was useless. Dan's a good cop and all. He does a hell of a job on the undercover work." Bobby hesitated.

"*But?*"

"But...Hey, you guys have some history together. I don't think I should be sayin' anything else."

"Dan and I *had* some history. He's a nice, sweet guy when he's not pretending to be Robert DeNiro. I don't mean to be trite because his work is *important*, but to him he's more like an actor in a movie. Only now I think he can't remember what's the movie and what's real life."

Bobby became serious.

"You're a real smart lady, Samantha. Dan's good at his work. He's just been doing it too long. We really try to be on the lookout for signs of burnout. There's lots of department horror stories about guys flippin' out an' eating' their guns, or goin' over to the criminal's side. You let me know if you think Dan is gettin' close to anything like that."

Samantha nodded. She decided to change the subject.

"I want to tell you about what I found last night at the *Baron's* apartment."

She described the apartment, carefully leaving out the cozy dinner for two with Dan. That could be just the burnout sign Bobby was talking about, she thought. She told him about her visit with the maid, and how the *Baron* had moved his grandfather clock from the apartment just three weeks ago.

Digging through her shoulder bag, Samantha retrieved the bundle of receipts she'd taken from the *Baron's* desk. Finding the pharmacy receipt, she showed it to Bobby, acknowledging there wasn't much to go on.

"But I plan to go over to the pharmacy today and find out what our friend bought," she said.

She showed him the yellow paper with the list of *HK* rhymes. He studied it for a minute, mystified.

"Ya know there's one possibility on these words which might relate to the investigation. Maybe they're connected with some bank accounts. I know part of the *Baron's* network involved banks in Hong Kong and Singapore. Can't hurt to check it out."

"That's what *I* was thinking," Samantha said.

"I've been talking a little with the group assigned to review the *Baron's* books. They're FBI agents. Accountants. And they're unraveling the money paths. They're holed up in this hotel room doing nothin' but pouring over ledgers and bank statements and computer files. They're happier than pigs in shit. That's a good time to those guys. But anyway, you're gonna love this part."

He kept his voice low so it couldn't be overheard.

"I don't know how they did it exactly, but somewhere in the money laundering chain, the *Baron* helped the feds set up these dummy accounts. They're all in the name of Elizabeth Ross Trust."

He waited for her response.

"Well, I didn't get it right away either. You know, Betsy Ross? The lady who sewed the first flag?"

"Yes, I know Betsy Ross. But I don't know what you're talking about."

"Instead of the government having to freeze the bank accounts where the money is traveling through so it doesn't get away, which would alert the bad guys, they're diverting the drug cartel money into these accounts. Then when the investigation is over, the feds have all the drug money before the cartel even knows it's missing. Pretty cool, heh?"

Samantha was impressed.

"Actually the *Baron*'s case is a challenge. He gave them the money flow chain up front, so the feds became obligated to stop the money as soon as they knew it was dirty. This way, with Betsy Ross' help, they've essentially secured the money without closing down the operation. Since the *Baron* didn't have enough time before he disappeared to give us the players, the bad guys, Betsy Ross buys us some time to maybe identify these guys."

Bobby hesitated. "But not a lot of time. That's why they're moving so fast on Alex. *And* his Navy stud brother."

"I guess it makes sense," Samantha said after a moment. "But there are still things I'm uncomfortable with. For instance, the *Baron* moving his clock out before he contacted Stuart. And the coincidence that the *Baron* had blood drawn just days before the bullet and the pillow were discovered. Without that doctor's appointment, the lab couldn't have positively identified the blood on the pillow as the *Baron*'s. And then there were the two men on the boat. I know they weren't lugging a *body*. Bobby, what would happen if the *Baron* wasn't dead?" she asked, trying to make the question sound nonchalant. She didn't want Bobby to lose confidence in her judgment.

He studied her for a moment, realizing that she was serious. He thought it over carefully.

"Well, let's see. Because of the blood and the bullet, the police think he's dead. So they're not going to look for *him*. Since the *Baron* disappeared about the time Dan got introduced to Alex and his organization, the cartel would assume Dan and Alex were responsible for his disappearance. Therefore the cartel wouldn't be looking for the *Baron*, either."

Bobby stopped, disturbed by the theory.

"And Alex, knowing he wasn't responsible, would assume the cartel had done it. He might even think he was next. That the cartel was eliminating their weaker links. Okay, so let's look at it from the *Baron's* perspective."

Bobby concentrated. A devious smile crept onto his face.

"This is pretty cool. We've already said the police wouldn't be looking for him. And the drug cartel wouldn't be looking for him. And Alex would probably be paralyzed by fear, so he wouldn't dare speak to anyone about it. The *Baron* would be home free."

"But for what? What would be his benefit?" Samantha asked.

"He'd be free and clear of the cartel. It's a dangerous business, and he's a smart guy. Maybe he didn't get into it without carefully planning a way he'd ultimately get out," Bobby said.

Samantha chimed in, "And, lest we forget, he controlled all the books. *And* knew where all the money was going. Maybe he took some of it, and devised this whole charade about his death to make his get-away."

Bobby jumped up from his seat, and crossed quickly to a bank of public telephones against the wall. He fished some coins from the pocket of his jeans, and punched in a phone number. Less than a minute later, he returned to the table.

"I just called the accountant's secret off-site. I'm heading over there now. I want to discuss this with them. I'm not going to mention our entire theory. If we're wrong, we'd look pretty stupid. I just want them to check for any skimming the *Baron* might have done."

Bobby winked at her.

"We'll keep this to ourselves for now. The momentum of this investigation is based on the *Baron's* murder. No one would be happy to hear our theory unless we have some evidence."

Bobby signaled for the check. Samantha bundled up her shoulder bag. Together they threaded their way through the cafe's tables to the street.

"I think I'll go over to the pharmacy and see what our friend bought. I also want to stop by the Waldorf again and check on that clock," Samantha said in parting.

"I'll call you later at home. Good luck, baby," Bobby said, and disappeared around the corner.

———

"Ya wanna know what I think, Birkwell? I think it stinks. Ya ever been in a war? 'Nam? The Persian Gulf? No, I din' think so. Ya ever serve our country in uniform? The reserves? The *Coast Guard*? Nah, I din' think so either. So ya can't know how much this is gonna mean to him...that some a' *your* guys just talked to his commanding officer. That some a' *your* guys are puttin' him under surveillance."

"Officer Lenihan..."

"That's *Detective* Lenihan to you, *Birkwell*."

Stuart Birkwell looked pained. He wondered if this buffoon in polyester might actually take a swing at him.

"*Detective* Lenihan, it's obvious why we haven't put you in charge of this operation. You have no investigative judgment. Perhaps Ethan Post is an innocent third party, but we have no way of knowing this. To *assume* that he is, simply because he wears a uniform, would be amateur. And I believe none of us on this assignment are amateurs. We damn well better not be."

Lenihan was so hot he could feel his armpits smell. But this piss ant attorney wasn't going to get to him, he vowed. He'd seen worse. Twenty-one years on the job had put him next to the vilest of human scum, and most of them were attorneys like this asshole.

"Okay, Birkwell. Just bring him in soon. Level with him. Do what his Admiral says an' stop wasting our time."

Stuart heaved a sigh. This was what he'd been waiting for. A concession. It was worth the agony of having to deal with the NYPD's under-educated echelon. They always fell into line. Poor toads. Always trying to *do the right thing* as they'd say, and look out for their partners and all that *bullshit*. A couple of minutes with an abrasive prosecutor and they were putty in his hands.

He said, "We'll take care of Ethan Post. Get hold of the Maryland agents. Tell them to step up their efforts. The quicker we clear this guy, the better."

Lenihan smiled triumphantly.

CHAPTER EIGHT

"Hey, Papa, remember me?"

The voice was scratchy through a poor telephone connection, but it was unmistakable.

"Remember you? It's about *fuckin'* time you called me! You think you're so *fuckin'* indispensable you can leave us hanging like this? I was jus' about ready to cut you off."

"Hey Papa, don't do that! I know I've been out of touch. I had ta lay low for a while. But now I got somethin' for you that'll make up for it. Hey-hey. Really Papa, don' cut me off. Ya know I got bills ta pay. My kid's tuition is due in a couple of weeks."

Papa growled.

"Princeton, right? How you figure those Ivy League punks would feel 'bout where that tuition money really comes from? They really think a New York cop can afford fifty g's a year?"

"But I don't have to, Papa. Not with what I got for you. Ya want ta know what I got? Check your books. They've been doctored."

"What the *fuck* ya mean, doctored?" Papa's interest piqued.

"Ten grand, and I'll explain."

"That's bullshit. Nothin' you got is worth ten grand."

"Okay, nine grand then, but that's as low as I go. You'll be buyin' me a gold watch on top of it, jus' to show your gratitude."

"Aw right. So what's this about my books?"

"We got somebody on the inside," he said, lowering his voice. Cradling the receiver, he crossed from behind his desk and swung the door shut on the detective bullpen.

"He lifted your books. Made some copies. Passed 'em on to us. Now we're working to funnel all that money into new accounts. *Our* accounts."

"That would put me out of business. Who's done this to me?" Papa asked quietly.

"Nine grand ain't gonna get you *that* information. Just take a look at where your money is really going."

"Who's done this to me?"

"If I were you I wouldn't worry too much about that. I thought you'd be more interested in the *money*. I wanted to save you some bucks."

"Vuillard has disappeared. Perhaps the one who has done away with him is responsible. Perhaps it is Alexander Post?" Papa asked.

"Hey, yeah, what the hell? Maybe it is. So, how about that nine grand?"

"Check your left-front tire when you get off work tonight. I think it might be going flat."

The phone connection went dead.

He cradled the receiver for a few seconds more, and then replaced it. He hadn't wanted to start Papa on a witch-hunt. People *died* when that happened. But what the hell. The nine grand would be hidden in the wheel well of his cruiser tonight, just in time for the first tuition install-ment. He stretched his arms over the old typewriter on his desk and rested his aching head.

———

Ethan Post drove absentmindedly into his parking slot, aligning the Jaguar's front wheels to the concrete slab labeled *RESERVED* in bright orange letters. He switched off the CD player and removed the keys from the ignition. He admired the sun's reflection against the automobile's rac-ing green paint.

Exiting the car, he stroked the new paint job, feeling for imperfections.

"God, Stan did a good job," he thought, feeling damned pleased with himself. He'd had the Jag in storage in his mom's garage. It had been a spur of the moment purchase during one of his infrequent trips home. He'd been in Germany that year, before his last stint at Riyadh. A classified ad under *classic automobiles* caught his eye.

"For Sale. Jaguar XJ6 convertible sedan. Mint condition. Low Mileage. Needs paint."

Ethan knew a classic Jag with the right amount of care could really be worth something. He had a beat up VW in Germany that got him around, but he'd always dreamed of piloting a classic Jag. Something about the smooth lines was sexy. *Exciting.*

The engine was in really good condition, but the body sure needed paint. The kid selling it had dreams bigger than his bank account. When he gave him cash on the spot, the kid almost jumped for joy. But when Ethan got in and started driving the Jag away, he could have sworn the kid was going to cry. He almost wanted to offer him visiting privileges, or something. Perhaps temporary custody every other weekend.

He'd parked the car at his mother's, planning to get it in shape his next visit. That was five years ago.

Last month Ethan ran into Stan at *The Mooring*, a local pub with a pool table and a jukebox that played endless jazz. It was a comfortable place. Nothing trendy. A good place to ease back into the American pace.

"Jeeses, you haven't changed at all," yelled Stan from across the room. His voice was loud enough that nearly everyone in the bar turned to look. Ethan glanced up from his place at the bar.

"Hey, hero! Are you home to stay this time?"

"You look great, buddy," Ethan said as they embraced. Stan immediately challenged him to pool.

After a few games, Ethan poured out his heart. He told Stan about his quest to get the Jag painted.

"Something tells me you're a perfectionist, my friend."

"Damn straight I am."

"You're going to have to trust somebody, *someday*. Or drive around in a dull gray Jag. Of course, *I* can do it for you," Stan offered, with a wink.

"Yeah, we'll do it *together*. We'll get a six pack, and a couple brushes, and do it ourselves."

"This isn't bullshit. When you were doing your college prep in high school, I was doing auto shop. Remember? And art classes. Well, I finally found a way to kind of *merge* my two talents. But I gotta *love* my subject."

Ethan smiled now, remembering that night. Stan was right. He was a true artist. Ethan gently massaged his masterpiece, the classic racing green paint evenly applied to every inch of sleek surface.

Tossing his keys into the air, Ethan walked toward the classroom building. He jumped over the curb and onto the sidewalk winding toward the pale brick structure. He looked up to the second floor and counted the windows from one end, settling on the one that belonged to his new office.

I can keep an eye on my Jag, he thought as he walked right past the dark blue Ford LTD, not even noticing its two occupants and their unusual attention to his movements.

He mounted the two flights of stairs quickly. Mail was already accumulating outside his office door. Ethan gathered it up before unlocking the old heavily lacquered white door to his office.

He switched on the overhead light, but it added little illumination. The sun's angle through the windows bathed half the room in daylight, but buried the other half in shadow.

Leafing through the mail, he found an envelope addressed to him from the Naval Academy. It was a form letter.

"Dear Commander Post. We are pleased to welcome you to the academy faculty. We look forward to a pleasant and constructive association. Very truly yours, Admiral Roger Massey, President, United States Naval Academy."

"Ol' Massey, huh? This is going to be fun."

Ethan tossed the letter onto his desk.

The next piece was an oversized, express mail envelope striped red, white and blue with a big eagle on the front. Ethan flipped it over. It carried a New York City postmark, but no return address. Ethan opened it with curiosity.

Inside was a piece of thin, onionskin typing paper tightly folded. An old manual typewriter spelled out a message that Ethan read twice and then a third time. Wadding the paper violently, he threw it across the room.

He paced the floor and then retrieved the wad from where it had landed near the bookshelves, opened it again and almost tore the thin paper.

"What the hell is Alex up to? And why warn *me* about it?" Ethan yelled. Walking back to his desk, he savagely punched the numbers to Alex's home into his phone. An answering machine responded.

"Alex, its Ethan. Some of your *friends* just left me a really cute message. At the *academy*! I don't know what the hell you're up to, but I promise you I'm going to find out."

The receiver slammed against its cradle. The onionskin paper sat crumpled on the desk. Ethan read the words again.

———

"What's he doing up there?" Agent McKenzie asked idly, lounging with his coffee cup against the blue Ford's driver's seat.

"Can't really tell. He was just walking back and forth a minute ago. I think he made a phone call. Now I can't see him anymore."

Agent Maxwell leaned against the car's dashboard, squinting through the glass to the building above.

"No trouble following him though. That Jag's pretty easy to spot. No many of *them* on the road," he said.

"Great car. What year do you think it is?"

"Don't know. Must be a new paint job, the way he's babying it. I recorded the plate number," Maxwell added, trying to anticipate the senior agent's next question.

McKenzie eyed the younger man with a mixture of humor and respect. Maxwell was a new, eager agent. A little over anxious, perhaps, but he wanted to do a good job. McKenzie remembered when he'd been the same way. So he didn't mention to Maxwell that he'd already memorized the plate.

The big Ford wasn't his choice in a surveillance automobile, but then, the surveillance aspect of their assignment this morning had been thrust upon them, *after* they'd reported to headquarters the results of the Massey interview.

"Set up on his office. Maybe he'll show up there," they were told.

"If he comes out and leaves, we'll have a hell of a time following him in this thing. He'll spot us for sure," Maxwell said, and looked at McKenzie, awaiting a response to his *wise* observation.

McKenzie smiled again, resisting the urge to say, "I've already thought about that." The kid is on the right track, he thought. Why stifle his eagerness?

"He's not going to be looking. Ethan Post is an innocent guy and innocent people don't watch for surveillance. We just want to make sure he's not some way involved with this. He doesn't have any reason to think he's being followed."

The two agents snapped to attention. Ethan exited the building, almost running to his car. He slowed momentarily to unlock it, making sure the keys didn't brush the paint around the lock. The engine purred. Throwing the car into reverse, he screeched from the parking slot.

McKenzie emptied his coffee out the window onto the concrete, threw the paper cup into the back seat, and turned on the big Ford engine. Maxwell was absolutely right. Anyone surveillance conscious couldn't help but hear that engine roar. A real criminal would be looking in their rear view mirror right about now. But Ethan Post wasn't a criminal, McKenzie remembered. With confidence, he maneuvered the large sedan out of its hiding place and pulled slowly in the direction of the Jag.

———

Ethan's temperature blazed. He removed a CD from the glove box, and pushed it into the stereo console. Ramsey Lewis' jazz piano poured from the speakers, soothing his agitation.

"So, where are you *going*?" he asked himself. Classes didn't start for another two weeks. He *could* focus on Alex. If he did, what should be his next step?

The sinister message had electrified anger deep inside him. His thoughts were a disorganized jumble. Memories of Saturday night and all those strange people surrounding Alex. The yacht itself and how Alex could afford it. And his own glorified fantasy of how he and Alex would finally patch up their differences. Alex was again making it impossible.

Ethan thought back to the night in Saudi when he'd learned he was finally going home. He'd lain awake thinking mostly of Alex. He'd envisioned them sharing beers and shooting pool. Starting over in their relationship.

Their father was dead, and couldn't come between them anymore. There'd be no more conversations at the dinner table directed only to him, as if Ethan was the only important one.

The one who'd followed in his father's footsteps. Who'd gone to the Naval Academy. Who'd been an outstanding football player. Who'd flown airplanes. Ethan was the perfect one. Alex was inconsequential.

Ethan remembered back to a time they were both in college. Alex had gone hunting and shot a three-point buck. He must have paid the taxidermist handsomely to get the rack mounted in time for Christmas. Alex had presented it to their father as a gift at Christmas dinner. He'd orchestrated it with Mom to coincide with the unveiling of the meal. Not turkey this year, but venison steaks. Mom had been pretty excited about the plan for Alex's sake but had been apprehensive about cooking the wild game.

The meal hadn't turned out well. The steaks hadn't marinated long enough, and tasted strong and gamy. Their father had accused Alex of ruining a special occasion, and walked away from the dinner table, announcing that he and Ethan were going into the library to discuss the Naval Academy.

Ethan always wanted to apologize to Alex for *that*, but Alex never gave him a chance. That night in Saudi, Ethan truly believed he and Alex could finally make amends. They could be brothers again.

But *now*?

Ethan headed back to the house. The anger abated and he started to regret the message left on Alex's machine. He'd sounded almost *violent*, spitting the words into the telephone. Maybe he should amend that message.

Pulling into the driveway, he didn't notice the blue Ford that drove past the house, and slowed at the end of the cul de sac.

Ethan poured a cool glass of water from the kitchen faucet, and walked into the library. He relaxed into his father's desk chair, and gathered his thoughts before lifting the receiver of the desk phone. Slowly he punched in area code two-one-two, and the seven digits. After three rings, the call connected. A momentary whirring sound indicated he'd once again reached the answering machine.

The recorded message came on. At the tone, Ethan took a deep breath.

"Alex, it's Ethan again. Listen, I'm sorry about the way I sounded earlier. I guess I was upset. I'm back at the house now. I really want to talk to you - about a lot of things. When you're alone and have some time, please call me back."

Ethan started to replace the receiver. He heard a *click*, then Alex's voice on the other end.

"Ethan, it's me. Are you still there?"

"Yeah, Alex. I'm still here. Did you get my first message?"

Alex's voice was tentative, almost nervous.

"I got it. I don't know what you're talking about. I wasn't sure I wanted to talk to you. That was why I let the machine run just now."

Ethan thought he detected fear in his brother's voice. He was torn between his previous anger and an overriding desire to understand Alex and calm the waters between them.

"Hey, maybe I overreacted. I wasn't expecting to find something like that in my office mail. It really wasn't all that threatening, I guess."

"What did it *say*?"

"Something like, if you know what's good for you, you'll stay away from your brother. That was about it."

"Don't give me bullshit, Ethan. *Read* it to me! I want to know *exactly* what it said!"

Reluctantly, Ethan removed the crumpled paper from his pocket.

"It says, save yourself and your career. Your brother is going down soon. That's it. Listen, Alex, I know you don't trust me to help you, but maybe you should. I have this bad feeling you may be mixed up in something you shouldn't."

"But that was *all* it said? So why did you immediately think I was up to something? You *immediately* thought I was doing something *wrong*, and that you were going to straighten me out. I think you took a leap of the facts this time, little brother. I'm sorry you got a note, and I'm sorry you just assumed it meant something threatening. Anybody could have written that note, Ethan. *Anybody*."

Alex's voice became loud through the receiver.

"You keep telling me you think I'm mixed up in something. Well, I'm *not*. And I don't need your help."

Ethan expected Alex to slam down the telephone. He didn't. The line remained open. Ethan could hear Alex's thin breathing through the phone line. He was sure Alex heard his, too. They sat like that for a few moments.

"Alex, I'm not like Dad. I don't know how to make you understand. I know he treated you like *shit*. God, I watched him do it for so many years. If you weren't a football jock, or flew an airplane, you weren't *anything* in his eyes. I know that. But I'm not like him. I don't know if you'll ever believe that."

Ethan waited for a response.

"Yeah, well," Alex began, and then stopped. Moments passed again. Ethan could hear Alex drumming his fingers against a table. He always did that, Ethan recalled.

"I guess I just want a chance to talk to you, when you're not angry. When you'll *listen*. Can I come up to New York? I could leave this afternoon. We could have dinner somewhere in Manhattan tonight. I haven't been there for a while."

"No! You shouldn't come *here*. I was thinking I'd come down to Annapolis Friday night. I've got to head back to New York Saturday because I have a big meeting scheduled for Saturday night. But maybe I'll try to come down early Friday and we can talk. Maybe there *is* something you can help me with. I've got to think about it, first, though. And Ethan, don't worry about that message. I'm sure it's nothing to get excited about."

Ethan slowly replaced the receiver. He stared at the telephone, thinking that maybe he'd gotten through to Alex. He wasn't concerned about the note. Ethan could take care of himself. But he doubted Alex could.

———

Outside and down the block, a small brown Chevrolet drove quietly to a stop next to the blue Ford.

"You've come to relieve us?" McKenzie asked. The Chevy's driver nodded.

"We're only going to stay until seven tonight. We're the only unit on him. I guess this guy isn't too important."

McKenzie nodded and shifted the big LTD into drive.

CHAPTER NINE

The tram taking tourists to the top of Victoria Peak was bathed in white hazy clouds this morning. The old man watched the clouds through his dirty apartment window lazily traverse the green peak, almost obscuring it. It may rain today, and that would be good because it will bring luck, he thought. And tomorrow that luck would be useful at the Happy Valley Racetrack.

He dreamed of this good luck, this *joss* as the Chinese knew it, as he dressed in a faded madras shirt and worn beige pants. The cuffs of the pants were frayed from where they touched the ground when he walked. He wedged his thin, long feet into brown sandals and adjusted his thick, black spectacles.

Outside the tall, rickety apartment building decorated with strings of laundry like so many brightly colored flags, the old man began his daily three-mile walk along Bowen Road overlooking Hong Kong Island, then down the great hill to the banking district.

As always, he passed groups of old Chinese practicing *Tai Ji Quan*, the ancient exercise, and European expatriates walking their domesticated animals. He walked briskly, thriving on this physical activity, keeping his body supple and vigorous.

At the entrance to the great building he paused. He noticed, seemingly for the first time, the flurry of activity that surrounded him. The taxicabs, the businessmen in fine suits, the women turned out in bright silk garments. To them he was invisible.

He entered through the large doors and approached the framed teller cages. Within minutes he had transacted his usual business. A withdrawal of $9,000, converted to traveler checks. As usual, no one noticed the small, frail looking Chinese man.

Next door to the great bank was another bank. And next door to that bank, another bank. And across the street yet another, and adjacent to it, another. He entered each one, his mind absent; his feet leading him through the repetitive steps learned from three years of routine.

To each teller he presented a deposit slip for $2,000. To the account of Wong Tai Chen at one bank. Long Kwok at another. Chung Hsiang-Tzu at another. Nung Wu received the last $2,000 deposit, and as was customary, he kept the final $1,000.

Each account carried a private number, a special authorization number that he didn't know, but that he knew he would be given very shortly. His friend Vincent would finally tell him. He must remember to telephone him as soon as he returned home.

There were five banks needed to complete each cycle, and each day he must move five cycles. Where else but in Hong Kong were there that many banks? Why not consolidate these actions, he had asked Vincent one day. Group them all at one bank? It was then that he learned about international funds movement and how banks track cash transactions over ten thousand dollars. His regular and repetitive transactions of nine thousand dollars fell below this monitoring threshold and the money was then free to move unobserved. It was during this conversation that Vincent had told him that he was a *smurf*. A funny word indeed. Listening to it in his head still made him smile.

That he was *this* close to his final assignment was also good joss, for it would mean the end of his daily routine. He could collect what remained of his fortune after losses at the racetrack, and there had been *many* losses these past three years, and retire. Perhaps he would buy a Rolls Royce like so many of the rich drove on Hong Kong Island. Or take a trip to California to see Disneyland.

The little man smiled contentedly at the thought, and began his climb back up the peak.

———

Vincent Vuillard tried not to act nervous, however he noted with consternation that he had checked his watch at least five times in as many minutes. The lobby of the China Regent was becoming noisy with mid-day traffic, and Vuillard wasn't sure he could usurp the hotel telephone much longer. Just as an elderly woman passed him for the third time, eying the inactive phone, it rang.

"Hai. Yes. It is done," said a quiet voice.

Vuillard smiled, and replaced the receiver. The final deposit had been made. Little could go wrong now, he realized. It was time to put the rest of his plans in action. He lifted the receiver and gave the hotel operator a local number.

"Victoria Harbor," a frail female voice answered.

"This is Monsieur Vincent, of Zud, Switzerland. I am calling about my shipment."

"Ah, yes, Mr. Vincent. It is arriving this afternoon."

"That is just wonderful. I wish to make arrangements for the second leg of its journey. To my home in Zud. I will be returning there within the next few days."

"But it has just come from New York, Master Vincent. Surely there was a more economical route than through Hong Kong."

The voice tried to mask its prying with sweetness. Vuillard was not fooled.

"I wish it to see the world as I have, Madame. I will be at your dock this afternoon."

With that, Vuillard pressed the disconnect lever. Waiting momentarily, he released it and requested an overseas operator. The number connected.

"It's the fuckin' middle of the night. You're supposed to be waitin' until I get up..."

"Your profanity is overused and inappropriate. I will call you at any time I please. That has always been the nature of our relationship. You exist in our little business equation because I *choose* to allow it. Now, please tell what was so urgent you left a message for me, in my name, at the hotel."

"*Papa* knows his books have been changed. They didn't fall for the ones you substituted. They're gonna start lookin' for the money soon."

Vuillard gasped. This was not possible. No one in the organization could be that smart.

"But, you must *fix* this. Your financial share in this event is dependent on my successful escape to Switzerland."

"Hey, listen. I'll do what I can. They think you've been *done away with*. I think I can encourage this line of reasoning, but it'll cost you a lot more."

"Is this just another of your attempts to extort more money? Haven't I already met your son's tuition needs?"

"Aw, ya got me all wrong. I was just looking out for your interests. I came upon this important piece of information and I had to give you a head's up. Besides, they think Alex Post is the one responsible for liftin' the books, not you."

Vuillard shook.

"Exposing Alexander to the wrath of this organization was never my intention. They are brutal. *Papa* will stop at nothing if he believes Alexander is behind the disappearance of any of his money."

"Hey, better *him* than *you*, don' ya think, Vinnie? Ol' Alex never endeared himself to *Papa*, anyway. It's his fault they suspect him."

Vuillard listened hungrily to this rationale. It wouldn't be *his* fault if Alexander were suspected of siphoning the cartel's funds. And on further thought, it would make things that much easier. While *Papa* and his band of thugs spent their time hounding Post, he would have more time to disappear. Actually, it wasn't such a bad turn of events after all.

———

The midday sun poured into Samantha's apartment through the big windows, baking her furniture. A blast of hot, stuffy air greeted her as she returned from the morning's investigation. Her chintz couch upholstery was fading before her eyes.

She turned the air conditioner on *high*, and peeled off her T-shirt and jeans. Walking around in her underwear, she felt a sense of freedom. She still needed to go to the Waldorf this afternoon, but that would require a change of clothes. It had already been three hours since her breakfast meeting with Bobby, and she wasn't yet hungry for lunch. Samantha checked her telephone voice mail. Nothing.

From her shoulder bag, she extracted the notes she'd made after the visit to the pharmacy. They'd been written hurriedly, with the notepaper propped against a mailbox down the street from the drugstore. She hadn't wanted the pharmacist to see her taking notes and be suspicious of her motive, after she'd given him such a convincing cover story about why she was trying to reconstruct the purchases on the *Baron's* receipt.

Trying to read her scribbles now, Samantha had to laugh. Her pen had lost ink in a few places because of the upward angle she'd had to write.

"I'm sure the pharmacist could have cared less why I was there," Samantha thought now.

She'd told the pharmacist she was keeping records for her taxes, and wasn't sure why she had saved this particular receipt. Perhaps she had purchased something that was tax deductible. Could he possibly check the inventory codes to see what she had bought?

The pharmacist was happy to do so. When he returned, he looked a little perplexed.

"Miss, our inventory shows you purchased six packages of wide sterile gauze, two rolls of wide adhesive tape and an antiseptic ointment. Are you a nurse by any chance?"

"No," Samantha said.

"Then I think you'll probably have some trouble deducting these purchases. Unless you were preparing for a war, or something."

Samantha figured she shouldn't look too surprised, or he'd suspect she hadn't made that purchase at all.

Looking back now, she realized the subterfuge probably wasn't necessary at the pharmacy. But it would be necessary at the Waldorf. She would have to ask some explicit questions there, about people who had visited the *Baron* and who would have moved his grandfather clock. They would want to know why she needed the information. Lying down on the couch, she concentrated on what she might say.

"I'm dying to call Bobby," she said aloud. He'd want to know about the bandages. Why would the *Baron* buy so much? Samantha had an idea about that.

"I'm wondering if Bobby will think it's too farfetched," she mused. He wasn't expected to call her for a couple of hours. She had his cell number, but decided to wait.

She wrapped her legs over the sofa's wide arm, feeling the cool material against her bare skin. Her mind wandered. She envisioned Ethan Post walking into the apartment, and finding her nearly naked. He strolled in unannounced like his appearance in the *Baron*'s bathroom, only this time Ethan was dressed in running shorts and a tank top. Samantha laughed. This was all getting out of hand.

A splash of cool water from the kitchen faucet and reality returned. Samantha cradled the telephone and dialed Bobby's cell phone.

CHAPTER TEN

"Anywhere in particular you want to go, lady?"

Samantha glanced sideways at her new chauffeur. "Let's go to the Waldorf," she said.

Bobby drove the surveillance car onto the street and headed uptown. Traffic was starting to grow heavier. Samantha glanced at her watch. It was almost three.

"You haven't asked me what I found at the pharmacy. I don't know whether to be excited about it or not. The *Baron's* purchase was really strange, but it might fit our theory."

Bobby turned to her from behind the wheel.

"So what did he buy?"

"Six rolls of wide gauze bandage and adhesive tape, and an antiseptic ointment. Now either he's stocking up, or he needed to dress a wound."

"Like a gunshot wound?"

"Well, that was what I was thinking. But I wasn't sure if it was possible to shoot yourself somewhere in the body, and fix it up yourself. Some place where it wouldn't hurt all that much, where it wouldn't touch any important organ or bone tissue. Is there such a place where you can shoot yourself like that? And would a normal person actually do something like that?"

Bobby thought for a few minutes.

"It's pretty farfetched, but it fits the evidence we've uncovered so far. You know what I'd like to do? I'd like to talk to Stuart. He was one of the first people to sit down with the *Baron* when he turned himself in and struck his deal with the government. I'd like to find out how the *Baron* acted. Was he scared? Was he calm?"

Samantha interjected. "Could he have done what we're now thinking he might have? Could he have set us all up to think he's dead? To have the government think he's dead. To have the *De Yambi* Cartel think he's dead. And he gets away with his life, his grandfather clock, and a bandaged hand or foot or shoulder or something."

Bobby snorted. "*Or something* is right. I think the *Baron* traded his sore foot for maybe eight million in cash he's been skimmin' off the books!"

Samantha caught her breath.

"You found something? In the books?"

"Don't know yet. I spent three hours poring over them with the task force weenies. They asked me a bunch of questions, like why I was so interested. But I finally convinced them to look for money going out regularly that the *Baron* hadn't explained."

Bobby was working his way uptown along the East River drive as he spoke. Traffic was stop and go.

"Seems the *Baron* was pretty thorough with the government. Explained all the big dollar transactions. Everything except for a little bitty amount going weekly to some foreign consultant in Hong Kong. He never explained that. Never even brought it to anyone's attention. Wasn't a big amount, but over the years, and with interest, it amounts to about eight mil. My guess is that at the end of this money, we might find our buddy."

"You didn't tell the accountants why you wanted to know this information, about the possible skimming?" she asked.

"God no, not yet. First off, as I said before, I don't want to look like an ass if we're wrong. Secondly, if we're right, I want to make sure I can back it up. Stuart will want some heavy proof. Then, I want to make sure you and I get credit for our fine investigative work, *partner*."

Bobby turned to her and winked.

Samantha smiled. *Partner.* She liked the sound of that.

———

Finding a place to park Bobby's undercover car was impossible at this hour. Yellow cabs rushed along the two regular lanes of Park Avenue, and occasionally formed a third lane where one would swear they couldn't find the room.

Nonetheless, Bobby slowed to a stop in front of the Waldorf Astoria's main entrance, cutting off one overly aggressive cabbie. A loud, sustained honk sounded his displeasure. Bobby raised his hand and Samantha thought he meant to flip the cabbie off, but instead Bobby just flashed a wide smile and waved.

"You drive 'em nuts when you're nice," he commented as he shifted the car into park and glanced at Samantha.

"Do you know what you'll ask?"

Samantha nodded.

"I've been practicing for this all afternoon. I need to find out two things. Did the *Baron* have any furniture or items moved from his apartment during the recent past? And if he did, what was the company that did it for him?"

"Maybe you'll get some answers. You don't look threatening. Just smile pretty and show him that great tan of yours. Can you unbutton a couple more buttons on that shirt? Show a little cleavage?"

"Bobby, please."

"Just trying to insure your success. Go do your thing, baby. I'll wait out here. Good luck," Bobby said.

Samantha jumped from the vehicle and crossed the sidewalk to the massive revolving brass door. She heaved her body weight against the frame and it swung her around into the lower lobby. Ascending the red-carpeted stairs, she headed toward the reception area.

Taking a deep, calming breath, Samantha advanced to the Concierge desk. A pert, young woman dressed in a trim black suit greeted her.

"May I help you, Madame?"

"I don't know. I'm on a mission for a friend of mine who lives in the towers. Vincent Vuillard. He lives on the thirty-seventh floor?" Samantha hoped she looked confused. She continued.

"Mr. Vuillard is gone for a couple of weeks, and I'm watching his apartment for him. He'd told me he wanted to move some furniture out while he was gone. A large grandfather clock, actually."

The woman simply stared blankly. The explanation sounded too long.

"I guess I just want to make sure it was done safely." Samantha stopped there. *Let's see what she says to this.*

"Oh, I'm not the person you should talk to. It would be Stephen Majors. He handles those things for our apartment guests."

"Where might I find him?"

"Stephen is on the desk here from seven each morning until three. I'm sorry but you just missed him. Perhaps I can take your name and telephone number, and he can call you tomorrow morning."

"No thanks. I'll just stop back tomorrow. You're *certain* he'll be here?"

The woman nodded, and answered the telephone jangling on the desk.

Bobby lounged against the huge octagon clock in the middle of the lobby, watching her. She sidled over.

"You found a parking place?"

"Not really. That's the beauty of being a New York City detective. *Any* stretch of concrete can be a parking place. You're only limited by your imagination."

"Maybe *I* should be a detective," she said.

"This week you *are*, sweet cheeks. Where are we going now?"

"Oh, I guess home. The guy I need to speak with won't be in until morning. We'll just have to wait."

The Waldorf's revolving door spit them onto the street. She caught her reflection in the glass as it spun by. Bobby's words echoed. *Maybe I even look like a detective*, she thought, enjoying the image.

CHAPTER ELEVEN

She didn't recognize the man's voice at first. It sounded familiar but her caffeine-starved brain couldn't piece it together. Besides, who'd be calling her this early in the morning, anyway?

"Hey, Jeannie, it's me. *Ethan*."

"Ethan?" she asked groggily.

"Jeannie, wake up. It's not *that* early. I already ran four miles, had breakfast, and did some work. Don't you have kids to feed?"

Ethan heard an audible gasp through the receiver.

"Jesus Christ! *Ethan*! Where are you? Are you *here*? God, you sound so close, you must be here! How long have you been here? Why haven't you called me before this? I can't believe it! It's so good to hear your voice."

Ethan smiled, holding the receiver away from his ear. Jeannie's voice pierced the silence of his mother's kitchen.

"So, how are the kids? Or did you give them away by now. You always threatened to do that."

"Oh, the kids. Ya, right. They're off to school. They get me up at six for breakfast then once they're off I sack out for a while. So tell me, are you here on a break, or are you going to stay this time? You always threatened to!"

"Yeah, well I'm making good on *that* threat. I've been back a couple of weeks. I've been doing so many things that I haven't had time to call. But you've been on my mind."

"You were never one to keep in touch with the ladies in your life. I guess I can forgive you. So how about that sexy body of yours? You haven't broken any important pieces with all your super sexy adventures, have you?" Jeannie asked.

"No, I returned completely intact. I have to admit, I began to think I was pressing my luck after fifteen years. I've grounded myself for a while. I'm teaching at the academy this semester."

"A *teacher*. Now, that would have been my perfect fantasy as a college student. To have a professor like you to stare at? I'd probably flunk the course."

Ethan laughed.

"I think I could have handled that. As long as you didn't blow me any kisses. Then I'd have to jump over my desk and come after *you*. I never could resist you, Jeannie. So how come you ended up with my brother?"

It was Jeannie's turn to laugh.

"*Ended up* is the correct term, all right. We officially *ended up* eighteen months ago. I guess you heard about that."

Ethan knew.

"So, how *are* the kids?"

"Well, Alexandra is twelve, and Steph is almost nine. They're such big girls now and they've taken the divorce pretty well."

Ethan sighed.

"Do they see their dad much?"

"*Ohhh*, now that's a long story. Are you at your parent's house? We're still close by. Why don't you stop by this afternoon? I'll make 'ritas and we can get smashed. Maybe I'll tell you all about it. How about three o'clock? The girls will be getting back from day camp. You can see them, too. "

Ethan agreed, and replaced the telephone. He smiled, realizing how much he was looking forward to seeing her. Alex's girlfriends had never much interested him. But Jeannie was different. Their father's attitude toward him had turned Alex into a competitive, driven man. With women, Alex was always domineering. But Jeannie was able to stand up to him. Ethan figured marrying her was the best decision Alex had ever made.

———

Driving to Jeannie's house was painfully nostalgic. I guess I convinced myself she and Alex were really happy, Ethan thought. It had been comforting those lonely nights in Saudi, to think that his brother had a good life with two beautiful daughters.

Ethan had thought their break up was sudden. After witnessing the changes in his brother firsthand, he wasn't all that sure.

The house she and Alex had shared loomed ahead of Ethan now. It was a split-level on an attractive side street in Arlington just over the river from Washington, DC.

He rang the doorbell. The front door hung open, allowing Ethan to peer in through the screen. A console TV at the end of the room was playing some sitcom. A young girl with long blond hair ran to the door. She looked up at him with wide eyes. Then she turned and darted into the house and out of sight.

Momentarily, Jeannie came to the door. She was short, and a little stocky, but still had the fresh washed looks of a high school cheerleader. She squealed when she saw him, threw open the screen door, and lunged.

"*Chrrist!* This is so great! I'm so happy to see you!"

Ethan peeled her arms from around his neck and surveyed his ex-sister in law.

"Jeannie, you really look great. Honestly."

She was wearing white Capri's and a pink T-shirt. Ethan assumed she wasn't starving for male company in Alex's absence.

"Come on in. I've made margaritas. *Frozen* ones," she added with a wink.

Ethan followed her into the house, threading his way around the incidental toys and books.

"Oh, don't mind those. Just give 'em a kick. Girls, come on out and say *Hi* to your Uncle Ethan!"

Ethan noticed his two nieces hiding behind the door. They stared at him with a mixture of excitement and awe. He lowered himself to one knee. They hesitated; then ran at top speed into his out-stretched arms. Bundling them together, he picked them up. Their arms clung to his neck and chest. Ethan buried his face in their hair.

"Boy, you two have sure grown. Jeannie, these two must be a real handful!"

He laughed, and lowered them slowly to the ground. They gave him one last look, and ran out of the kitchen. Ethan watched them depart. Jeannie had poured the frozen margarita into a glass and pushed it into his hand. Ethan took a sip. His lips puckered at the taste of lime and tequila.

"Thanks, I needed that," he said, and took a seat at the kitchen table. Jeannie poured her own, and took a long, cool drink. She seated herself opposite him.

Ethan caught her up on his past month, and his assignment at the academy. Jeannie admired his Jaguar, so he told her the long story surrounding its paint job. Jeannie made another blender of margaritas.

"You must be wondering about Alex. I know you've probably noticed something different about him since you've been back," Jeannie said as she deposited another drink into Ethan's outstretched hand.

He didn't know how honest to be. He hesitated.

"Don't try to protect my feelings, Ethan. I've watched Alex change these past five years after he took that job in New York City. It was tough having him gone three days out of each week. Then three days became weeks at a time and he started to change. He started having all this extra money. I knew he couldn't get it from his job at the bank. That is, unless he was *stealing* it. I always thought you could straighten him out when you got back home. I didn't know then and I don't know now what he's up to. He started tuning us all out a long time ago. I finally couldn't take it anymore, so I asked for a divorce. I thought maybe it would shake him up."

Her expression saddened, and she looked out the window, not meeting his gaze.

"But it didn't work. He must have thought it was a *good* idea."

Her voice drifted off. She swirled her drink.

"Did Alex ever mention anyone he was working with? Anyone that seemed like they didn't belong to his group at the bank?" Ethan asked.

Jeannie thought for a moment.

"At first he introduced me to some people. But then he stopped taking me with him when he went out," she said. "I did meet a very interesting guy at the beginning. He was European. Very dignified. I thought perhaps he might be gay."

"Do you remember his name?"

"You know, maybe I *do*. I liked him, so I remembered him while the others are only a blur. His first name was Vincent. He pronounced it with a French accent. Alexandra heard it, and it became her favorite word for an eternity. *Vin-sohn.* He may have given me his card. I think I still have it."

Jeannie stood up and walked into the bedroom. Ethan heard her closet door open and close. She returned carrying a cigar box.

"If it's anywhere, it'll be in here. I don't really know if he's involved with Alex now. Alex talked about him a lot at first, but hasn't mentioned him recently. As if we've even talked much for the past year or two. After he bought that yacht and his big house. Oh, *here* it is."

Jeannie handed Ethan a small white calling card.

"Vincent was very nice. I'd be surprised if he were involved with anything illegal."

Ethan read the finely scripted name. *Vincent Vuillard. Suite 3704, Waldorf Astoria Hotel.* Ethan placed the card in his wallet and rose to leave. He smiled reassuringly at Jeannie.

"I'll see what I can find out," he said.

It was after five o'clock; too late to drive to New York and drop in on Alex. Besides the margaritas had left him buzzed. He'd drive to New York City tomorrow. Thursday morning. He'd drop in on Alex and this guy, Vuillard.

The Jaguar's engine purred as Ethan backed from the driveway. Alexandra and Steph waved from the front porch as the Jag disappeared from sight.

CHAPTER TWELVE

Pump. Pump. Pump. Pump.

Samantha's arms propelled her body forward, willing her legs to follow. She could swear her running shorts were made of cement. Effort contorted her brow into deep furrows, giving her a headache. One mile down, two to go.

This is normally so easy, she thought with disgust. She tried coaching herself, but it was no use. Surrendering to the earth's gravitational pull, she allowed her legs to stop their motion. She turned around and walked slowly back home.

Thursday morning had dawned peacefully enough over the Hudson River. Red light shining through thin layers of clouds disappeared when the sun found its place on the horizon. A faint yellow-pink glow was now all that remained of the beautiful sunrise.

Samantha willed herself to enjoy the early morning, but the short mile course had failed to exorcise the sleepiness from her brain.

She dragged herself up her apartment stairs, clinging to the railing for strength. "How the hell did I get in such a foul mood?" she wondered, as she flung herself face down on the bed.

Her kitchen table was still covered with papers from last night. A half-sketched science lesson plan and some software specifications for teaching remedial math.

She'd called it quits at midnight, promising to be superwoman today and get it all done. She wasn't off to a good start.

With energy gained from her moment of self-pity, Samantha pulled herself up from the bed. In the bathroom, she shook off her running shoes and turned on the shower. Once the stream of water reached an acceptable temperature, which was a long time in the old building, Samantha climbed in, running clothes and all.

The soggy T-shirt clung to her like a warm, comforting hug.

———

The sunrise over Chesapeake Bay bathed the waterside park in soft pink and yellow light. The water rolled in a gentle rhythm, emulating Ethan's movements. Sweet, late summer smells of grass and flowers greeted each unlabored breath. It was a five-mile run to the park and back, and he was on the return leg.

His mind had wandered since the first mile, rehashing the plans for today. Drive to New York, check in on Alex; then a little investigative adventure to find this Vincent Vuillard at the Waldorf Astoria Hotel and back home again.

Ethan finished the quarter mile back home at a sprint. Inside, he poured himself a large glass of orange juice. Invigorated, he showered and dressed.

The drive to the city would take almost four hours. The Jag could make it in two and a half, he figured, but the speed limits and tolls along the way would slow him down.

It was nearly eight o'clock when Ethan climbed into the Jag to begin the trip.

———

Samantha's soggy running clothes sat in a seeping pile at the end of her bathtub. She didn't have the strength to wring them out and hang them to dry. She'd get to that later.

Her closet looked like an unfamiliar jumble of mismatched garments. Her mood suggested she select something black and dull, but it was probably going to be a warm day.

She would need to make it to the Waldorf sometime before three to make sure she caught Stephen Majors. But beforehand, Tisha Adams was expecting her up in Washington Heights. Tisha had asked for a special meeting to discuss curriculum.

Samantha could get away with shorts for her meeting with Tisha, but she'd need to wear something sexy to the Waldorf if she hoped to con the concierge into giving her information on the *Baron*. Her eyes settled on a short blue sarong and sleeveless chemise top. She could wear the skirt with flats and a white T-shirt for the subway trip uptown. After her meeting with Tisha, she could substitute the T-shirt for the chemise. Perfect.

The outfit looked good in the mirror and improved her mood, but her eyes looked saggy from too little sleep. Reluctantly, Samantha dug foundation from her makeup drawer where she'd retired it for the summer and applied it sparingly to the corners of each lid. That was better. She brushed on extra mascara and blush and then put all three items into her shoulder bag, knowing the look would probably fade by midday.

A bowl of *Wheaties* and half a grapefruit sufficed for breakfast. She made coffee. It was already after nine o'clock when she bolted the door to her apartment.

A tall, handsome man in a business suit passed her as she crossed to the subway entrance. His eye caught hers briefly. Samantha felt the warmth of his admiring glance. This might be a good day after all, she thought.

———

Ethan paid the toll off the New Jersey Turnpike and joined the long, disorganized line of cars awaiting entrance to the Holland Tunnel for the two-mile trip under the Hudson River. He checked his watch. It was eleven-thirty. It had been years since he'd visited Manhattan but he felt he could still find Alex's office without much difficulty.

Passing Barclay Street, he saw the modern building looming to his left. He dropped the Jag at the closest parking lot and jogged the two blocks to the offices of Federated First Financial Group.

He'd visited Alex five years ago when his brother's office was nothing more than a cubicle hidden within a prefab labyrinth. Alex had just taken the job after over a decade in DC working for the international monetary fund. Now his office occupied the southeast corner of the twentieth floor. A young male office assistant met him. A large oak door bore a brass nameplate, *Alexander Post, Senior Vice President*.

"Wow, from staff accountant to *S-V-P* in just four years! I should be working for you guys," Ethan joked. The assistant glared.

"If *you* can attract important clients and millions to the bank like Mr. Post, I suppose you *should* work here. Can I help you?" he asked, tightly.

"Would you tell Mr. Post his brother is here?"

"Mr. Post is with someone right now. Would you like a seat?"

Ethan sat on the corner of an overstuffed leather couch and checked his watch. Almost noon. He watched the office assistant remove a small brown paper lunch bag from his desk drawer, and saunter off down the hall without a glance in his direction. Quietly, Ethan rose from the sofa and approached the oak door. Raised voices could be heard from inside.

Suddenly the door burst open. Ethan took three steps back just in time to avoid being run down. That pock marked thug from the boat yelled some obscenities over his shoulder as he stormed to the elevator.

I should have broken his arm when I had the chance, Ethan thought. He heard Alex in the office stomping around and for a moment Ethan thought Alex would pursue that Julio character. But he didn't. Instead he slammed the office door. Ethan thought for a moment and took off after Julio.

———

The hot, smelly subway nearly wilted Samantha's upbeat attitude, not to mention her outfit. Walking toward the Waldorf, the noontime sun beat hot.

Samantha smiled to the uniformed doorman at the Park Avenue entrance and pushed hard against the heavy brass revolving door. Air-conditioning greeted her with a surprising rush.

Samantha frowned as she approached the concierge desk. The woman from yesterday was still there. She checked her watch. It was twelve-thirty. What if she'd missed Stephen Majors again?

Tourists and business people milled about the hotel's reception area. A long line formed at the check-out desk. Samantha moved past these people and walked intently to the concierge desk.

"Excuse me. I'm looking for Stephen Majors."

The woman looked up brightly.

"Oh, yes. You were here yesterday. Stephen is having his lunch. He should return any moment."

Samantha breathed a sigh of relief. She wandered about the reception area. In the center of the room stood the huge octagonal clock. She studied its intricate brass and marble details for a moment and then wandered in the direction of the Peacock Alley lounge. It seemed like ages ago that she and Dan had met there. She hadn't even spoken with him since.

A tall slender man in a navy blue crested blazer approached the concierge desk. Samantha drew in her breath, and walked provocatively to the counter.

Stephen Majors was very tall. He moved gracefully. His thin, manicured mustache moved briskly when he spoke.

"Well, madam, what can I do for you?" he asked, barely noticing her appearance. Nuts, she thought. Seduction won't influence information from this guy. She shifted gears.

"I'm a friend of one of your tower guests, Vincent Vuillard. My name is Sammy Wilde."

"Ah, yes. Mr. Vuillard." Stephen Majors said the name with affection. Perhaps they knew each other more than casually.

"We haven't seen Mr. Vuillard around for quite a while. I assume he is on one of his regular trips to Europe?"

"Sure. In fact, that's why I'm here," Samantha said. "Mr. Vuillard asked me to look in on things for him while he was gone, and I have a question."

Stephen Majors regarded her coldly.

"Mr. Vuillard has been a resident here for many years. I don't believe I've seen *you* here before. However I was told a young lady visited him earlier this week. I suppose that was *you*?"

Samantha removed the keys Bobby had given her from her bag and jangled them in front of Stephen Majors. She smiled with a confidence she didn't feel.

"Yes. I *was* here earlier this week. I have Mr. Vuillard's keys."

Majors looked skeptical. Maybe the *Baron* had never given his keys to anyone before. No, that couldn't be it. Dan having keys hadn't raised concern earlier. Maybe he's just jealous, Samantha thought. She envisioned

Stephen Majors being miffed that the *Baron* had entrusted her with the protection of his apartment.

"All right. How might I be of service?" Majors asked.

"Mr. Vuillard had his grandfather clock removed a while ago. He was concerned that it had been taken care of professionally, but he didn't know the moving company. He thought perhaps you might know."

The cover story sounded rehearsed and a little wooden in delivery but Samantha smiled sweetly, hoping Majors hadn't noticed.

Stephen Majors moved to the far end of the desk and extracted a large register from a drawer. He displayed it in front of her and began leafing through the pages.

"Do you recall the date it was moved, or the general time frame?"

Samantha's mind raced. Now, what had the maid told her?

She smiled again.

"I'm really not sure. Would it be way too much trouble to check this past month?"

Major's expression indicated it probably would be too much trouble but he leafed back over the pages anyway. After some time, he emitted a nasally grunt.

"I think I've found it. The Steinman and Sons Moving Company were here for a pick up on August fourth. They reported to the thirty-seventh floor. That would probably be Vincent's apartment."

"Do you have a telephone number or an address for Steinman and Sons?" Samantha asked with anticipation. Majors withdrew a yellow notepad from the desk, and jotted the phone number and address. He gave it to Samantha.

"Thanks."

"Will you be going up to his apartment now?" Majors asked.

Samantha hadn't really thought about it. It could be a good place to telephone the moving company and ask a few questions. Like when and to where they had moved the clock?

"Yes, I think so. And thank you very much for your time. I'll tell Mr. Vuillard how helpful you were."

The last comment was an ad-lib, but it was obviously the right thing to say. Stephen Majors' beamed.

"Do give Vincent my best."

Samantha entered the hallway toward the Apartment Towers. She smiled at the elevator man as they rode up to the thirty-seventh floor. The abandoned stillness in the *Baron's* apartment hit her again as she entered. Heaving her belongings onto the living room sofa, she withdrew a Diet Coke from the apartment's mini-bar.

———

Stephen Majors busied himself at the Concierge desk, organizing tourism brochures into separate piles. He didn't immediately notice the man standing before him until Ethan Post cleared his throat.

"Yes sir, what I can I do for you?" Majors asked with an efficient enthusiasm.

CHAPTER THIRTEEN

The wiry man behind the Waldorf's concierge desk looked gawky and prim, reminding Ethan of an ostrich. He rolled the business card Jeannie had given him around in his palm, eyeing the name one more time.

"I'm trying to find someone who may be a resident of this Hotel. Vincent Vuillard." Stephen Majors raised an eyebrow. He studied Ethan noting the strong build barely camouflaged beneath the deep green button down shirt and khaki slacks. The scrutiny made Ethan uncomfortable. He shifted his weight and began again.

"I've been referred to Mr. Vuillard by a business associate. Do you know where I might find him?"

Majors sniffed. "Mr. Vuillard is indeed popular today."

"Then he *does* live here?"

"Yes. He's been a resident of our apartment towers for years. But I can tell you he's not there now. He's in Europe."

Majors could tell Ethan was disappointed and his manner changed.

"You're an associate of Mr. Vuillard's?"

"As a matter of fact, I'm a *close* associate of Mr. Vuillard's. I hadn't known he was off to Europe. When do you expect him back?"

Stephen Majors smiled.

"Are you a *personal* friend?"

Ethan was about to answer *yes*. Noticing Majors' obvious interest he reconsidered. He cleared his throat in his most manly way.

"Ah, no, we aren't *personal* friends. *Really.* Not like *that*. We're business associates."

"Oh," said Majors. He drew himself up to his full height, and regained his professional demeanor. "I suppose I can help you either way."

"Does anyone know him around here? Anyone I might talk to?" Ethan asked.

"We keep a visiting list for our tower guests. Perhaps I can refer to that?" Major suggested. He removed another long register from a desk drawer and turned its pages.

"What is your name, sir?"

"Ah, Ethan Post."

Majors reviewed a selected page.

"We have an Alex Post listed here."

Bingo, Ethan thought.

"Yes, I'm Alex's *brother*. Who else is on Mr. Vuillard's list?" Ethan strained to peer over the register.

"We have a Daniel Giacometti listed here."

Giacometti was the guy from the boat! The guy with that blonde, Ethan thought. Vuillard *was* his link to Alex's underworld. Ethan started to walk away from the desk, but Majors drew him back.

"There's a lady upstairs now in Mr. Vuillard's apartment. She seems to know his whereabouts. Perhaps you should speak with her?"

Ethan stopped. Why not?

"Who is she?"

"She isn't on the list but she visits him often, I'm told. She gave me her name just a few moments ago." Majors stopped to concentrate. Nothing came. He looked disappointed.

"I'm sorry I can't recall. I must write it down the next time. But she's quite pretty. Rather tall. Blonde hair."

Ethan froze. Now this was interesting.

"You know her, sir? Perhaps I can ring her," Majors offered.

"Ah *no*. Don't call her. I think I'll just go up and surprise her. We *do* know each other."

"You'll want to take the elevators under the Apartment Towers sign over there. Apartment 3704."

———

From the desk at the window, Samantha dialed the Steinman and Sons number. After a brief conversation, she replaced the phone. They'd picked up the clock on August fourth. They'd moved it from the Waldorf and deposited it at a warehouse in New Jersey for storage until shipment overseas. The clerk gave Samantha the warehouse address and phone number and she wrote it down.

The warehouse was next. The secretary offered to search their storage records for Vincent Vuillard, and placed Samantha on hold while she looked. *"Up, Up and Away"* wafted through the receiver as Samantha waited staring out the large picture window, admiring the afternoon sunshine.

The doorbell rang. She let it ring again. She didn't want to hang up on the warehouse, but who could be at the *Baron's* door?

It's probably Maria, the maid. She hung up the phone and wandered to the door. The ringing had stopped. Peering through the little peephole she could see the lower portion of a man's body.

Bobby was the only one who knew about her Waldorf investigation. Neither Dan nor Stuart knew she would be here. What if it was either of them? How could she explain herself?

Carefully she opened the door a couple of inches. The body turned.

"Well, hello. I was told I'd find someone up here. Can I come in? We met on the yacht. I'm Ethan. Alex's brother."

He extended his hand and smiled.

"Can I ask what you are doing here?" he said.

Samantha stood very still. Ethan's hand remained suspended, waiting for her to acknowledge it in greeting. All she could do was stare. Ethan gave her a wink, and pushed past into the apartment.

Slowly he circled the living room. Samantha followed, not yet able to speak or sure whether she should. She needed to find *Sammy's* character but it was lost in her confusion. She glanced at herself in a hall mirror. What the *hell* was he doing here?

In near panic, she remembered what Bobby had told her. That Ethan Post was under surveillance. And he'd led them straight to the *Baron's* apartment!

Ethan leaned against the mahogany desk, eyeing her scribbled notes strewn on top. Notes about the moving company and the warehouse. He picked up one page, glanced at it and then tossed it back onto the desk.

Samantha stood awkwardly in the open room. She was barefooted. Her leather sandals lay where she'd kicked them, next to the sofa. A strap from her silk top fell down over her shoulder. Self-consciously she shrugged her shoulder, returning it to place. It slipped back down again.

"Can I get you something to drink?" she heard herself ask. It was Sammy's voice, thankfully. Charming and light. Ethan shrugged.

"That depends. I was in the neighborhood and thought I'd find Alex here. What do you have?"

Samantha crossed to the bookshelf bar, and swept her hand *Vanna White*-style over the liquor array.

"Anything you see here is available."

Ethan sauntered toward the bar. He stopped next to her, picked up a bottle of Scotch, and appeared to study it.

"Even you?"

"*Excuse me?*"

Ethan replaced the bottle.

"You told me anything here was available. Does that pertain to you, too?"

His silky tone unnerved her. She was suddenly warm and flushed. Hugging her arms to her chest, she took a few steps away from the bar.

He's flirting with *Sammy*, not with you, she told herself. He remembers Sammy from the yacht. What would she do? Sammy would flirt right back. Summoning her character, she turned toward him.

"What kind of a question is that? You already know I have a boyfriend. You met him the other night on the boat."

Ethan shrugged and replaced the bottle of Scotch.

"Sure, I noticed. You two made the perfect couple. He looked like a great guy."

"You *liked* Dan?"

"Sure. Why not? Any friend of Alex is a friend of mine, ya know? Hey, maybe I didn't have the whole picture that night. Now I understand what's going on. So, you're a friend of Vuillard's?"

"Yeah, I guess so. What do mean, you now *understand* what's going on? How did you gain such wisdom?"

Ethan smiled omnisciently.

"I just *know*. So, let me ask this again. What are *you* doing here?"

"I could ask you the same thing. What made you think you'd run into Alex here?"

Ethan pulled himself up to his full six foot-three height and towered above her.

"He visits Vuillard a lot. I wanted to have a talk with him."

He brushed past her and began wandering about the apartment, first surveying the dining room, pulling out the chairs and studying the upholstery. He wandered along the hallway, noting the artwork. He could feel her walking behind him.

Samantha hoped her confusion wasn't obvious. It was all she could do to keep Sammy in focus. Ethan stopped outside the opulent bathroom, and switched on the light, illuminating the marble. He wandered inside.

Samantha stood at the doorway and watched his hand gently caress the sunken tub's cool surface. He sat down, facing her, at the front of the tub and turned on the golden faucet.

Slowly he began unbuttoning his shirt, the green cotton folds parting to expose tanned, smooth skin. His electric blue eyes ricocheted off the marble. Slowly and deliberately, he pulled the shirt from his pants and unbuttoned the bottom button.

Jeeses. This is exactly what I imagined him doing, Samantha thought. Cool water streamed from the spigot. She watched him splash it on his face and forearms. Taking a white washcloth from the ledge, he immersed it in the water. Slowly he squeezed the excess water from it and rubbed it against his neck and across his chest.

"Pretty hot outside," he said.

Samantha's knees weakened. She propped herself against the door jam. The little camisole strap dangled off her shoulder.

"I was hoping that you might join me," Ethan said with a smile, his lips parted only slightly over perfect white teeth. He laughed at her expression.

"*Downstairs.* In the bar. For a *drink*?"

Samantha could only shake her head slowly in disbelief. What is happening here, she wondered? Why is he doing this to me? The look on his face was intentionally seductive. Her intelligence told her to run away. *Fast.*

She threw her head back and stared up at the ceiling, gathering strength from the tiles' mystical powers.

"Sure. I was almost done here, anyway. Let me get my stuff."

Walking weakly into the living room, Samantha gathered her notes and stuffed them deep inside her shoulder bag. She gazed momentarily out the window. She wanted to jump but that would be messy and over dramatic. She had to play this out.

Looking up, she saw Ethan standing in the middle of the living room floor. He'd re-buttoned his shirt, and tucked it back into his pants. At this distance it was safe to look at him.

God, am I in trouble, she thought. Ethan was easily the handsomest man she'd ever seen.

Samantha crossed the room and stopped. Their eyes locked. Ethan looked back unblinking, but he could feel her eyes bore into his soul. This is a very dangerous game indeed, he thought.

With great effort he peeled his eyes away from hers, and together they exited the apartment.

CHAPTER FOURTEEN

He'd been staring up at the same clock for almost ten minutes now. Occasionally someone would pass an inquiring glance his way, making him feel uncomfortable in his worn tennis shoes and fraying jeans. He hefted the backpack to a better position, all the while staring at that damned clock.

The camera equipment was heavy and was supposed to stay in the car. Why the hell he'd grabbed it at the last minute, he didn't know. Paperwork, probably. Too damned much paperwork to do if somebody stole it. So now it was hanging from his shoulder, cutting into his skin disguised in its navy blue backpack.

Sweat dripped down his back. The hotel lobby was air-conditioned but the black windbreaker he wore was like a rubber suit, baking him in his own body heat.

Casually he took a few steps to the right. Not too far, though. Otherwise he'd lose his view of the hallway. What the hell was *Bluebird* doing up there all this time? And where the hell was his back up? He couldn't stand here all day. Particularly dressed the way he was. He knew he was attracting attention.

If he made a move for that swanky gift shop, he knew he'd have half the hotel security guards on him in a second. But he didn't intend to go near the gift shop. Unless of course, *Bluebird* did. Then he'd have to follow.

He took a few more steps back to the left, wondering as he did if he was wearing an arc in the carpet below his feet.

He also had to take a piss. He had to ever since *Bluebird*'s car lined up at the tunnel. That was almost two hours ago. This surveillance shit could be brutal.

"So, where is he?" a voice whispered.

"Jeeses, thank god you got here," he said to his back-up. "I gotta make a pit stop." He signaled with his eyes toward the hallway on the other side of the big pedestal clock.

"He went down that hall about ten minutes ago. There are elevators that take you to the apartment towers. I couldn't go with him. I would've gotten burned. So why do ya think he's here?"

"Damned if I know. Have you attracted any attention?"

"I think that gay guy at the concierge desk is eyeing me."

"Maybe he thinks you're cute."

"*Bluebird* talked to him for a couple minutes when he first came in. Then he made a beeline for that hallway. You gotta cover me for a minute. I gotta pee."

He counted his steps out of the lobby, diverting his attention from his full bladder and concentrated on the Men's Room sign twenty yards away. He looked over his shoulder at his partner. Shit, he was moving away from the clock, watching something. *Bluebird.*

He had to decide. How fast could he make it to the Men's Room? How fast could he pee? He could do it in thirty seconds. That was his fastest time so far. If *Bluebird* was moving, how far could *he* get in thirty seconds? Far enough that I'm out of the surveillance, he thought.

Nature's call won out. He darted around the art deco entry to the Men's Room, past the tall potted fern. He leapt over the three steps leading to the private stalls, and swung his equipment through the first open door.

In one motion, the backpack was hurled to the floor and his pants were unzipped. He winced, feeling the immediate relief from his bladder, but wondering if he'd done permanent damage to the camera.

Fucking paperwork. Paperwork if you lose it. Paperwork if you break it. And even more paperwork if somehow you end up actually taking pictures with it.

Relieved, at least physically, he zipped up and loaded the pack back over his shoulder. The stall's washbasin mirror reflected straight hair crushed by a black Washington Redskins baseball cap, the bangs plastered to his forehead with sweat. His thin mustache, grown less to make himself attractive and more to disguise the baby face underneath, looked wilted.

He flew from the stall, nearly careening into a bathroom attendant in a white coat and leapt down the steps.

He took the corner at a full run and stopped suddenly. His knees almost buckled under him. His partner was at the corner of the lobby, gesturing violently in his direction. *Slow down!*

He tried to recover some nonchalance to his stride and eased himself the forty feet to where his partner stood. Look at the pretty pictures on the wall. Admire the big gold frame around that mirror over there, he told himself. My, isn't this carpet thick and nice? His partner swung his head in the direction of the Peacock Alley lounge.

"*Bluebird*'s over there. In the lounge. He came down a minute ago with some blonde."

"What the fuck? You mean we followed him all this way so he could pick up some ass?"

His partner shrugged.

"You stay here. I'm going to call in."

His partner crossed the lobby slowly, along the farthest wall from the Peacock Alley toward an alcove. He glanced in *Bluebird*'s direction. *Bluebird* was leaning forward with both arms folded on the table, hovering over the blonde. He faced the lobby but the woman's back was to him. He couldn't see her face.

Grabbing the cell phone from his pocket, he speed dialed the number to the Command Center.

"This is Yankee-Four. We've got *Bluebird* and some blonde in the Waldorf's lounge. Looks like they're going to have drinks. Should we break off?"

He was thinking of the long drive back to Maryland and the fact that his seven-to-three shift would be ending long before he got home. Sometimes, overtime just wasn't worth it.

"Stand by, Yankee-Four," he was told. A few minutes passed.

Jeeses, these New York guys take things so seriously, he thought. Can't they just make a quick decision?

"Ah, Yankee-Four, can you describe the female?"

Why do they care, he thought belligerently. If this guy was so unimportant, why did we follow him all the way to New York? And why do they care who he's with now?

"She's got her back to me but I got a pretty good look at her when they came out of the Towers area. She's tall, blonde hair, longer length. Good lookin'. Great legs. Maybe early thirties. He's hanging all over her right now. Has he got a girlfriend up here?"

He reserved his comments about her being a *piece of ass*. Talk like that was appropriate on the street, but not when you check in with the Command Center.

"Ah, Yankee-Four, did you say they came together out of the Towers area?"

"Yeah, that's right. She must have been upstairs and he came to meet her."

Yankee-Four heard muffled conversation and wondered if maybe this was significant after all.

"Yankee-Four, how many people you got with you?"

"There are just two of us inside and another unit in a car on the street."

"Okay, stay where you are. Keep out of sight. And if they move, don't lose them."

"What if they split up?" he asked, wondering how their few troops could follow two people going different directions through the streets of New York.

A few more minutes passed.

"Ah, Yankee-Four, we're sending some people up to meet you now. Just stay with *Bluebird* and the girl and keep in regular contact."

The Command Center hung up and Yankee-Four cursed under his breath. These guys don't give out too much information. He walked slowly to a corner diagonally across the lobby from his partner and lounged against a wall. His twenty-ten eyesight allowed close scrutiny of *Bluebird* and the girl, despite the distance. *Bluebird* was holding a drink glass but his fingers were gently massaging her arm.

Nice *move*, Yankee-Four applauded. Nice *tan*. It was like watching Ken seduce Barbie.

———

Lunch at the Peacock Alley had been over for a while. The crowd had thinned dramatically when Ethan led Samantha to the front table, behind the fern. The same place she and Dan had sat a few days earlier.

He slid effortlessly onto the upholstered cushion. Before he could invite her to sit next to him, Samantha had taken a chair at the end of the table. She was still close to him but not as close as being on *that* cushion.

A waiter in a white dinner jacket had materialized from out of nowhere. Samantha ordered Chardonnay.

"I'll have a dry martini," Ethan said.

They sat in silence for the moments until their drinks arrived. Samantha's smile was almost frozen in place. She was trying desperately to relieve the sexual tension Ethan had stirred in her upstairs. Her mind strained to find an appropriate, safe opening to conversation. Her eyes scanned the seats in the lounge and the lobby, looking for any familiar face from the surveillance team. She saw no one she recognized.

But that doesn't mean they're not here watching us, she thought. She wondered how she would explain this tonight. When Dan or Stuart, or even Bobby questioned her about what she was doing with Ethan Post at the Waldorf.

Samantha knew Bobby would get in trouble. He'd appropriated keys to the *Baron*'s apartment for her. He wasn't supposed to have them, much less lend them to her. They'd have to explain to Stuart about their private investigation. And they weren't ready to do that yet.

Then there was the problem about Ethan. His mere presence here would raise suspicion. She hoped they weren't under surveillance.

Ethan took a long sip from his martini. The cool, potent liquid jolted him. He leaned forward toward Samantha, their arms almost touching on the table's surface. He studied her hand as it reached nervously for the wineglass. He looked at her face. Nonchalantly he began tracing the muscles in her forearm with his fingers. The skin was smooth and warm.

Samantha took a long sip of wine.

"So, why did you think you'd find Alex here?" she asked.

Ethan smiled, pleased that she had initiated the conversation. And pleased that she hadn't pulled her arm away from his touch.

"He comes here a lot. He's known Vuillard for a number of years. I stopped by his office but he was out," Ethan lied. "So I figured I'd stop over here."

"You and your brother are really close?" Samantha asked.

Ethan shrugged, but continued massaging her skin.

"Well, I've been away for a while but now that I'm back we've grown closer. That thing you saw on the boat the other night? That was just sibling stuff. You know, between brothers. I wasn't really *that* angry with him. Actually, we've been talking about going into business together. He's told me a little about what he does and I'm interested."

"Oh yes. And what kind of business would that be?" she asked him.

Ethan took a drink of the Martini and chose his words carefully.

"Alex has been doing some free-lance work outside of his job at the bank. It's been really lucrative for him, so he thinks I might, shall we say, *benefit* from it, too."

Samantha listened, wondering what the hell he was talking about.

"I've given fifteen long years to the U.S. Government. All I have to show for it is an old sports car. I want *more*, and I think Alex and his friends can help me get it."

He tasted the Martini again and smiled at her conspiratorially.

"I like yachts. I like money. I like *beautiful women*."

He leaned closer to her with that remark. Samantha felt her knees weaken.

"And you'd give up the Navy? I would have thought it was something you loved."

Ethan frowned. "I guess my priorities have shifted lately. I got pretty lonely sitting around those deserted airfields. When I got back to Annapolis I realized that I'd had a lot of fun flying airplanes, but I had nothing to show for it. When I saw you on the yacht, I realized the things that could make me happy. And what I should do in order to get them."

Samantha almost choked on her wine. "What is it you think you *should* do?"

"I think I should go to work with Alex and your friend Dan. I've spoken with Alex about it already. Tell me, do you think Dan would accept me into his operation?"

His eyes implored hers, but Samantha could think of no response. He leaned closer.

"*You* could fix it for me. *You* could have Dan introduce me to some of his friends."

His fingers gripped Samantha's arm insistently.

"And just what is it that you think Dan *does*?" Samantha was becoming concerned. Maybe Ethan Post wasn't such a good guy after all.

Ethan paused for a moment. Alex was probably into money laundering. Giacometti was probably into drugs. He looked the type. But these were all just assumptions.

"I know that Alex handles the money for Dan's people. If Dan could introduce me, I know that I could be helpful. Tell me what I should do."

His fingers again massaged her arm. She stared into her wineglass, wishing that she wasn't a public school teacher. Wishing that she *were* an undercover agent trained to handle this situation.

"I really don't think Dan would ever consider working with you and I don't think this is something you should get involved with."

She allowed her words to hang in the air between them, hoping he would believe her, hoping he'd take her advice. Samantha watched him closely. His body continued pressing toward her. She took another sip of wine and changed the subject.

"What was it like in the Navy?" she asked. Whether or not this was a wise question didn't matter. This undercover repartee was exhausting. Could she ask him things that were really on her mind? That *Samantha* wondered about? Could she tell him things about herself without undermining her undercover role?

Ethan shrugged.

"For the first few years, it was really exciting. All I wanted to do was fly. My father introduced me to it. He retired a Captain. Some people think he pushed me into it, but I really chose it for myself."

"Did Alex ever want to be a pilot?" Samantha asked. The massaging of her arm stopped as Ethan looked into space.

"I suppose he did, but probably for the wrong reasons. He would have done it simply to get my father's attention. He rebelled instead. Then he became a banker. He's the smart one."

Samantha replied, "I felt that way when I first came to New York. I was really excited at first. Everything was so new. So many things to see. But now that I've been here awhile, I'm remembering all the things I left behind."

WILDE AT THE WALDORF

Ethan nodded, wondering where she was from, but afraid to ask. Afraid that more personal information from her might distract him from his purpose. But it was nice sitting here, talking. It had been a long time since he'd done something like this. It felt natural, comforting.

"Don't you think you'd miss the Navy if you pulled out now? After all, it's been your whole life."

Her question was intriguing. His eyes caught hers, and lingered there.

"Oh, I don't plan to give up flying. I own an airplane now. It was my father's. It's a Beechcraft turbo-prop that seats six. I'm actually trying to sell it."

"Why would you sell your father's plane?"

Ethan swirled the ice cubes in his glass.

"It's not what you're thinking. I'm not trying to get rid of everything that was my Dad's. The plane was a wedge between Alex and me. My father bought it for me, exclusively. He had no problem showing favoritism. Alex always hated the Beech. So, when I got back, I put it up for sale. I plan to buy one that we both can use. I even think that he'll let me teach him to fly."

When he gets out of jail, Ethan thought bitterly.

The waiter returned. Without looking up, Ethan ordered another Martini and another wine for Samantha. He leaned toward her, and brushed his face against her hair.

"I can't believe your friend Dan really appreciates you. It just seems like such a waste."

Ethan felt the words hang between them, surprised he had uttered them. He'd been speaking from his heart. He remembered her lonely figure walking along the dock the other night. He eased himself closer until Samantha could feel his breath against her cheek.

Tentatively he placed his hand on her knee and felt her skin's coolness. Unconsciously he began moving it up her thigh.

"I watched you two on the boat."

With one hand, he brushed the hair from her eyes.

"He doesn't take care of you, does he? Guys like him never do. They're too caught up in themselves. They really can't love a woman like you. The way she *deserves* to be loved."

The waiter delivered Ethan's second Martini. He sat back and took a long drink. Samantha's leg burned under his hand. Carefully, she shifted her weight and moved the leg away from his immediate reach. His fingers were now fondling her hemline, but somehow she felt that was safer than before. She nursed her glass of wine, resisting the overwhelming urge to turn her face toward his. Knowing if she did this his lips would be millimeters from hers, and then it would be all over.

Ethan was right. Even at his best, Dan had never really taken care of her. He'd never been a good lover. He *was* too caught up in himself. She relaxed for a moment, allowing herself to feel and enjoy the sensation of Ethan's hand near her leg. And the rest of his warm, powerful body only inches away. So what if this was an undercover fantasy? She thought. It sure beat the hell out of reality.

She relaxed her neck, and allowed her head to turn ever so slightly toward him. His fingers wrapped around her chin, tilting her face upward.

Samantha's surroundings disappeared. Her entire world was this face in front of hers, the lips whispering something she couldn't hear.

Ethan lowered his face toward hers, until there was no space left between them. His tongue reached out toward her, gently encircling her mouth.

His mouth was soft and hot against hers, but deliberate and powerful. She released her hold on the wineglass, and raised her hand to his face. Her fingers traced his hair, threading themselves through the soft, brown strands. The room blurred around her until it disappeared entirely. Until her only reality was his mouth on hers.

Then abruptly her surroundings returned. She pulled her head away. What had been a passionate blur now focused into wallpaper and plants, and people. Nausea almost overwhelmed her as she realized she might have just blown *everything*. Blown her cover as Dan's girlfriend, blown any respect the task force could have for her, if they were under surveillance. Blown her objectivity to this man who, only moments ago, confessed his attraction to joining a drug underworld. Blown it all in exchange for the most *incredible* kiss she'd ever received.

Samantha pulled herself up and groped for her shoulder bag. It was close by but her motor reflexes weren't working. She reached for the bag and knocked it over into a pile. On the second try, it was safely within her grasp.

"I have to *go*," she stammered.

With more strength than she knew she possessed Samantha rose from her chair and fled into the hotel lobby. She ran down the escalator steps and through the brass doors into the afternoon sunlight. She darted up Lexington Avenue and into the subway station.

Thankfully, the underground station was crowded. She searched in her wallet for a subway pass. Her hands were shaking almost violently, but she managed to find it and thread it through the little slot. She walked quickly to the far end of the platform and hid behind a tall column. She peered out from behind, eyeing the platform for anyone who might be following. There was no one.

Moments later a train approached and Samantha boarded it, her hands still shaking. She wasn't sure if it was going uptown or downtown and she didn't care.

CHAPTER FIFTEEN

Yankee-Four dropped the cell phone into his pocket and ran to the edge of the alcove. He'd only caught a glimpse from the corner of his eye, but he was sure the blonde had just run past him. What the hell was going on?

He searched the lobby for his partner and found him hiding again behind the big pedestal clock. Someone from the Command Center was yelling. A little voice scratched from inside his pocket.

"Hello! Hello!"

Yankee-four retrieved the phone frantically.

"Yes, hey listen, the woman just moved. She ran out of the hotel lobby. *Bluebird* is still in place but I think we've lost *her*. You guys have any idea who she was?"

The person at the Command Center was swearing into the receiver.

"*Son of a bitch*! We've got a guy on his way up there now. He's the one who could've made the I.D. Son of a bitch! Damn traffic!"

"So what do we do now?" Yankee-Four asked.

"Aw, hell. Just stay with the *Bluebird*. He's still sittin' there, right?"

"Right."

"The New York guy should be there any minute. Look for a black guy. Name is Bobby Washington. He's bringing some additional surveillance. When they get there, you guys break off and go back home."

"Roger, Command Center," Yankee-Four responded, and hung up. He walked slowly over to his partner, trying to avoid the *Bluebird*'s line of sight. His partner laughed.

"She's gone, huh? Wonder what he said to her."

"I can't figure this one out. One minute they're in a lip-lock. The next she's beatin' hell out of the hotel. The guy who could ID her hasn't made it in time, so maybe we'll never know who she was."

"He looks pretty upset though, doesn't he?"

The partners looked over toward where Ethan was sitting. A waiter arrived and he ordered another Martini. His expression was glum.

The surveillance team retreated into the lobby shadows to wait. Five minutes later a black man entered the hotel wearing jeans and a red and white striped rugby shirt. He wandered slowly around the lobby, then stopped and retrieved a stick of gum from his pocket. He whispered into the shadows behind him.

"*Bluebird*'s covered. Follow me outside. I've got a car waiting."

After he had cleared the lobby, Yankee-Four emerged from his hiding place and followed Bobby Washington's exiting figure down the escalator and out of the hotel. His partner followed moments later. The three climbed inside Bobby's gray Caprice and pulled away from the Waldorf into New York traffic.

"You guys have had a long day. There's a coffee shop up here. We'll stop for a cup and you can tell me everything that went on. Then I'll drive you back to your car," Bobby said with a smile.

The Maryland FBI agents thanked him, grateful they could soon start for home. Bobby pulled the car into a bus lane, positioned the Police Parking plaque in the front window, and exited the Caprice into a Greek diner.

The trio took a booth next to the street and ordered three cups of coffee and some French fries.

"I'm Bobby Washington, NYPD," he said and extended his hand to the agents. "Task force."

"I'm Jim. This here's Timmy. We're part of Washington Field Office SOG."

Bobby smiled a toothy grin. "So, tell me about the lady."

"Damnest thing we ever saw," said Timmy, shaking his head. The thin mustache hid a face not more than twenty-five.

"One minute they're all over each other and the next, she's running out of the hotel. We got a good description of her. Any idea who she might be?"

"Not the *faintest*. Anybody else get a good look at her?"

"I think I could identify her if I saw her again. We were hopin' you guys would get here in time to take a look at her," said Jim.

"Just our *bad luck*, eh?" Bobby chuckled. "You said they were all over each other. Just what did you mean?"

Both Jim and Timmy laughed.

"Well, it looked like they were talking for a while. Then he started putting the moves on her. I could see pretty well from where I stood. Just how much detail do you want, anyway?" Jim asked.

"As much as you can give me, boys," laughed Bobby.

"He seemed pretty cozy with her. He's a good lookin' guy. What is he, some kind of drug dealer?"

Bobby shook his head.

"Actually he's a Navy pilot. That's why his code name is *Bluebird*. We didn't think much about him until he showed up here today. Doesn't make too much sense."

"Maybe he was just meeting the girl," Timmy offered.

"*No.* I'm fairly certain the girl was a surprise to him. That's why we're a little interested just how he acted toward her."

"Well, she had wine but *Bluebird* ordered two Martinis. He was on his third when you showed up. I couldn't see her face, but he was really coming on strong. She held back for a while, but I guess he kinda got to her. Wore her down."

Yeah, that probably didn't take a whole lot of doing, Bobby thought, and smiled again.

"But he kissed her really hot and heavy," Timmy said with enthusiasm.

"And she seemed to enjoy that?" Bobby asked.

The two agents laughed again.

"I was thinkin' they were gonna get a room afterwards but then she just stopped real sudden, jumped up and ran out of the hotel," Timmy said.

"I was on the phone to the Command Center when she left. They were so cozy I thought they'd be there awhile. Figured it was a good time to call in. I was wrong. Hope I didn't screw anything up for you guys," Jim confessed.

"Hey, don't worry about it. How were you going to follow her anyway? There were just two of you, and a car outside. Never would have worked in Manhattan," Bobby concluded. He dropped ten bucks on the table and they walked out.

Bobby drove the two agents back to their illegally parked car. A red light stuck to the dashboard was the only indication it was a police vehicle. Three parking tickets were wedged under the windshield wipers. Bobby pulled them out and tore them up.

"Let the parking authority try to find you, eh? With luck, you'll never come back to New York in this car."

"With luck, we'll never have to come back to New York," Jim said.

Bobby watched their car drive away. He pulled out his cell phone and poked in Samantha's number. More beeps as he waited while the message machine issued its instructions. Putting his two middle fingers between his lips, Bobby emitted a high-pitched wolf whistle into the mouthpiece.

"I guess you had a *fun* afternoon. Jeeses, baby, I got *hot* just listening' to them tell me about it. Can't wait to hear your version. But don't get nervous. You made a clean get away. Nobody can identify you, thanks in part to your ol' pal, Bobby. I'll call you at five as planned. Dan and Stuart want to have a tea party tonight. You might be thinking' how much of this you want to tell them. Bye bye."

———

The humid air wafting off Sheepshead Bay clogged Arturo's sinuses, making his whiny voice even more high pitched. He squeaked a "Ha-choo" and blew thin bursts of mucous into his over-used white handkerchief. It made Julio want to vomit. But the guy was invaluable. Nobody else in the organization was as singularly loyal, and brutal. So Julio put up with Arturo's frequent sinus congestion and plotted his eventual murder.

"So, yous think Vincent is dead? Man that sucks! That really sucks! An' Post did it to steal Papa's money?"

Julio laughed at Arturo's firm grasp of the obvious.

"Yeah, well, it could be that way, but I think what we got is a problem with that theory. See, if *you* got it, means *anybody* could figure it out. So I think maybe there's somethin' more going on. Like ol' Vinnie sets Post up to take the heat, and disappears with a couple a million. What you think?"

Julio waited for the delayed light of comprehension to illuminate Arturo's huge steely eyes. Gradually it came.

"Sure, I see wha' you're sayin'. Fuck an A, Alex is too much of a wimp. Vincent did it himself. Hey-hey! The skinny ole fag fucker pulled one over on Papa!" Arturo attempted a laugh that decayed to a wheeze.

"So I ask myself, jus' where could he be? I figure Switzerland, an' if thas' right, we're royally fucked..."

"Why are we fucked if it's Switzerland?" Arturo asked.

"Hey, you know anybody can do us a favor in Zurich? How 'bout Geneva? *No*, right? Bunch of self-righteous bastards. My second guess is Hong Kong, and if he went there I could check with the Tongs in Chinatown here. Maybe they could find 'em for us. Not much gets past those guys. Finish your coffee and we'll take a drive downtown."

———

Samantha switched trains twice to get one that would take her close to home. Walking the four blocks to her building, the hot afternoon sun beat down upon her shoulders, baking her like a convection oven. By the time she got inside her apartment, she looked like a crime victim.

She flung her belongings on the sofa and opened the windows wide. The air conditioning hadn't been run all day, and it would now take too long to cool the entire apartment. What she needed was a cold shower, and a stiff drink.

The light was flashing from her message recorder. She rewound it and listened. Her mother had called around ten just to say hello. Then she heard an ear-piercing whistle. Samantha jumped. Then she heard Bobby's voice. He was *laughing*.

Samantha listened in horror to his message. They *had* been under surveillance! God, she *knew* they were. Why had she walked out of the apartment with Ethan? Why had she gotten a drink with him? And god, why had she let him kiss her, right there in front of the *FBI*?

But how could they *not* know it was *her*, she wondered. She was sure Bobby was lying. She'd ruined everything.

She lingered in the shower as long as possible, then filled the bathtub and shaved her legs. With a towel wrapped around her, she collapsed onto the couch. A gentle breeze wafted through the apartment. It was four twenty-five.

She grabbed her purse from beside the couch, retrieving the notes from her phone call at the Waldorf. Carefully she punched in the New Jersey warehouse telephone number. The same woman who had been helping her hours ago answered the phone.

Samantha apologized for hanging up earlier, saying she'd gotten involved in an emergency situation. The woman chirped on. Yes, she *did* have the information Samantha wanted. The shipment for Mr. Vuillard had been scheduled for delivery to an address in Hong Kong. It had left on a ship August 17th, and was scheduled to arrive any day.

"Will Mr. Vuillard be picking it up?" Samantha asked.

"Not according to the shipping documents. A *Mr. Hua* is supposed to take delivery. There is a contact number for him. 852-791-4453."

Samantha scribbled the name, address and telephone number and then thanked the woman. When she hung up, she wondered why she'd been able to get all that information so easily.

I might be good at this yet, she thought.

The phone rang just as Samantha was pulling on blue jeans and a T-shirt. It was Bobby.

"Hi, baby. How's my lover girl?"

"Don't say another word. I'm not in the mood. I have some important information for you. When can you get here?" She hoped her tone sounded professional and in control.

"Okay. I won't kid you now. But you're in for it later," Bonny replied. "We have to meet with Stuart and Dan at seven thirty. I could come by in an hour. Will you cook me dinner?"

"I'll cook you dinner as long as you behave yourself about this afternoon. Are they coming over here?"

"Nah, we have to drive over to a greasy spoon in Brooklyn. But it's not far from you. Just over the bridge. It won't take us but fifteen minutes, so we'll have enough time to talk. Should I bring some wine?"

Samantha smiled. "Red would be nice. I'll make pasta."

———

Bobby arrived ten minutes early. Samantha put the pasta pot on to boil, stirred her homemade pesto sauce and extracted a wine bottle from the long paper bag Bobby had brought.

"Hey, it's got a cork and everything! You've got class. And it's a Super Tuscan. My *favorite* Italian wine," she cried.

Bobby took the bottle and deftly removed the outer wrapping and inserted the corkscrew. In one motion the cork was released. He filled the bottom of two glasses and offered her one.

"I was a waiter before I joined the police force. I love wine. This here's one of my favorites."

Their glasses clinked in a toast.

"To your big day." He took a small sip of the deep red liquid and rolled it around his mouth.

"Mmm, mmm, that's *good*."

Bobby lounged against the kitchen counter top and watched Samantha as she prepared a spinach salad.

"Okay, so I've been here for almost ten minutes, and I've been a good boy. When are you going to tell me what happened this afternoon?"

"It seems to me that you *already* know more than I do. Except about the important stuff. My investigation at the hotel was successful, although perhaps a little too *eventful*. It seems that the *Baron*'s clock *was* transported from the Waldorf on August fourth to a shipping warehouse in New Jersey. It was loaded on a ship to Hong Kong on the seventeenth and will be delivered to a Mr. Hua in Hong Kong any day now. I have his address and telephone number."

Samantha looked at Bobby smugly. "As an investigator, I'm pretty good, huh?"

"Yeah," he said and smacked his lips. "And as a *woman*, I understand you're *dynamite*. Your lover boy had to sit for twenty minutes before he could recover from your hot, steamy presence. He also needed another Martini. What the hell did you *do* to that poor boy?"

"It wasn't me! Bobby, it was all *him*. He was coming on to *me*. Relentlessly."

Bobby feigned disbelief.

Samantha shrugged. "Well, *maybe* I enjoyed it a little bit. Just how much *did* the surveillance see? It was mostly Ethan. That's what I couldn't figure out. That's what I wanted to discuss with you."

She shoved the salad at him and pointed to the table.

"It took him twenty minutes to leave after I ran out? Really?"

"Yep, darlin'. *Twenty whole minutes*. And he didn't look too happy about you goin'. I watched him for a few minutes after I called off the Maryland feds. That's why nobody can identify you. They were all out of state guys followin' him. Never saw you before. But I recognized your description right away. Yep, the minute they sent your description over the radio."

"Oh, my god! Over the *radio*!" Samantha shrieked.

"It's okay, baby. I saved you. I just picked up my radio and made some real raunchy comment that he probably picked you up in the bar. That hotel's known for that kind of thing. Lots of working girls hoping to meet rich, traveling businessmen. Everybody just accepted what I said as the truth."

"And that's supposed to be *helpful*, making out that I'm some kind of *prostitute*! I'm a teacher. An underpaid, overworked but *dignified* teacher!"

"I told ya don't worry, baby. Besides, the description wasn't that good anyway. They said you were heavier and that your hair was a bleach job."

Samantha almost scalded herself with the pasta pot.

Bobby sidled behind her and gave her neck a kiss.

"Relax, babe. I just made that last part up. I love getting a reaction from you. It's better than watching TV. Anyway, nobody downtown really cares about some girl *Bluebird* was sittin' with at the Waldorf. They were more interested in just why he was there in the first place," Bobby said. "I'm the only one who knew you were going to be there. That's how I knew it was you he was with. I don't want your cover blown any more than you do. I did what I had to do and it worked. At least for now."

Bobby took his place at the table.Samantha brought the pasta dishes and poured herself a hefty glass of wine.

"So, tell me, why was Commander Ethan Post at the Waldorf in the first place and how does he know about the *Baron*?" Bobby asked.

Samantha idly mixed her sauce over the pasta.

"That's what I was hoping you could tell me. He mentioned he was there to find Alex. That he'd stopped by his offices, but Alex wasn't around. So he figured he'd find him at the *Baron's*. That's what he said. "

Bobby swirled the linguine onto his fork and took a big bite.

"That's a lie. Alex *was* there. Not at the Waldorf. *Bluebird* drove from Annapolis directly to Alex's office. Surveillance was with him all the time. He hung outside Alex's office, even listened at the office door. Then when Alex finally opened the door, Ethan hid behind a water cooler. One of our surveillance ladies was watching from the elevator bank. Your pal Julio marched out, really pissed, and headed for the elevator. *Bluebird* tried to follow but lost him right away. We sent a few troops with Julio just for fun."

Samantha listened closely.

"Bobby, Ethan knew Vuillard's name, and I don't think he got that from the front desk. They're very careful. They might have given him the apartment number, but he'd have to have known the name first. How would he have known about the *Baron*? He even knew Vuillard and Alex had been working together for a long time," Samantha said.

"Beats me, babe. Maybe he's doing some investigation of his own. That could be pretty dangerous for him. I hate to tell you this, but as of this afternoon, your lover boy is now a target of this investigation."

Samantha shook her head. "Are they serious?" she asked.

"Probably not really. Couple of the PD guys want him brought in. He's a military guy and there's lots of vets on the police force. You know, cut the surveillance bullshit and give him the straight story. Start him working for *us*," Bobby said.

"Against his own brother? Would he do that?" Samantha asked.

"It'd be pretty messy. But it's pretty messy any way you look at it. He's makin' all the wrong moves right now an' before too long he's gonna be in way over his head."

Samantha thought back to the Peacock Alley restaurant and Ethan's kiss.

"I think I would trust him to work for us. But some of the things he said to me today, I, uh, well…"

"Go on."

"He said he was sick of not having anything material to show for his life. That all he could afford after years in the Navy was an old sports car. That he wanted money and that Alex had agreed to take him into his operation."

"Did he tell you exactly what he thought that operation *was*?" Bobby asked.

"Actually, no. He seemed to be baiting me for that information. Whenever I asked him for details, he'd say something like, maybe I had more details than he did. Then he'd smile, and, well, once he actually rubbed my leg."

"Your *leg*! You let him rub your leg? I'm surprised at you. I thought you were raised better," Bobby chided.

"Stop kidding me about this. I'm really honestly trying to figure it out and I need your help. Every time he would ask me a question about Alex or Vuillard, he'd lean really close to me. I can't tell you how tough it was. Bobby, I don't think he knows anything. I think he was just pumping me for information."

"No shit, sweetheart."

"So maybe he isn't involved after all?"

"Of course he isn't. I've suspected he was clean from the beginning, but you confirmed it for me just now," Bobby replied confidently.

"I did? How can you be so sure?"

"The Jag."

"The Jag?"

"Yeah. It's a *guy* thing. You remember those feds that followed him out to the academy? The same ones that nearly got tossed by the Admiral? Well, I talked to them. Your stud worships that car. Checks it for scratch marks all the time. Strokes the paint job. They saw him do it twice. He'd never call it an *old sports car*. He values it. He was lyin' when he said he wanted money, and yachts and that kind of stuff. My guess is he doesn't care about those things. He's a *good* guy. And after what he did to you this afternoon, I'll bet he feels real guilty. You might want to remember that tomorrow night when you see him again," he added.

"Oh shit, that's right!" Samantha exclaimed. "If he's there."

"Oh, he'll be there, all right. Commander Post is conducting his own investigation. Regardless of what happened between the two of you, he's on a mission. My guess is he's going to study all Alex's friends tomorrow night and lock onto whoever looks like Mr. Big and get cozy with him. And that's dangerous turf. Word is that Alex is expecting some heavy cartel hitter to show up, an' those guys know when they're being pumped for information."

The dinner was over. Samantha put on a pot of coffee. Bobby relaxed on the couch, studying her notes from the afternoon.

"Do you think we have a connection with all those Hong Kong rhymes we found the other day?" she called from the kitchen.

Bobby looked pensive.

"Hey babe, have you paid your phone bill recently? I want to run it up a little. An' I don't want my office to know who I'm calling. Ya mind?"

He didn't wait for a response before dialing the international operator.

"Hong Kong Police. The Central office."

He waited; then scribbled down a telephone number. He glanced at his watch. It was a few minutes to seven.

"What time do you think it is in Hong Kong?" he called to her. "I can never remember if they're twelve or thirteen hours ahead of us."

He punched in the international access code and the 852 area code for Hong Kong.

"I got a friend of mine on the Royal Hong Kong police. A Brit. Great guy, but he can't drink beer to save his life."

Bobby waited for the pickup then enunciated slowly into the mouthpiece to a receptionist. Detective Inspector Jim Kilgowan didn't come in until nine in the morning he was told. Bobby left his name and asked that Kilgowan call him back in a couple of hours and hung up.

"Time to go, darlin'. Can't keep Stuart waiting. He's one of those Type-A guys. Always on time."

CHAPTER SIXTEEN

Stuart Birkwell arrived first at the deli cafe. It was seven twenty-five. He ordered a meatball hero with extra green peppers and onions and a diet cream soda. He carried his dinner to a rear table, furthest away from the counter and out of sight of the windows.

He ate the messy, greasy sandwich ravenously thinking it was the best he'd tasted in weeks. It was the first thing he'd eaten today, anyway. Maybe that just made it taste better.

A number of years ago, seven to be exact, his wife would cook for him in the evenings. He'd walk home after a long day at the law office and she'd have a casserole, or maybe even roast beef waiting. On Wednesday they'd have lasagna. She wasn't Italian but neither was he, and it had always tasted great to him.

That was before he went to work for the Brooklyn U.S. Attorney's Office and started prosecuting the really big cases. Before he knew it, he was running the Organized Crime Task Force. And his wife was gone.

He figured he missed the cooking the most. And the furniture. It had been three years now, and his studio apartment still held only a double bed and a deck chair. The deck chair was superfluous. He'd bought it for company, but he rarely had people over. He just went to the apartment to sleep. During the day, he lived at the Federal Building. And dined at the nearest deli counter.

But hell, he was only forty-two. He would build his reputation first, then join some big time law firm in Manhattan and defend the same kind of people he now put in jail. Then he'd buy furniture, he thought. Maybe an oak dining room table with chairs. He liked that idea.

Dan arrived next. He wore a tight black T-shirt that stuck to his big muscles. He wore no belt with his Levi's and his boots were old and scuffed. He needed a shave.

He stopped at the counter and ordered corned beef on rye. Two sandwiches. And a liter of Pepsi. He clutched the warm food to his chest and sauntered over to where Stuart was eating. He dropped the Pepsi bottle on the Formica tabletop, and straddled a chair.

"Hey Stuart, how's it goin'?"

"Great," Stuart replied between mouthfuls. His enthusiasm was real, even though he looked like he hadn't slept in days. He'd forgotten to wash his hair that morning and he was starting to regret it now.

Most of Stuart's days were spent in his office, on the phone. The only people that came by were other attorneys and they'd gotten used to him by now. Or federal agents and they all looked about like Dan. No suits. Nobody to impress.

The attorneys that worked the bank crimes or public corruption, now, *they* wore the suits. Stuart worked Organized Crime and drugs, and that was messy work. He didn't have to dress up.

But tonight he felt like a slob and he was suddenly self-conscious. He didn't think too much of Dan's undercover girlfriend. He would have preferred a trained FBI agent. He also thought she had a big mouth. But she was cute. And he wished he looked better.

"When are the others coming?" he asked.

Dan needed tonight's meeting. It was a formality – an official interdepartment briefing on the status of the undercover operation. Dan wanted to make sure the objectives were clear. Stuart wanted to make sure he retained absolute control over the operation.

Stuart was uncomfortable no FBI agents had been able to penetrate undercover to Dan's level, or to that blonde's level either. There just hadn't been enough time. But he had to go with what he had. This thing was moving too fast.

Tomorrow night they would be at another party; this time at Alex Post's home in Manhasset. The code name was *the carnival*. It was certainly shaping up to be just that.

The DEA said it was working quickly on the Columbia Cartel end, but Stuart doubted it. The DEA said they knew the De Yambi's pretty well. They knew they were a wealthy group, funneling drugs into the United States and Europe. But their information to date had been periphery. Stuart thought it was all crap. Nobody in the DEA could put names to the faces his people were seeing and so as far as he was concerned, they didn't know *shit*.

Stuart needed Giacometti and his blonde to help him identify people he could build criminal cases against. People he could put behind bars. He'd never had to work an investigation *backward* before. He knew he would get the cartel's *money*. The *Baron* ensured that. But he wasn't so sure about the convictions.

———

Bobby dropped Samantha off a block before the deli so she could walk in alone. It was a benign Brooklyn neighborhood during the day, but at night it turned sinister. He watched closely until she walked through the door and then drove the Caprice four blocks in the opposite direction. He parked and waited for a few minutes, then walked down the street and into the deli.

It was deserted except for the small table in the rear. He ordered a cup of coffee and wandered to the back. They were waiting for him.

Samantha sat to Dan's right. Bobby pulled up a chair at the end of the table. They'd decided not to mention Samantha's meeting with Ethan at the Waldorf. Eventually it would come out, since it was dangerous keeping information from Stuart. But not yet.

Dan started the ball rolling.

"There's a lot of tension inside right now. Alex is really nervous. That's part of the reason tomorrow night has become more important. When Alex and I discussed getting together last weekend, it was mostly going to be social. Everyone getting to know each other better, ya know? Bring in some big wigs and *schmooze* a little. But the *Baron*'s disappearance has made everybody jumpy. I think Alex is worried because Vuillard introduced him to this outfit. He's never really fit in, and doesn't have the personal style the *Baron* has, so some people think his position has been elevated since Vuillard's disappearance. Particularly Julio." Dan gulped Pepsi from the wide-mouthed bottle.

"Julio is the cartel's muscle on the East Coast. Alex has told me in confidence that Julio has killed a lot of people. I don't know how many details he has about these murders. It may just be propaganda to keep Alex in line and out of Julio's hair, but I guess it's got him pretty nervous."

"It seems Julio thinks maybe Alex knocked off the *Baron*. And because Julio knows Alex doesn't have the ability to do that kind of dirty work, Julio thinks maybe *I* did it."

Dan laughed.

"I can see his point. I appear on the scene, chummy with Alex and Vuillard. Then Vuillard disappears. And it's just Alex and me. Alex is really stupid. In five years he never formed any personal alliances with the De Yambi's. He depended on the *Baron*. Now he's depending on me. That's good for us, but I don't think it's too good for Alex."

Samantha listened intently. Bobby rested his head in his hands. She wasn't sure if he'd heard this before. Stuart just stared into space.

"Alex has the ear of a cartel honcho, street name *Papa*. The guy apparently controls Julio, if that's possible. Alex has pleaded with this *Papa* to come by tomorrow night. Meet with everybody and maybe reassure Julio that Alex is okay. So he's coming, I guess."

"Who do you think this *Papa* is, and how will we recognize him?" Bobby asked.

"I'm going to try to get him to take a walk with Alex and me. Outside. On the porch, around the house, around the neighborhood. Something like that. Just keep an eye on me. I'll do the best I can. I don't think it'll be a problem."

"Does anyone suspect the *Baron* turned informant?" Samantha asked. Stuart shot her a glance, as if to reprimand her for speaking. Dan smiled.

"So far, no. At least I don't *think* so. Alex and Julio got into a shouting match today at Alex's office. We had surveillance close by. Some pretty brutal language was used. Julio has been going over the bank records, and found some money going out to a company based in Hong Kong."

Samantha and Bobby exchanged glances.

"It's a little uncomfortable for me, because it's the same company I was supposed to be linked with. That's how the *Baron* introduced me, as somebody he'd worked with through this company. A consulting firm, so to speak. These guys have all kinds of consulting firms that handle the money as it gets washed through banks. Vuillard gave us the name of the firm, and we used it. I hope he wasn't setting *us* up," Dan breathed.

Bobby leaned forward to join the conversation.

"I spoke yesterday with one of the FBI accountants looking into the records. They found money being diverted to that Hong Kong consulting firm on a regular basis. Not a lot, by cartel standards, but over the years it would add up nicely,"Bobby said.

Stuart looked interested.

"So we think Vuillard was siphoning off cartel funds?" Dan said, "Yeah, him or Alex. Maybe both. I wouldn't put it past either of them. Julio doesn't really understand the bookkeeping stuff, though. He's no accountant. Hell, I don't think he even graduated from high school. But it's just another reason to distrust Alex, and me. An' Julio's in tight with some really bad asses."

"Besides, Julio's our primary suspect in Vuillard's murder, *after* Alex," Stuart interjected.

"Do you think you'll be in danger tomorrow night?" Samantha asked with concern.

Stuart gave her a nervous look and ran his hand through his hair.

He said, "Look, Dan's gonna have to play a lot of this by ear. It's not the ideal way, but everybody's in too deep to back off now. Ideally we'd like to know exactly who will show up. We normally have time to run some background checks on *Papa* and his pals, but we're not going to have time with this one. Dan's a little exposed. We have to live with that."

The table turned solemn.

Stuart continued, "We followed Julio from Alex's offices in New York to a brownstone in Queens this afternoon. Surveillance has been with him ever since. We're hoping he might pick up this *Papa* from the airport or something. That would be best. Then we'd get a good look at him. But none of us believe in Santa Claus anymore."

The deli door jingled as two Hispanic girls in purple bike shorts entered and ordered something from the counter. They were talking loudly in heavy Brooklyn accents.

Stuart and Bobby began discussing the surveillance coverage for the following night. It would be a risky operation, since Post's home was in a quiet residential area. The presence of any unknown vehicles would generate suspicion.

Dan listened in solemn silence. Tonight he was the consummate professional undercover man. No wonder they keep choosing him for these assignments, Samantha thought. She watched as he sketched out the surveillance plan on a napkin.

The meeting broke up a few minutes later. Dan was the first to leave. He barely looked at her as he stood, gathering up his sandwich wrappers and Pepsi bottle. With the confident stride of a bodybuilder, he exited the deli and disappeared into the Brooklyn sunset.

Bobby left next. His plan was to retrieve the Caprice and meet Samantha on the same corner where he'd dropped her an hour before. Samantha and Stuart stared across the table at each other, neither one knowing what to say.

Stuart thought of asking her if tomorrow night's plans frightened her. But she wasn't acting as if they did, so he kept his mouth shut.

Samantha wanted to reassure him she would do a professional job, even though she was still such an amateur. She thought back to the spectacle she'd made of herself that afternoon at the hotel and determined that any comments on her professionalism were premature.

They sat in silence, counting out the five-minute interval before she could leave. At four minutes and thirty seconds, she excused herself and walked out of the deli. The door jingled as she walked through. Bobby's car was double-parked in front of a rundown row house. A few neighborhood women sat on their stoops. They studied her as she walked by. A tall, blonde white woman getting into an old Caprice with a black man.

Bobby drove her directly home.

"I need to use your phone," Bobby said as he parked the car. Once inside Samantha's apartment, he dialed an international number.

"Detective Inspector Jim Kilgowan, please," Bobby pronounced slowly into the mouthpiece. It was nine in the morning, Hong Kong time.

"Thought you might still be out in the bars," Bobby jibed as Detective Inspector Kilgowan answered.

"Oh, no, no. Not anymore for me. Found myself far too lucky in those haunts, I'm afraid."

"Too much luck? You're tellin' me the women wouldn't leave you alone?" Bobby laughed.

"Well, actually it was a couple of well-placed women who sort of had the *eye* in for me, if you know what I mean. I suppose I got a little tired of trying to out run them. It's fine, actually Bobby. I'm sober and fit and don't miss it at all. Now what can I do for you, old friend? Something about a shipment? Is it cocaine?"

Bobby laughed. "Not this time. It's a grandfather clock."

"*Packed* with cocaine?"

"No, just a grandfather clock. The guy who's receiving it was the moneyman for the De Yambi cartel. We think he's staying in Hong Kong until lots of shit blows over here. Do you think you could check him out?"

Bobby gave him Vuillard's description, and Hua's name and address on Bowen Road, and the shipping company accepting the delivery. Kilgowan agreed to get back to Bobby as soon as possible.

CHAPTER SEVENTEEN

The Xcel Energy truck moved slowly along the residential streets. The driver and passenger had their windows rolled down, and the smell of fresh cut grass and late summer flowers filled the cab. The driver sneezed once, then two more times.

"Damned hay fever," he cursed.

It was four o'clock Friday morning. Sunrise was a couple of hours away, but the sky would start to lighten before that. They had about ninety minutes to work.

The truck meandered quietly down the cul de sac, its occupants admiring the stately brick homes they passed. Each house sat on a double lot, surrounded by well-manicured, mature landscaping. Behind was a small, thickly foliaged wood.

The large brick colonial, second from the end, had huge, white Greek columns. Tall pine shrubs provided a privacy fence from the street.

"Shit," muttered the driver, seeing it all for the first time. "We'll have to go pretty high."

The truck followed the circular pavement around the cul-de-sac and then headed back up the street. It pulled to the curb in front of a power pole and stopped. The passenger, dressed in white overalls and an old orange T-shirt, exited and opened the truck's rear doors. He extracted a large yellow sign that read *Men Working* and placed it conspicuously next to the van.

The driver pulled a lever inside the van, and slowly raised the large cherry-picker cage toward the top of the power pole. Confident he had it lined up correctly, he lowered the cage.

Both men climbed into the rear of the truck, pulling the doors closed behind them. From two separate foam boxes, they extracted a camera, a high-power lens, and a black metal sheath. Carefully they placed the expensive equipment in a bright orange toolbox.

In silence, they donned their radio headsets, and climbed from the truck. The driver returned to the cab. His partner hefted himself and the toolbox carefully into the cherry-picker cage.

Slowly the cage was raised to where the power lines met the power pole. A black metal power box protecting the electrical monitors sat on a wooden ledge. Working quickly, the black metal sheath was placed on top of the power box, secured by black duct tape.

With painstaking care, the remote controlled camera was slid inside the sheath, its toggle switch adjusted and taped to the *on* position. Next the high-power lens was carefully inserted into the camera.

"I'm going to eyeball the placement now. Tell me how it looks," the man in the cage whispered into his headset.

The driver rolled up the windows in the van, and picked up his headset.

"Blue One to Outpost. Blue One to Outpost."

"Go ahead, Blue One."

"The unit is placed and is functioning. Tell me what you've got. We need the big house with the white pillars."

There was a moment of quiet as the Outpost adjusted their monitor screen.

"It looks like we've got one white pillar to the far left. See if he can improve that angle."

"Larry, try moving it thirty degrees to the right. They've only got the left pillar."

"How's that?" Larry asked a moment later.

"Give us a read now, Outpost," Blue One requested through the console microphone.

"That looks pretty good. We've got the front door now, or at least the top half of it. Those damned shrubs are in the way. See if he can angle it downward a little, and more to the right. We want to see the front porch and driveway," responded a female voice with a heavy Brooklyn accent.

After fifteen minutes, the fine-tuning adjustments had been made. The view wasn't perfect, but perfection, or lack of it, was something they all took in stride.

Blue One lowered the cage, and Larry jumped out. He collected the large yellow sign, and loaded it and the toolbox into the rear of the truck. As quietly as possible, Blue One started the truck's motor and drove up the street, away from the cul de sac.

Tall brick stanchions guarded the entrance to the elite subdivision. As the cherry-picker turned north, away from the neighborhood, another Xcel van approached from the south. It rounded the corner, past the stanchions and in the direction of the cul de sac. It stopped curbside, fifty yards from where the cherry-picker had sat. The men inside wore white overalls and faded orange T-shirts. They sipped coffee as the sun began to rise.

———

A bright morning sun poked through tiny slits in the Venetian blinds. Ethan noticed the yellow streaks only half-consciously, and rolled toward the pattern they cut in his mattress. He lounged in their warmth for a moment; then sat up with a jolt.

The alarm clock on the ancient oak dresser read half past five in the morning. There shouldn't be this much sun, he thought. He fumbled on the nightstand for his wristwatch. Through sleep-fogged eyes he studied the face. The time it showed matched the angle of the sun. Eight thirty.

Confused, he rolled out of bed. He oriented himself. Where was he? Oh yes, at Alex's new house. He remembered the drive out last night and his exile to the little bedroom at the back of the house. He pulled on his running shorts and a T-shirt. He slipped on his Nikes, and padded out into Alex's second floor hallway, and down the oak staircase. Everything was silent.

He checked the clock on the microwave. It was flashing wildly. Outside the sun was already heating up. He hated to run when it was hot.

He did a couple of cursory leg stretches; then set out up the street toward Manhasset Bay. He passed an Xcel Energy truck midway up the block. A guy in overalls sat on the truck's rear bumper, fiddling with a tool.

As an afterthought, Ethan circled back to the truck, jogging up to the worker.

"Did something happen last night?" he asked, his feet still moving at a stationary run.

The worker looked up slowly, his studious eyes masked behind reflector Aviator sunglasses.

"Yeah, I guess so," he answered in a deep, slow southern drawl. "Damned if I know what it is, though. We may be here most of the day tryin' to figure it out. Power should be back now, I guess."

"Thanks," Ethan said, as he resumed his run up the street.

The worker chuckled to himself.

"Our guys at the power company must have been flickin' the hell out of this neighborhood last night, givin' us our cover story. *Everybody's* stopping to ask. That's our boy, ain't it?"

His partner adjusted the camera secured within the wire mesh cage inside the right rear door panel. It pointed directly toward the driveway from which Ethan had just exited. The truck's left rear panel was open to public view, exposing a hefty supply of authentic Xcel electrical gear.

"Yeah," the federal agent chuckled again, "Ain't no tellin' how long we're gonna have to be here today."

————

Detective Ralphy Villanueva adjusted the over-stuffed lounge chair until it was almost horizontal. A huge coffee mug sat on a white mesh lawn table next to her. She allowed her lids to close, relishing sleep's promise.

Across from her stood a long table with a color monitor and next to it a Mission Control mixture of recording devices and amplification boom microphones.

Almost drifting off, she was brought back to consciousness when the gazebo's metal screen door squeaked open. Steve Maxwell stood above her, holding a fresh pot of coffee, and a box of chocolate covered donuts.

"Mrs. Pollard made you coffee. I told her you probably wanted to get some sleep, but she insisted," he said.

Ralphy laughed, and sat upright.

"I don't know about the coffee, but I could eat that whole box of donuts!" she said in her thick Brooklyn accent.

Steve took three from the package, and pushed the box toward Ralphy. He sat opposite her on another lounge chair, and ate his donuts hungrily.

The screened gazebo occupied a place at the rear of the Pollard's huge backyard. It was thirty feet from the tiled kidney-shaped pool. The bright blue chlorinated water glistened in the morning sun.

"Mrs. Pollard said we could use the pool if we wanted. I don't think it's a bad idea, really. It'll make us look like real houseguests. Besides, by noon I think this gazebo will be like an oven," Steve said between bites.

The Pollard's backyard was surrounded by a stockade privacy fence obstructing any view the neighbors on either side might have. The backyard ended at the small, heavily foliaged woods. One eighth of a mile on the other side of the woods, and at a forty-five-degree angle to the gazebo, stood Alex Post's home.

On the other side of the Post home and up the street, in direct line of sight of the gazebo, sat the remote controlled camera perched atop the power pole. Its signal was beaming strongly into the receiver.

"*Bluebird* went for a jog a few minutes ago. He stopped by the truck, too. Guess he overslept. The whole neighborhood overslept," Ralphy laughed.

"I don't know why he decided to stay at Post's house last night. It's just our luck that he did, though. I'll watch for a while. You take a nap. It's going to be a long day," Steve said.

———

Samantha hadn't slept well. She awoke at eight thirty, feeling restless. A gentle late summer sunshine eased its way into her apartment. City street sounds comforted her. Cars honking. A garbage truck belching as it traveled up the street.

Normally these sounds assaulted her consciousness, reminding her again of reasons she did not like living in New York City. But this morning, they were familiar and safe.

In the kitchen, she extracted a box of corn flakes from the shelf and dumped a huge portion in a bowl. She was starving. She finished it quickly, searching with her spoon for the last flake, and drinking the remaining puddle of milk. As an afterthought, she poured herself another bowl full.

She paced slowly around the apartment. Her leather duffle bag was already packed for the weekend. A garment bag hung from the bedroom door. Shaking off her pensive mood, Samantha took a fast shower and washed her hair. Her face looked drawn and tight, and her tan was fading. Carefully she applied foundation, blush, eyeliner and mascara. She looked better.

At ten-thirty, she hefted the luggage bags over her shoulder, locked the apartment, and struggled down to the street. A taxi stopped almost instantly. She gave him instructions to the Marriott Hotel at LaGuardia Airport.

Twenty minutes later, the taxi dropped her in front of the Marriott. Early check-in had been arranged under the name Karen Aldridge. The room was already paid for, so she didn't have to produce any identification or credit card. A bell captain transported her luggage to a small single room. She asked him directions to the outdoor pool.

Changing into a one-piece, nautical striped tank, Samantha took the elevator to the tenth floor and followed the arrows to the swimming pool. The building cast a shadow so Samantha selected a lounge chair on the sunny side and spread out a large hotel towel.

She checked her watch. She was early.

Shortly after noon, a woman in khaki shorts and a pink blouse entered the pool area. She carried a large canvas shoulder bag. She walked casually to the chair next to Samantha's.

"Hi, I'm Karen Alexander," she said. Samantha recognized her. Karen had been the woman on Alex's yacht, in the flowered dress. The one she had seen later in the Denny's parking lot. A FBI agent.

Samantha sat up and smiled. Karen was about her age.

"Are you nervous?" she asked.

Samantha nodded. "I haven't slept much."

"I know how it is. I'm always a basket case just before an under-cover. Then I relax once it's underway. You just have to remain extremely calm. Slow down your reactions. Don't say anything until you've thought it out first. No one will notice that you're not being spontaneous. The worst they'll think is that you're an airhead, and that it takes you longer to understand what they're saying. But that's your role, anyway, so don't sweat it." Karen gave her a reassuring smile.

Karen removed a cardboard jewelry box from her canvas bag. It was tied securely with a red ribbon. Inside, thoroughly wrapped in cotton, was a gold locket and chain.

"This is yours for the weekend. You'll put it on just before you get to the Post home. Do it in the car, on the highway to Manhasset. It has a little microphone in it, so don't let anybody come up and try to open it. Tell them it's an heirloom and the hinge is broken."

"It's beautiful," remarked Samantha, studying the intricate engraving on both sides of the heart shaped locket.

"Thanks. It was my grandmother's," Karen said. Samantha was surprised.

"We had a little trouble figuring out how we'd have you wear the microphone. It's a pretty delicate piece of electronics, so we didn't want to put it in something you'd have to carry. A piece of jewelry was the best option. Our radio tech guys felt the locket would be perfect."

"I'll take good care of it," Samantha promised.

"It operates on line of sight radio waves so there's no wires for you to wear. We have a radio receiver set up nearby the house to pick up your transmissions. In the backyard your signal will be the strongest. In the front yard it won't be too bad but not as good as the backyard."

Samantha asked about inside the house.

"It should work okay in most of the rooms, at least better than not having any microphone at all. We won't be able to pick up anything inside a bathroom, so you have a little privacy. Something about the tiles. We'll be recording continually from the time you and Dan arrive at the house. Doesn't matter how long you're there. Overnight or over the whole week-end. We've borrowed the home of a former Naval Intelligence officer in the neighborhood, so we'll be close by."

"Is Dan wearing one of *these*?"

Karen shook her head. "That's too risky. We didn't want any equipment near him. Our targets are too sharp for that."

Karen retied the cardboard box and gave it to Samantha.

"You'll do just fine," she said and walked casually away from the pool.

Ten minutes later, Samantha gathered her towel and strolled back to the hotel room. She felt better now. Calmer. She carried the box carefully, and placed it into a side pocket of her large shoulder bag.

She dumped the purse's other contents on the bed, and sifted through them. Everything identifiable with Samantha Wilde was taken out. She put the credit cards, her driver license and some leftover notes and receipts from her week of investigation into a cosmetic pouch and then returned the edited contents to the purse. From the garment bag, she removed a white slip dress with rhinestones on the straps.

After a quick shower, she assembled her hair into a loose bun. She applied some make-up sparingly. The thin white sandals completed the outfit. She was ready.

But what about the locket? She wanted to try it on, but decided against it. Best to keep it safe and secure in its cardboard box.

The same bellboy who had brought her bags to the room now transported them for her down to the lobby. Samantha paused at Hotel Reception and registered for a safe deposit box. Inside it she placed the cosmetic pouch with all her identification.

A black Mercedes 450 SEL waited outside the hotel. Her duffle bag and garment bag were loaded into the trunk, and Samantha slid into the fawn leather passenger seat.

Dan smiled at her from behind the wheel. He was dressed elegantly but simply, in starched white trousers and a green Ralph Lauren polo shirt. Slowly he drove the luxury vehicle away from the hotel, past the airport, and onto the Grand Central Parkway.

———

The walls in the bedroom were bare, except for a thin brass crucifix nailed above the bed. The metal springs supporting the twin bed moaned as Julio rolled over. Reaching absently to the windowsill, he pulled a graying tassel string. Sunlight instantly bathed the tiny room as the shade flipped up.

He dressed quickly in black bike shorts and a blue V-neck t-shirt. His image, reflected in the full-length mirror propped against the wall, brought him satisfaction. His body was tight and compact. He liked the way his heavy gold chains nestled in the dramatic *v* at his collarbone. He liked the way the bike pants hugged his short, but muscular legs. They stopped at the knee, showcasing his muscular calves.

His face wasn't pretty, and he liked it that way. The pocks and scars made him look tough. He'd been a Golden Gloves featherweight boxer during high school. That was his only interest.He'd broken a guy's nose and ruptured his spleen in a fight his junior year. The kid almost died and Julio had been expelled. He never went back.

In the old neighborhood, people learned early not to mess with Julio.

His loose shirt covered the Lycra waistband. He stuffed his automatic pistol in the cleft of his back, grabbed his keys and exited the apartment. Garlic permeated the dark hallway as he jogged down the stairs. He passed the rear entrance to the cheap Italian restaurant, into an alley.

The stench of decaying garbage wafted from a huge green dumpster. Two scrawny cats pawed at a paper bag protruding from the metal lid. Julio hurried down the alley and into the street. In a place where he knew the signal was strong, he extracted his cell phone and dialed a number, waiting impatiently for it to connect.

"What did 'ya find out?" he barked into the phone.

He slammed his fist against a wall.

"I fuckin' *knew* it. What'd I tell you? So, *Papa's* comin' for sure?"

"Good. Good. So we take care of 'em tomorrow?"

Two kids rode by on bashed up bicycles. Julio lowered his voice.

"Yeah, start the plan. I'm leavin' in about an hour. Be ready."

Julio hid the phone in his shorts and shook his head.

"*I fuckin' knew it*," he mumbled again, and retraced his steps back to the brownstone.

———

The white Saab drove past the cyclone fence, and along a quarter mile of pavement to the small prefab shack labeled *Office*. A wooden sign stood outside, the picture of an animated airplane etched into the weathering wood. The airplane had a smiling face.

Beside the tarmac, a variety of small aircraft were tied to red anchors in the ground. A metal hanger had been erected further out into the field.

Dressed in blue jeans and a white button down shirt, Arturo exited the Saab and adjusted his sunglasses. Slowly he sauntered to the office screen door.

A petite girl of about fifteen sat at the office's only desk. She looked up brightly as he entered.

"May I help you?" she asked brightly.

Arturo looked around. The office appeared to have two other rooms, but she was alone. He smiled.

"I heard there might be a plane for sale out here. I came to have a look."

"Oh, that's great! Are you in the market for a rehabbed Beech? Or a little Piper Cub? That's about all we've got now."

"How many seats in the Beech craft? I need it for business," he said.

"Seats six. It's in really good shape. A pilot from the Naval Academy owns it. It used to be his dads', but he died."

Arturo frowned.

"Too bad he has to sell. I would like to take a look at it."

The girl rose from the desk and walked past him through the screen door. She pointed in the direction of the hanger.

"It's in there. Normally, I'd take you out to look at it, but I'm alone. I have to stay here."

She looked him over, marshaling the wisdom of human nature gained from her fifteen years. He was actually quite attractive, but she didn't like the Latin look. She preferred blonds. And his head looked too big for his thin body. Other than that, he looked harmless.

"I think I can trust you to have a look yourself. You'll find the hanger open. The Beech is the only one inside right now."

She watched as the man walked to the Saab and drove slowly along the pavement to the hanger. He opened the hangar's large steel door, returned to his car, and drove it inside.

"Hmm. Wonder why he did that?" the girl thought and then returned to her desk.

———

"Hey, Jeannie, it's me. How are the kids?"

It took a moment to identify the voice. It wasn't that the voice was *unfamiliar*, just that the call was *unexpected*.

"The kids are fine, Alex. Why are you so suddenly concerned?" Jeannie said and the wished she hadn't.

"Oh, I was just wondering if they'd like a visitor."

"Like a father kind of visitor? When?"

"I was thinking I'd drive down Sunday," Alex said.

"You need to see them this weekend? Is anything wrong, Alex? Are you in some kind of trouble? Your voice sounds funny."

"Why the hell would you ask something like that? All I want to do is see my kids. Is there a problem with that?" Alex yelled.

Jeannie pursed her lips.

"Calm down, daddy. It's okay. I think we'd all like to see you, too. Why don't you give us a call tonight, and we'll plan something?"

"Okay. Good."

"Alex, have you spoken with Ethan? He came by here the other day."

Jeannie listened. Alex's breathing labored.

"I know. He told me. He's here now."

"Good. So you guys are getting along?"

"I don't think Ethan wants to get along as much as *pry* into my life," Alex responded, and hung up the phone.

Jeannie stared at the dead receiver, mystified.

CHAPTER EIGHTEEN

When she was ten years old, her mother had bought her a white organdy dress with a stand-out slip and big pink satin sash. She wore it to her first real piano recital. She would have to play three pieces of music this time. Not one, like at her other recitals. But *three*.

In the car, going to the church hall, Samantha wasn't sure she could remember them all. Her father drove the big Oldsmobile, and kept looking over the front seat at her, sitting primly in the back, her hands folded and head down.

"Don't worry, little chicken," he'd said. "You'll do just fine. I'm really proud of you."

As she sat in the Mercedes now, her hands folded tightly and head down, she thought of his words. The white dress she wore today was a grown up version of the organdy, but she still felt like that little girl. Then, as now, she wasn't sure she could remember everything she had to.

The locket hung loosely from her neck.

Dan drove the Mercedes through the tall brick stanchions into the Manhasset neighborhood. He made a few turns and then pulled the car to the side of the street. He shifted it to park, and turned to look at her.

With his left hand, he smoothed the hair from her face. They stared at each other for a long moment.

"You'll do great," he said.

"You'll do great, too," she whispered back. She hoped they were both right.

Dan pointed down the road to the large brick house with the white columns.

"That's the place."

"Where is the surveillance?" Samantha asked. She couldn't see any cars nearby that resembled police or government vehicles.

Dan looked at her and squeezed her hand.

"They're around. Don't worry. We're not alone out here."

He wanted to show her the power company van across the street, and the video camera on top of the power pole. Or point through the woods to the big white house, barely visible through the trees. But he didn't. She didn't need to know that much. Dan discarded his ponderous look, put a confidant smile on his face and shifted the car into drive.

"Let *the carnival* begin," he said.

Dan parked the Mercedes next to Alex's BMW, and exited the car. He walked around for a minute, stretching his arms and legs, ensuring that the Outpost recorded their arrival.

Samantha was just exiting the car when Ethan materialized from the side yard. He stopped, and watched as she swung her long legs from the car and onto the pavement. Gracefully she stood; then saw him watching her.

Taking Karen's advice, Samantha arrested her suddenly racing pulse. She leaned against the open car door for support and took a deep breath.

She thought that a coy *Sammy* smile was called for, but she wasn't up to it after yesterday and their wild meeting at the Waldorf. So she chose a confident, assured look and hung onto the car door for dear life.

Ethan was naked from the waist up, the elastic band of his gym shorts discolored with perspiration. His piercing blue eyes enveloped her.

"Hey Dan. We've got a greeting party," Sammy called, smiling slowly.

The muscles in Ethan's jaw tensed.

Dan turned and saw Ethan standing on the grass. Quickly he crossed the driveway, grabbed Ethan's sweaty hand and began pumping it.

"Well, if it isn't the white sheep of the Post family, How's it goin', Ethan? Dan Giacometti. Met ya' on the boat. And you remember Sammy?"

Ethan clasped Dan's hand, wanting to appear friendly. He apologized for his appearance.

"Probably won't get any complaints from Sammy here. She loves to see guys sweat," Dan said.

Samantha smiled slow and easy, but her eyes were stuck on Ethan's chest, and the tiny rivulets of sweat swimming among the brown curling hairs. With effort, she tore her eyes away.

"Alex is inside," Ethan said, after a moment. "He's been here about an hour. Come on in and I'll mix you both a drink. You can probably wait for him by the pool. I'm helping him out with some stuff in the yard."

They followed him through the garage. The smell of lasagna wafted toward them as he opened the side door and escorted them through the kitchen, into the sunroom and onto the screened patio.

Samantha walked slowly, impressed by her surroundings. She loved the oversized country kitchen. *Was Alex a gourmet cook or did he just want us to believe so?* The hallway was tiled in Mediterranean marble. Italian faux texture adorned the walls. Heavy gilt frames bordered Michelangelo sketches. Reproductions probably, but nice nonetheless.

"I have to finish up the yard," Ethan said after depositing them pool-side. Samantha watched him walk away.

"Let's get a drink," Dan said.

———

A silver Pontiac Grand Am flashed its left directional signal and turned past the tall brick stanchions. It paused momentarily. An older man in the front seat bounced a huge cigar against the car door, spraying ashes into the roadway.

The fading sun reflected off his dark sunglasses. He dipped his white Panama straw hat toward the light, further shielding his eyes. The car continued slowly up the street, its occupants studying the stately homes. The cigar's owner puffed thoughtfully, blowing fat clouds into the descending summer twilight.

Like tourists, the driver and the cigar meandered through the neighborhood past the well-manicured lawns, past the large house with the pool and gazebo in the backyard.

At the end of the street the car turned around and repeated its movements down another street, and then another.

The car returned to where it had started. A large gold lighter ignited and sent sparks into the fading light. Thick lips encircled the tobacco tube, directing it toward the flame and puffing until the end glowed amber. With a nod of his Panama hat, the man signaled his satisfaction and the driver proceeded to the Post home.

———

"Outpost, look sharp. I like the looks of this one."

Gradually, the Grand Am entered the camera field. It parked near the end of the wide driveway behind the black Mercedes. The driver exited first and surveyed the Post home, turning around a full 360 degrees.

"We'll send that picture home to his mother," Ralphy said.

"You got him?" asked the truck lookout.

"Hey, we're better than *Sears*," she laughed.

The passenger with the cigar was less accommodating. He exited the Grand Am, his back to the camera, and walked deliberately into the open garage, his Panama bobbing with each step.

———

Once again there were no clues from Dan what she should do. He'd settled into conversation with Alex in the library, away from the other guests. Her gut told her it was best to disappear. The kitchen seemed the most interesting and safe place; the huge steel oven intriguing. Alone with the aromas of the pending buffet, Samantha grabbed a wooden spoon resting on a saucer and stirred a vat of sauce. She jumped back when the kitchen door slapped open.

"Have I got the right house? Are you Alex's wife?" His words clipped in a heavy Spanish accent.

Samantha shook her head.

"His sister?"

"My boyfriend is a friend of Alex's," Samantha offered.

"*Ahhh.* And you can cook? Your boyfriend is indeed a lucky man."

The man before her had thick, gray wavy hair curling beneath the white Panama hat. His face was large and sagging, with deep pools of skin under each eye.

His head sat nestled between wide, rounded shoulders, the jowls resting upon a barrel chest. His short, squat legs, humorously clad in Levi Dockers, provided inadequate support to the lumbering frame. Huge arms protruded from a white knit golf shirt and swung in wide arcs at his side. In one massive paw he twiddled a cigar stump.

Lifting through his heels, he walked toward her, bouncing the hat from side to side. His grin revealed perfect rows of stained teeth.

He crossed behind Samantha to the oven, pulled open the door and stretched half his body into the heated cavern. A gust of tomato and ricotta cheese escaped. He withdrew, a content expression on his face.

"My dear, you can call me *Papa*. Everyone does. Now, where might I find Alex?"

"I think he's in the library," Samantha replied. She swallowed. Was this the one they'd been waiting for? Who *else* could he be?

Papa bowed. "Show me the way," he instructed.

Samantha led him down the hallway and stopped at a tall mahogany door with ornate brass knobs. She signaled to the closed door and again *Papa* bowed. Loud voices emanated from within.

"Do you want me to knock?" she asked, perplexed.

"Yes, please. And *announce* me," *Papa* replied, smiling.

This wasn't going to go over well, Samantha thought as she rapped softly against the library door. The voices inside quieted. Momentarily the door swung open.

Alex stood before her, faint strands of receding hair crisscrossing his forehead. He was sweating. Before he could protest the interruption, Samantha stood aside and revealed *Papa*.

Fear and relief immobilized Alex. Then something Samantha recognized as cold dread settled across his features. Samantha's skin crawled. *Papa* read Alex's look and smiled even wider.

There had been no invitations for her to stay so Samantha turned to walk away. Suddenly Dan ran from the library and grabbed her shoulder, pushing her backwards down the hallway, away from the others. Ignoring her surprised expression, he pinned her against the hallway wall with his body and ran his hand over her rear and down her leg. He buried his head in her neck in what probably resembled a passionate kiss.

"This is going *great*," he hissed into her ear, not loud enough for the others to hear but probably audible to the locket. "Alex is a mess and now we have *Papa*. We need to be left alone for a while. Keep Julio away from us if you can."

Dan removed his head from her neck, gave her a big smile and a slap on the butt. *Papa* watched this display, intrigued and approving. He clapped Dan's back when he returned to the library. The door closed behind them.

Samantha was dumfounded. She wanted to renegotiate her under-cover contract right then and there. And *Papa* was eating that macho crap up. It was disgusting. She was about to say *fork you* when she remembered the locket and the surveillance crew listening on the other end. Instead Samantha shook her fist toward the library door. Turning, she saw Ethan leaning against the wall, watching her.

"How long have you been standing there?" she asked.

"Long enough. How can you let him get away with that crap?"

"He's harmless. Besides, he had something to tell me."

"Well, there are other ways to deliver a message. Like writing it on a piece of paper and slipping it to you. Or talking to you like a regular human being," Ethan said.

Samantha shook her head. She walked past him back toward the kitchen.

"Listen, that's not Dan's way. He's not a Boy Scout like you. He's *raw*. It's his *style*."

"And you just go along with it?"

Ethan followed her into the kitchen and leaned against the counter top.

"Sure I go along with it. I *love* it."

"*Bullshit.*"

Samantha watched him, recalling the twenty minutes it took him to leave the hotel yesterday and liking the thought.

"Why? Didn't it look like I loved it?"

Ethan shook his head. "Actually, you looked pretty pissed."

Samantha laughed.

"Well, what if I was? The way I see it, it's *our* business."

"I think you should find another guy," he said, resting his elbows on the countertop.

Samantha contemplated that thought.

"Like *you*?"

Ethan looked down.

Have I embarrassed him, Samantha wondered.

She said, "Isn't that what you want? That's what it seemed you were saying yesterday. When you were whispering in my ear and rubbing my leg, and pumping me for information."

Ethan raised his eyebrows. Samantha smiled sweetly.

"You didn't tell your boyfriend about yesterday. Why not?"

"Let's just say I was curious."

"About what?"

"About what you were up to. About why you thought I would help you."

Ethan regarded her closely. She was more intelligent than he'd given her credit. Or perhaps his objective was more transparent than he realized.

"I told you all that yesterday. I'm interested in going to work with Alex and Dan. I like what they're doing."

His words sounded hollow.

"You don't even know what they're doing, Ethan. That's why you questioned *me*."

Ethan's eyes dropped to the countertop, studying the granite patterns.

Samantha continued, "That's why you came onto me yesterday. You figured you could get me all hot and then I'd tell you everything I know. Well, I don't appreciate your tactics. Sure, I'm attracted to you. Otherwise things wouldn't have happened like they did yesterday. But I don't like being used."

"I know," he said. "I didn't mean yesterday to happen the way it did. I'm sorry."

Ethan looked at her, his Wedgwood blue eyes sad. Samantha reached out and took hold of his arm. Slowly she began massaging his skin. His lifted his free hand and covered hers. Her breathing slowed as she concentrated on the warmth radiating from beneath his hand, creeping up her arm and across her shoulders. It was all too familiar. Too *powerful*. For a moment she was back in the Peacock Alley lounge.

With great difficulty she pulled her hand from his grasp and squared her shoulders.

"Don't be sorry. Just stay out of their way," Samantha said.

"I can't."

"I guess I know that."

"What should I do?" Ethan asked.

"Go back to the library and introduce yourself to the old guy in the Panama hat. They call him *Papa*. He runs the show. Alex is terrified of him. Maybe you can help your brother out."

"Thank you." Ethan smiled and walked away. Looking down to straighten her dress, Samantha caught sight of the locket against her skin. *Shit.*

———

Laughter brought tears to Ralphy's eyes.

"Hey Steve, you're missing the best part!" she yelled through the gazebo's screened walls.

Steve Maxwell was lying in a lounge chair beside the Pollard's pool. A large beach towel covered him against the cooling night air. He made a move to get up, but Ralphy told him not to bother.

"I'll replay it for you later. But we've identified our mystery woman from yesterday!" she called.

"The blonde bimbo at the Waldorf? The one Bobby figured for a hooker?"

"That'd be right," Ralphy laughed.

CHAPTER NINETEEN

This morning there would be time for Tai Ji Quan, and that was good because the clouds around Victoria Peak had cleared, and that would make the exercise even more enjoyable. The old man dressed in the same faded madras shirt and fraying beige pants. He slipped into the ugly brown sandals that he did not notice to be ugly, and walked slowly down the concrete stairway. Nine flights. His muffled steps echoed in the cool, narrow stairwell.

The park beside Bowen Road wasn't really a park, but a grassy overlook that no one had thought to turn into a parking lot. It overlooked Central, Hong Kong. Looking down he could see the Star Ferry on its regular exodus to Kowloon. Looking up he could see nothing but blue sky and the grassy peak. And the tourist tram.

He began the measured contortions that were Tai Ji, the silent positions which brought a mystical contentment and exhilaration to his aging body.

How much time passed was immaterial. The ancient morning rite brought peace to his soul and calmed the excitement rising within. Soon, he would make his walk down the peak and to the many banks. His final journey in servitude.

Over an hour later the exercise was complete. He looked out over the crowded space below him. Tiers of tall buildings graduating down to Victoria Harbor. He exhaled and felt again in his pocket for the small, folded pieces of paper. They were still there.

Carefully he had copied the numbers this morning. The telephone call had come on time, as expected. His friend was quite prompt. But then, this was an *important* message.

There was greater lilt to his steps as he wove the three miles along the paved road. When he finally descended into the streets of Hong Kong Central, he was smiling broadly. An elderly Chinese man in heavy black spectacles.

There would be no withdrawals today from the great bank.

No traveler checks to purchase. He made his way to the four others banks, the banks into which he had made deposits nearly every day for four years.

Producing identification for Wong Tai Chen and the secret authorization number, he directed a wire transfer of all funds to an account held with the First National Bank of Fort Lauderdale, Florida. The account balance after four years had grown to two-point-two-million dollars. The bank officer merely nodded and completed the transaction in silence.

Long Kwok required different identification, and another number at the next bank. He provided it to the bank officer and directed the funds to the Landmark Bank in Boca Raton. Two-point-four-million. He liked this second bank. They had a better interest rate.

The money from Chung Hsiang-Tzu's account was directed to the Bank of Miami. Two-point-one-five million.

At the last banking institution, the little man identifying himself as Nung Wu produced the necessary authorization number, and directed a wire transfer of funds in the account to the Bank of Commerce in Miami. He waited.

The young Chinese woman in Western dress smiled at him happily. She was proud that a man of his age could be as industrious and frugal as to have amassed this fortune. She was from Hong Kong but had been raised in Southern California, she'd told him, and obtained her business degree from UCLA. She admired the modest life-styles of her heritage and felt guilty that she didn't save her money like her mother and her grandmother had but spent it on fine clothes and a new car.

She spoke Cantonese and attempted to converse with the elderly gentleman while she recorded the details of his transaction. Will he be moving to Florida? Oh, yes, quite soon. Yes, actually he *was* purchasing a business. The recipient of the wire transfer is his business partner. Yes, he had worked very hard his entire life. Yes, he was quite happy he had all this money to show for his efforts.

Her questioning and the truth in his answers galvanized his decision.

"How much will you be transferring?" she now asked. The balance read two million three hundred five thousand dollars.

Without further thought, he replied, "One million five hundred thousand."

"And you will be leaving the balance with us?" she asked hopefully.

The little man removed a separate piece of paper from his shirt pocket. He had prepared it this morning, just in case his courage prevailed.

"The remainder should be transferred to this account," he said, pushing the paper toward her. This time the information wasn't fraudulent.

"He is Mr. Hua. My *brother*," he told her.

No matter that his brother had been dead for twenty years and the account was now his. *This* information he did not share with the lovely young woman.

She returned moments later with his transaction receipt and smiled.

"Mr. Wu's one million five hundred thousand dollars will be credited tonight due to the time change. Mr. Hua will have his money posted to his Hong Kong account this afternoon."

He thanked her and exited the bank. It was difficult to control himself. He was having trouble breathing. He took a seat on a nearby bench and mopped his forehead. He was suddenly quite warm. His heart was pounding in his ears but it didn't matter. He had done it!

He knew his friend would be upset but what could his friend do to him? He couldn't go to the police.

He also knew that the money was *clean*. There was no way it could be traced to him or to his friend. No one could trace the money to the Florida accounts, because no one could trace it to the four Hong Kong banks in the first place.

And because his friend was safe, so was he. And eight hundred thousand dollars richer!

Recovered now from his fantastic ordeal, Mr. Hua rose from the bench and turned north toward Victoria Harbor. He had one final duty to accomplish for his friend before he was done. Before he too, could disappear.

He had memorized the address earlier. He knew the cargo handling basin of Causeway Bay but it was too far to walk. He entered the subway system. Ten minutes later he emerged, walking toward the water and the shipping business.

The delivery was waiting for him. He signed the bill of lading and cursed when he saw the size of the packing crate. His friend was crazy! All this effort for a stupid *clock*.

Two young Chinese stood next to a dilapidated truck. He approached them. He would need help getting the clock to the next pier. They argued for a few moments about price, Mr. Hua walking away twice, throwing his hands in the air. But eventually they agreed. It took the three of them lifting together to get the huge carton into the truck.

At the next pier they unloaded the crate, and Mr. Hua paid the exorbitant sum. Inside the shipping office, he prepared a new bill of lading, directing the carton to Mr. Vincent in Zud, Switzerland. He advised the woman Mr. Vincent would pick the carton up if she could tell him the expected arrival date. The woman was old and used to dealing with men of the docks.

"Contact number?" she barked.

"I have none," Mr. Hua said. She eyed him suspiciously and put down her pen.

"Old woman, you do not need a contact number," Mr. Hua said. This time she began to crumple his bill of lading.

Reluctantly he gave her his friend's telephone number. It did not matter, he told himself. No one could connect this clock to his friend, much less to his friend's money laundering activities. It would be fine. The old woman scowled.

Exiting the building into the afternoon sun, Mr. Hua felt like a young man. He would have to get busy now, he thought. He would have to determine a way to get his money out of the bank. He couldn't just come there with a wheelbarrow. And he would have to act quickly or else his friend might find it and take it. Mr. Hua wasn't exactly sure how his friend might do this, but he was worried nonetheless.

The old man adjusted his spectacles and returned up the long aluminum ramp. It would take him the rest of the afternoon but he decided to walk back to his home from Causeway Bay. It would be good exercise. It would give him time to think.

He crossed many streets before he came to the tall stairway which rose, concrete step upon concrete step, up the big hill. With measured steps he began his climb.

The roadway below was teaming with automobiles and pedestrians. A middle aged Chinese man stood at the bottom of the long stairway and gazed upward, studying Mr. Hua's progress. The compressed stub of a cigarette hung from his lips. The tails from his faded yellow shirt fell limply against his light blue trousers.

When he was confident Mr. Hua would not be turning back, the man took a final drag from the cigarette and flicked it into the gutter. Dodging between cars, he crossed one street, and then another to where the Citroen was parked.

Opening the driver door, he climbed inside. He sat for a moment, staring out toward the cargo basin. Two large ships were in dock. He could see many others threading their way along the horizon, through Victoria Harbor enroute to the South China Sea. Across the harbor he could see the rising, disheveled tenements of Kowloon.

He glanced back over his shoulder. In the distance, the small lone figure still marched upward to the heights of Hong Kong Island.

As an afterthought, he exited the vehicle and followed the long aluminum ramp to the shipping company. The old woman behind the desk was overcome with work and personal bitterness. He approached her cautiously and took out his badge.

In rapid Cantonese, he extracted from her the details of her last transaction. The cargo information. The delivery instructions. The contact number. He looked at the crate. It was tall and wide and marked *Fragile* in Chinese characters and English.

Should she ship it, she asked. Was the crate full of contraband? He did not know. He would call her later.

The old woman stared at him expectantly. He knew that look. As a policeman, he saw it every time he asked for information. Grudgingly, he extracted one hundred dollars Hong Kong from his worn billfold and passed it into her anxious fist.

She grabbed it hungrily.

Forty-five minutes later, he wheeled the Citroen into the elevated parking garage of Government House. Detective Inspector Jim Kilgowan was seated at his desk. He received Officer Wu's information and thanked him for his time. He reimbursed him the one hundred dollars Hong Kong.

He checked his watch. It was one thirty in the afternoon. It would be half past midnight in New York City. He could telephone now and leave a message for Bobby Washington at the police department.

Or he could wait until tonight and telephone at a time closer to morning in New York. Perhaps that would be the best plan.

Standing, Kilgowan adjusted the creases in his smart, gray gabardine slacks. He ran his fingers through his thin blond hair and straightened his shirt collar. He considered the risks of waiting until tonight to call and smiled with pleasure at the possibility he may be too distracted to remember.

He would have to thank Bobby later for the opportunity to perform this favor. The young Chinese woman at the bank had been exceedingly helpful. So concerned about the old man and yet so excited by the intrigue of Kilgowan's inquiry.

She was so vivacious and so American, yet very Chinese. Such delicate bone structure and porcelain skin.

After he had completed his questions at the bank, Kilgowan had asked her to dinner. They would meet at eight and Kilgowan anticipated the night would last much longer. Better safe than sorry, he thought. Lifting the telephone receiver, Kilgowan requested an international number.

―――

How could things have gone so far? Alex wondered as he fell into his leather chair. Where the hell was that money? How could he have been so close to Vuillard and the cartel's books without realizing the money was being diverted? He'd tried to tell *Papa* it wasn't him. That Vuillard must have been responsible. But he knew *Papa* didn't believe him.

Where the hell was Vuillard? Alex's face contorted with desperation. Vuillard could have assured *Papa* that it was all a misunderstanding. But Vuillard was gone and Julio was the only one *Papa* was listening to.

And Julio's convinced him *I* took the money, Alex thought, and that I then got rid of Vuillard so I could keep it all for myself.

How could they think I'd be that stupid? He cried to himself, wrestling back tears. I'm a banker for god's sake. I'm not a criminal. I'm not like Julio or *Papa*. I don't have anything to do with drugs or selling them or taking them. I'm a banker. That's all I am, a stinking banker.

He wiped his sweaty palms against the armrests and studied his hands. They were small and pale. How could anyone think these hands could kill? It was ludicrous.

Swinging the chair around to the desk, he picked up the telephone and dialed Jeannie's number. After seven rings, she finally answered. He listened to her voice. She'd been reading to the girls.

He thought back to a safer time, when the girls were little and he was having trouble making ends meet at the bank. He'd felt like a failure then. So, this was *success*?

If Jeannie noticed the tension in his voice, she didn't comment. He would drive down Sunday and they would all go to the zoo. Alex hung up slowly, wondering if Papa would be gone from his house by then.

Pulling open a desk drawer, Alex found the telephone directory. He flipped to the blue pages in the back, leafing through the city and county government listings. His hands stopped at the Federal Government page. They started to shake.

Slowly he picked up the telephone, and cradled it in his hand. What would he say, he wondered? Then he realized it was too late to call. Maybe he'd tell Jeannie everything tomorrow, and they'd telephone together from her house. That was safer.

He replaced the receiver, wondering if he was doing the right thing, but knowing he had no other choice. It was all over.

CHAPTER TWENTY

The video picture was granular and dark gray. Adjusting the small knobs, Maxwell made it brighter. Despite the darkness, he could now see the fuzzy figures of two men standing on the Post's front porch between the two large columns. He added a green tint to the screen and that seemed to draw in more light. He pushed a black button at the rear of the monitor and produced a digitized photograph off the screen. Then he ran to the gazebo door.

"Stuart, come here!" he yelled, hoping afterward his voice wouldn't carry too far in the quiet night air. Jerking around, Stuart Birkwell dumped coffee down the front of his shirt. He sloshed more from the mug as he pushed past Maxwell to the video monitor.

Twisting the knobs violently back and forth, Stuart fought to focus the picture. The screen turned from black to gray fuzz under his awkward adjustments. Maxwell reached over to help, but Stuart batted his arm away. Then he settled on a picture no better than before, but this time good enough for Stuart.

The short chubby shadow wore a white Panama hat. The screen sparked a stream of yellow light when the shadow lit a match and held it to a large cigar. Stuart exhaled audibly, hugging the instruments.

"Jeeses, it's *him*," he whispered.

"Who?" asked Maxwell cautiously, gazing over him to the screen.

"Enrique Bodero. The head of the DeYambi's. *Papa*. Get Bobby Washington for me *now*."

Maxwell jumped to attention and ran from the gazebo, leaving Stuart still hugging the monitor.

Bobby and two of the surveillance crew were watching television in the Pollard kitchen, waiting. Their cars were secreted in the garage. Maxwell roared through the sliding glass doors and stood breathless.

"Bobby, come *on*," he cried, gesturing to the backyard. Bobby swung his legs from the kitchen table and followed Maxwell to the gazebo. Stuart pointed to the vague figures on the screen.

"It's Bodero. This is big! Did anyone see where he came from?" Stuart barked.

Bobby studied the screen, recognizing the partial description of the man arriving in the Grand Am an hour ago.

"They got him on tape when he arrived. But they didn't get a look at his face. Couldn't be anyone else, though. Same hat. Big cigar."

Bobby looked closely at the second figure standing on the porch.

"Who's that with him?" Stuart asked, still trying to focus the screen. Bobby hesitated. Somebody who *shouldn't* be, he thought.

"It's Post," Bobby replied.

"Alex Post. *Great!* This makes our case. Alex is Bodero's henchman. I knew it! And we've got them *together*!

Bobby shook his head.

"No. Not Alex Post. Ethan Post. *Bluebird*."

Stuart looked at him, baffled.

"What the hell is he doing talking to the head of a Columbian cartel? I thought he flew airplanes. I thought you told me he was *clean*."

"Yeah, I did, sir," Bobby said, pulling back from the screen. He knew in his gut Post wasn't involved. He'd stake his reputation on it. Maybe he already had.

———

Did I just send an innocent man into a dangerous situation? Samantha wondered. She couldn't accept that possibility. Ethan was bound to go anyway, right? She'd just mapped his way.

Had she just screwed up the task force investigation? Probably. They didn't need another player in the mix, mucking things up for Dan and complicating an already complicated situation.

Guests were enjoying the pool and hot tub outside. It seemed safer to be around people right now, Samantha thought, than off on her own where trouble could find her. She would need her swimsuit and a cover-up from her suitcase.

Mounting the staircase, Samantha padded softly down the hall to the room she was a sharing with Dan. Gently opening the door she saw Dan outstretched on the four-poster bed, staring at the ceiling. The room was pleasant but sparsely furnished with a dresser and a chair, and a yellow-fringed rug. A halogen lamp lighted the room in a soft, comforting glow, but her two bags from the car weren't there.

She wanted to ask Dan how things were going, but he looked too deep in thought. Instead, Samantha retrieved the car keys from the night stand and let herself out of the room.

She slipped back through the kitchen and out into the garage. The air was cooler there, but it smelled of gasoline and stale exhaust. She squeezed past a late model Buick and a lawn mower, trying to avoid smudging dirt on her dress enroute to the Mercedes in the driveway.

Voices from the front porch stopped her before she emerged from the garage. She could smell cigar smoke and hear *Papa's* thick accent. Listening closer, she heard Ethan's voice. "I've played some nice golf courses around Myrtle Beach, but I've never spent much time in North Carolina," Ethan was saying.

Papa replied, "Oh, what a shame. When I first come to America I spent all my time in Miami. But lately I better appreciate the quieter, slower life. I have a large house on a bay in North Carolina."

Papa puffed audibly on his cigar.

"And I have my own golf course."

"Eighteen holes?" Ethan asked.

"Eighteen *beautiful* holes, my friend, with two of them right on the water. Only special friends of mine play this course with me. But I *like* military men. Pilots *especially*. I would consider it an honor if you come to my house to play my golf course."

Ethan pondered the proposal. *Papa* continued.

"That is where I come from today; from my North Carolina compound. I am meeting more friends tonight, and we are flying back tomorrow to play golf. Perhaps you and your brother could join us?"

Samantha strained to hear Ethan's reply, but none came.

Papa continued, "I have a private plane for myself and my friends, but you have a plane too, do you not? I believe Alex told me that once. You could fly down with Alex and we could all have a *wonderful* time."

Samantha shifted her weight, and nearly fell against a garden rake. She caught it just before it hit the garage floor.

"We can even have more fun. We can invite Alex's friend Dan and his lovely lady companion. How many seats your plane?"

"It seats six," Ethan replied.

"Wonderful. That would work, hey? We have a party!" *Papa* flashed a big smile.

"It *could* work. My plane is outside Annapolis. It's a four-hour drive from here," Ethan said.

"So, we get up early and have pancakes! Then you drive down there tomorrow morning. Simple! Good plan!" *Papa* laughed and slapped Ethan on the back.

———

Stuart fumbled violently with the monitor's tuning knobs again, ripping the screen from black to bright green and back again. Maxwell grabbed his hand this time and firmly pushed him away from the delicate machine.

"Boss, ya gotta let me do that," he said, as he regained the fuzzy picture. Stuart wanted to call Maxwell an asshole, but Bobby grabbed him before he could open his mouth.

"Hey, come on Stuart, he's *responsible* for these machines," Bobby whispered in his ear. Stuart shrugged off Bobby's arm, but didn't say anything. He just glared at the rookie agent.

"What were you trying to find?" Maxwell asked, his eyes glued to the screen fearful of meeting Stuart's.

"There's a shadow in the corner of the garage. It wasn't there before. It looks like a person just walked up and is standing there. I wanted to see who it was."

Maxwell toyed with the contrast and enhanced the screen's resolution until the figure became clearer. Bobby whistled and clapped Stuart on the back.

"That ain't a *person*, Stu! That there's my *partner*, and she's *on the job!*"

———

Papa's cigar smoke clouded Ethan's mind. On one hand he couldn't believe his good luck. Here was his big chance. Of course he couldn't expect a cartel kingpin to outline his drug operation between golf strokes, but here was the opportunity to gather intelligence. If *Papa* was really so enamored with pilots, maybe he could become his friend, at least for the weekend, and maybe *Papa* might open up.

Yes, this could be a great opportunity. But he didn't like the idea of that asshole Dan coming along. And he didn't like the idea of Sammy being there, but for a different reason.

Ethan scuffed the porch's concrete floor with his shoe.

"Sure. What the hell. Let's do it," he answered.

Papa smiled broadly.

"But how will I find your compound?"

"Not a problem. My pilot will outline the flight plan for you tomorrow morning over breakfast. I have a small airfield nearby, so easy, see? It's only a four hour flight from here for me and what? Two hours for you? We be there no time, you'll see. My driver will meet you when you land."

"Sounds great," Ethan said, although his stomach felt queasy.

A white Saab gunned its engine and raced up the street, pulling to the curb in front of the Post home. Julio opened the driver side door and climbed out. He kicked his pant legs free of his topsiders and adjusted the gun at the cleft of his back.

Papa took off his white Panama and waved it to Julio. The signal. Julio turned to Arturo who was just exiting from the passenger side.

"The plan is on," Julio said, pleased.

Julio and Arturo walked side by side up the driveway. Samantha plastered herself against the garden hose. She clung to the metal garage door tracking for support and crouched down out of sight.

Julio's eyes darted back and forth over the parked cars, lingering momentarily on the open garage. Samantha held her breath. His gaze bypassed where she hid and focused on the front porch. He climbed the two steps.

"Julio, you will be pleased. Ethan Post has agreed to join us for the weekend," *Papa* said in greeting.

Julio shook his boss's hand and smiled oddly at Ethan. Ethan wondered if he'd been too hasty.

Julio's friend wandered off the porch and over toward the garage. Stopping next to the open door, he lit a cigarette and tossed the match to the ground. It fell next to Samantha's foot. He took a long drag and leaned against the doorframe, looking out into the street. Julio joined him momentarily.

"It's all set. Fucking bastard Post. I knew he took the money."

Julio paced between the parked cars. With each footfall, Samantha had the feeling of impending doom. Julio paced until Arturo finished his cigarette. When done, he flicked it aside and walked to the front porch. Julio followed and together they entered the house.

Samantha waited for a minute, counting the seconds off in her mind until she felt safe enough to stand up. Her knees were stiff and she smelled like gasoline. Slowly, she massaged the feeling back into her legs.

She waited for another minute before walking to the Mercedes. It was completely dark now and the street was quiet. She hefted her bag and Dan's from the trunk; then loaded the straps onto her shoulders until she looked like a pack animal.

———

"Why are you still up here?" Samantha asked Dan as she struggled in through the bedroom door.

"Alex asked me to disappear for a while. The meeting didn't go too well and he said he needed time to think. I did, too. Besides, I needed a little nap. How is it going downstairs?"

"Should I tell you now or should we take a walk in the backyard?"

Dan thought for a minute.

"Let's meet outside in an hour. By the pool. The guests should be pretty much gone by then and we can talk privately." Samantha nodded and rubbed some grease from her arm and left leg.

"How'd you get so dirty?" he asked.

"That's part of my story. I need to take a shower."

She gathered her overnight bag, and disappeared into the bathroom.

———

The pool was built twenty years ago when kidney shape was the rage, before people used their outdoor pools to swim laps rather than as a cool diversion and a nice place to entertain. It was deep blue with bulbs around the rim that sent shimmering ripples of light through the water. The tall fence surrounding it was high enough for privacy. Large slate tiles formed the patio. Wire mesh garden tables and chairs decorated the tiles. The cool night air made Samantha's powder blue jeans and cotton sweater all the more appropriate. The shower dissolved the layer of garage grit from her skin and she felt refreshed. She was anxious to speak with Dan.

———

The digital clock on the dresser read eleven thirty. Ethan checked it against his watch. No more power outages tonight. The Excel Energy van had left from across the street sometime earlier. It hadn't been there when he and *Papa* were on the front porch. I guess they solved their problem, he thought.

Slowly he pulled his shirt off and unbuttoned his pants, thinking about tomorrow. A light breeze blew through the window screen. He leaned forward against the windowsill to smell fresh flowers and catch the moonlight on Alex's pool below. At the pool's corner stood a lone figure, bending toward the water. Ethan quickly turned off the room light, allowing him to watch. His heart skipped. It was *her*. *Alone.* Could he run downstairs quickly enough to intercept her? Would she follow him upstairs to his room if he asked?

Ethan lunged for the shirt on his bed, but stopped as he saw a second figure emerge from the sun porch. With a disappointment that throbbed throughout his entire body, he recognized the second figure. He watched as the man walked to a chaise lounge and lay down. Samantha walked toward him and sat at the corner of the chair. In one motion the man's arms enveloped her, and pulled her down next to him. She went willingly.

———

"For God's sake, Dan, do you think this is *necessary*?"

Samantha squirmed to fit next to him on the chair. The armrest cut into her shoulder blade and her left arm was twisted.

"Yeah. Relax, baby. By the way, do ya feel like a trip to North Carolina tomorrow?"

"So, we're going?"

"How'd *you* know about it?" he asked.

Lifting her locket, Samantha told Dan the whole story.

CHAPTER TWENTY-ONE

Wind chimes caught a gentle breeze, filling the gazebo with a tranquil, melodic shimmering. A clear full moon bathed the backyard in a restful peace.

Bobby Washington listened to the two hushed voices amplified through the small, black speaker. His head was hot in his hands. Slowly he massaged his temples, listening to Samantha's hushed voice describe the conversations overheard in the garage. He couldn't believe she'd had the nerve to stand there and listen. She was a real pro.

He looked at Stuart's solemn face as he sat across the screened porch; his face glued to the video monitor.

Dan's voice was quiet but excited as he outlined the benefits to the North Carolina trip. He'd be *in* with the De Yambi kingpins, particularly *Papa*. He could cozy up to Julio, too. Who knew the extent of *his* crimes?

Describing the closed-door meeting in the library between him, Alex and *Papa*, Dan's voice hardened.

"Alex is a dead man. There's over eight million dollars gone, funneled to some bank accounts in Hong Kong. *Papa* had total faith in the *Baron* so he suspects Alex. Period. Alex was sweatin' like a pig."

"Alex is ready for us, I tell ya," Dan continued. "After this weekend, his nerves will be shot. Hell, they're pretty much gone right now. All you guys will have to do is pick him up, take him down to the precinct and shine a light in his eyes. I bet he'll tell us everything."

"When *Papa* told Alex about the North Carolina plans, Alex looked like a starving little rat that someone just threw dinner scraps. He hadn't expected a second chance. But *Papa* just smiled at him like Santa Claus and before I knew it, Alex was pouring drinks. *Papa's* a sly piece of work. You can see he's toying with Alex. I've got a feeling they're going to want to rub him out sometime soon, but the way I figure, *Papa* needs him for now. I think *Papa*'s worried about Julio and his pals. If *Papa* makes a move against Alex right now, that will leave no one from the De Yambi cartel on site in New York. He'd be relinquishing the control of his organization to Julio's group and it's obvious he doesn't want that to happen. I think *Papa*'s beginning to trust me. I'm going to try to get closer to him when we play golf."

Samantha listened intently to Dan's litany, propping the little locket against her shoulder, closest to his mouth. She envisioned Stuart listening to this, somewhere nearby. She looked at the little gold piece of jewelry and wanted to open it to see the microphone inside. She wondered if it was working. Maybe we're sitting out here talking to ourselves, she thought, and laughed.

Dan glared at her, annoyed. He paused, and Samantha took the opportunity to speak.

"When I was in the garage, Julio told the guy he came with, the driver of the white Saab, that the *plan* was on. At first I thought he was referring to the trip to North Carolina because Ethan had just agreed to go, but now I'm not so sure. Julio came back to the garage and whispered to the guy that Alex had taken the money, so I started to think that maybe there might be another *plan*."

"What kind of a plan?" Dan asked.

"I'm not sure. I'd hate to go on record with this, because what if I'm wrong? I'm not a professional, as you all know. I'm remembering that Julio fought with Alex earlier this week about the money disappearing to Hong Kong. And Dan just said *Papa* is convinced Alex took the money, or at least knew about it. Therefore, common sense tells me that no one trusts Alex anymore. Both Julio and *Papa* would want him out of the picture, *permanently*. If we assume that Julio's reference to the plan meant the trip to North Carolina, then it wasn't a spontaneous invitation that *Papa* cooked up while talking to Ethan about golf. He'd already had it in his mind to bring Ethan, Alex, and probably Dan and me to his compound this weekend."

She looked to Dan for reinforcement. He looked tired, but nodded for her to continue.

"What I can't understand is what benefit this trip would be to *Papa*? We're all talking about how it would benefit *Alex*, and how it would definitely benefit our investigation, but I just don't see what *Papa* would get out of this. I guess that's all I have to say. I think there's danger here somewhere, and I believe we might be walking into something bigger than a golf game."

Samantha was surprised when Dan didn't answer right away. Somehow she'd expected him to discount her suspicions immediately.

Dan shifted his weight in the lawn chair, pinning Samantha's back severely against the wooden armrest. His left arm slid over her hip to her waist, as he pulled her and the locket closer to him. She could feel his moist breath against her face. He appeared to be selecting his words carefully.

"I know we've talked about this before, Samantha. About the danger of doing these undercover assignments. You're in a pretty tough spot right now, and we put you there. But I know I speak for everyone involved in this investigation, that we'll do everything in our power to keep you safe. We're professionals. We know our job."

Samantha wanted to scream.

"That's not what I'm *saying*. My concern is for the *investigation*. I have no worries for my own safety above yours or Alex's. I have misgivings about these plans and I wanted to bring them to your attention," Samantha protested.

Dan picked up the locket between his large fingers. She felt his body tense and knew if she could see his eyes, they'd be hard.

He said, "Alex wants to visit his ex-wife tomorrow before we fly out. It's harmless, I think. Ethan Post keeps his plane somewhere near Annapolis so we're headed in that direction anyway. I presume you'll be around to give us surveillance. Good night."

Dan dropped the locket and stood abruptly. Without looking at Samantha, he advanced toward the house. She watched him walk through the sun porch and disappear into the shadows of the Post home.

The pale blue glow from the immersed pool lights comforted her. She raised her hand and gently covered the locket, muffling the sounds of her agitated breathing.

Bobby paced back and forth over the green feathery AstroTurf. Stuart sat silent in his wicker chair hugging the video monitor, his head resting against the blurred screen, listening and thinking.

"Get everyone together in the house in five minutes," he instructed Bobby without looking up.

The screen door squeaked as Bobby pushed it open. The sound suspended in the midnight air, accompanied him as he walked toward the Pollard house.

He's gonna do it, he thought. He's going to let them go.

Five minutes later Stuart stumbled through the Pollard's sliding glass door. His wrinkled white button down shirt still held the remains of the spilled coffee from hours ago. The collar drooped below his thin, pointed chin where dark stubbles now grew. He ran his hands threw his wiry hair, and poured himself another cup of coffee from Mrs. Pollard's perpetual pot.

Around the oval dining table were assembled his surveillance crew. He regarded them now, and wondered if he looked as tired as they did. Maxwell had managed a shower between the end of Alex's party and Dan's briefing, but it failed to refresh his appearance. He sat now in faded red running shorts and a frayed white cotton t-shirt, its faded letters spelling out a now unreadable message.

The two radio technicians, minus the Excel Energy overalls, lounged back against one wall. Karen Alexander refilled her coffee. They all looked expectantly at Stuart.

"Maxwell, do we know where Ethan Post keeps his airplane?" Stuart barked, his words cutting through the air, jolting them all to attention. The rookie agent looked confused, caught like a schoolboy without his homework assignment.

"I think it was in his file at the academy. I think I wrote it down. It'd be with my notes in the car."

"It damn well better be. Get your notes. Now," Stuart snapped.

Maxwell's chair almost tipped over as he pushed from the table and ran out of the room. Despite his absence Stuart began laying out the plans for the next day.

Bobby's cell phone rang. Heads turned to him. He glanced at the number. "Excuse me, but I have to take this," he said, backing out of the room into the hall. A sweet female voice greeted him.

"Detective Washington? This is the Command Center. There's a message here for you. It's marked *urgent* so I figured I better call. It's from an Inspector Kilgowan of the Royal Hong Kong Police. He left two numbers where you could be sure to reach him."

Bobby shifted the telephone to his other shoulder, and hunted through his pocket for a pen and scrap of paper. He copied the numbers down carefully.

"I hope you don't mind that I called. I figured it might be important."

"Thanks, baby. No trouble at all. When did he call?"

The woman paused. "*Ohhh*, looks like sometime this morning."

"*This morning*? Like in twelve hours ago?"

"Yeah, looks like it. You have a nice night, okay?"

The woman hung up quickly anticipating an outburst and hoping to avoid it. Bobby cursed the incompetence of his office and checked his watch, praying Kilgowan would still be at one of the numbers.

He dialed the first, and was connected to Royal Hong Kong Police headquarters. No luck. He punched in the second number and waited. After two rings, Jim Kilgowan answered.

"Don't tell me you just got the message, old chap. Your department is a finely tuned machine, as always," Kilgowan said.

"Yeah, I trained them myself. They told me it was urgent. This better be good."

Bobby thought he heard a woman's voice through the telephone lines.

"Did I catch you at a bad time, buddy? Sorry."

"Hey, no problem. I should be thanking *you*. I had quite an adventure conducting your little investigation."

The female voice whispered something inaudible and Kilgowan covered the receiver. Bobby heard muffled laughter.

"By the way, old chap, is anyone on your end missing eight million dollars? We have a little Chinese man who seems to have been laundering it for about four years over here. He wire transferred most of it earlier today to a Mr. Vincent at four different banks in Florida. Does this sound interesting?"

Bobby whistled through his teeth. He scribbled down the information excitedly. It was all there. The eight million plus that the De Yambi cartel was missing, that they'd pinned on Alex. The Hong Kong bank that the FBI accountants saw the money going into. The accounts at the four banks in the names of Wong, Long, Chung and Nung, matching the Hong Kong rhymes Samantha had found in the *Baron*'s apartment. The laundered money wired to a *Mr. Vincent*. The *Baron*'s prized clock destined for delivery to Mr. Vincent in Switzerland and even a contact telephone number for him.

"So tell me, old chap, are these criminals simply sloppy, leaving such a trail, or are you simply very good to have found them?" Kilgowan asked.

Bobby whistled again. "We're the fuckin' *best*. An' don't you forget it. The NYPD may be shit at passing on phone messages, but we do a hell of a job when it counts! I owe you a big one, Jimmy. Jus' name it. What can I do for you?"

Kilgowan laughed and the female voice joined in.

"You've done enough, my friend. You'll have my help anytime," he said, and hung up the telephone.

Bobby returned to the kitchen, anxious to tell Stuart the information. *Now* was the time. *Now* he had his proof. He wished he could tell Samantha, too. Frowning, he realized it could be two more days before she would find out.

 Leaning against a wall, he listened distractedly as Stuart wound up the assignments for the next day. One by one the FBI agents straggled past him to their sleeping bags in the living room.

Bobby crossed to the refrigerator and retrieved two Budweiser's. He twisted the caps off and put one on the table in front of Stuart.

Stuart looked at him, solemn and exhausted.

"Boss, I think we need a drink," Bobby said and clinked his bottle against the other in a toast. Stuart picked the Bud up slowly and took a swallow.

"I've got some important information for you, but you might not be too happy about how I got it, and that I didn't tell you about it sooner. So just sit there for a minute and let me tell you. An' enjoy your beer."

Stuart finished the beer and got two more from the refrigerator for them both as Bobby told the tale of his and Samantha's suspicions and their ensuing investigation. Reluctantly, he told him how she had ended up with Ethan Post in the Waldorf's Peacock Alley lounge.

"So *she* was the blonde?" Stuart asked.

Bobby shook his head.

"She's really embarrassed about it, though, so please don't tell her I told you."

Stuart thought for a minute. "I'm surprised at you Washington. Word was you stopped working when you got your gold shield. That you'd done some heroics up to that point but that I was inheriting a burned out detective happy to wait out his remaining days until retirement doing surveillance. So what's happened?" Stuart asked, taking a sip of his beer.

Bobby smiled and shrugged. "I guess I'm inspired again."

"Well, keep it up," Stuart said and offered Bobby a high-five.

Bobby finished up the story with the details on the money transfers to the Florida banks and the contact telephone number.

"My guess is the *Baron* is alive, and at the other end of this telephone number. If we find out who owns the telephone and pay them a visit, our missing informant will probably answer the door and some part of his body will be bandaged from a gunshot wound. A .22 gunshot wound to be exact," Bobby concluded.

Stuart sat back in his chair, filtering the information.

"You said that all of the eight million, except for some eight hundred thousand was wire transferred to the *Baron*. Who got the eight hundred?"

Bobby laughed. "I guess everybody's got an angle, boss. The Chinaman kept it for himself. The Hong Kong PD put a hold on his personal account. The *Baron* was ripping' off the De Yambi's and Mr. Hua was ripping' off the *Baron*. Seems fair to me."

Bobby sat forward, suddenly solemn.

"I know you were discounting what Samantha said tonight, Boss. When she talked about her suspicions of *Papa*. I know you and Dan don't give her much credit because she's not a cop or an agent, but she's got damned good instincts. Hell, she's the one who got us started on the

Baron's disappearance in the first place, after she saw all that stuff on the yacht. An' she's the one who got me excited about investigating the possibility he'd faked his death in order to steal the cartel's money and disappear. And now it looks like she was right."

Bobby sat back and took a long drink from his beer.

"You know, I've been content these past two years to just sit on my butt and watch other people investigate. Waiting for retirement, that was me, and I'm only forty-four years old! She got me excited about this work again. But she's a little afraid of you, Stu," Bobby said and winked.

Stuart laughed.

"So you think we've got something to worry about tomorrow. Is that what you're saying?" Stuart asked pointedly.

"Yeah, I really think so, boss," Bobby replied, shaking his head. He just wished he knew what he was worried about.

———

Samantha climbed the stairs to the second floor quietly. The thought of crawling into a comfortable bed enticed her, beckoned her. Without much sleep last night, she'd plunged her body into overdrive to endure until now. But her energy was ebbing fast and she needed at least six good hours of sleep to revive.

And I'm not going to get it sleeping next to Dan. Her stomach tightened with that thought. Even if he didn't *try* anything, just lying next to him, feeling the tension between them was too much to deal with right now.

They're not paying me enough to go through this, Samantha thought. Just how much are they paying me? She wondered. *That* hadn't even been discussed.

She paused at the top of the landing, hoping Dan was asleep already. Padding down the hallway, she noticed the open door next to their room. Taking her hand from the knob, she tiptoed to the next room and turned on the light. It was empty. Two twin beds were placed against a wall papered in a lively rose floral. A nightstand was set between the beds and on it, an alarm clock.

Quietly she entered and closed the door behind her. The room faced out onto the backyard allowing her to navigate by the faint light of the moon. She crossed to the nightstand and picked up the clock. It was one of the simple, old style alarms that required no computer training to set. She turned the knob on the back until the tiny alarm hand read six thirty, and pulled the alarm button to *on*.

Slipping off her tennis shoes, she turned back the covers on one bed and crawled in.

CHAPTER TWENTY-TWO

Ethan slept fitfully. After his midnight surveillance of Samantha, he'd lain awake for at least an hour, wondering if he'd ever find a woman to walk with late at night or crawl up next to on a lawn chair in the dark and just talk.

He awoke before the alarm and listened as the gentle morning breeze rustled against the half-drawn shade. Rolling over toward the window, he smelled the fresh morning air. It was moister than yesterday, heavier and more fragrant.

Discarding the sheet, he swung his legs over the side of the bed and peered through the window. The sky was a cloudless early morning blue, but Ethan wondered how long that would last. The moistening air signaled a possible weather change and he hadn't planned on flying in the rain.

He crossed the room to his overnight bag and extracted a T-shirt and worn shorts, white cotton socks and his old Nikes. It was still early as he walked quietly into the hall.

The second door down the hall was open slightly. He paused outside and pushed it open further. On the twin bed closest to the door Sammy slept. He watched her gentle, peaceful breathing and her arms as they hugged the pillow. He closed the door and retreated down the stairs.

Setting his stopwatch, he forced the moist outside air into his lungs and took off on his run at a sprint. Concentrating on his breathing and his strong momentum his mind had no room for distracting thoughts.

———

The first thing Samantha noticed was the soft white material against her face, like a pretty veil through her half opened lids. Then a jingling sound invaded her subconscious. The jingling sound continued, not loud enough to be startling but enough to drag her from her sleep. Burying her head deeper into the soft pillow, she willed the sound to stop, wondering if it was in her imagination.

The pillow felt comforting and familiar but she had no idea where she was. Pushing herself up with her elbows, Samantha looked around sleepily, trying to make sense of her surroundings. The little alarm clock on the nightstand came into focus. Ahh, that was the source of the jingling. She gathered herself up, smoothed out the bed where she'd slept, and tip-toed out into the hall and into the adjacent room.

Dan was stretched diagonally on the double bed, his legs and striped jockey shorts visible from where he had kicked off the sheets. One pliable soft pillow was stuffed up against his cheek, and he breathed rhythmically, but loudly through his mouth.

She lay down on the rug. If Dan awoke and wondered where she'd been all night, she could tell him she'd been sleeping on the floor. She rolled onto her side, and felt the bones of her shoulder smash against the hard wood beneath the rug. Happy that she hadn't slept on the floor all night, she closed her eyes and drifted back to sleep.

———

Alex awoke with a headache, and for a brief moment he was happy because it was the only thing on his mind. He rolled over and buried his head into the pillow. The inside of his mouth felt thick from the heavy liqueur he'd drunk with *Papa*, and his stomach felt stale and queasy. *Papa's* face popped into his consciousness and his body shuddered involuntarily. He could almost smell *Papa's* cigar breath and he thought he might throw up again. Forcing himself from the bed and downstairs to the kitchen, he hoped coffee would relieve his anxiety and improve his focus.

The first coffee mug fell from its wooden tree and crashed against the sink's stainless steel sides, the sound echoing through the empty kitchen. Alex looked down, and noticed his shaking hands. Grabbing the mug to stifle its sounds, he felt the clanging continue to reverberate inside his skull. He filled the mug and stared out the window, blind to the early morning sunshine. He didn't even hear the side door open and Ethan walk in.

"You're going to need steadier hands than that to handle *Papa*. You're a wreck. Didn't you get any sleep last night?" Ethan asked, watching his brother.

Alex turned from the window.

"Can't you even manage a *Good Morning*, or something pleasant? Whatever happened to light conversation?" he barked.

Alex's worn T-shirt clung to his soft middle and his legs looked like white sticks protruding from under his shorts. The sunshine against his face made him look older and drawn.

"What I do about *Papa* is my own business," he continued. "Your business is to fly us to North Carolina. You don't see me asking whether you're up to the trip."

Ethan ignored him and walked to the sink to pour himself a cup. For a moment they stood on opposite sides of the kitchen, glaring at each other.

"Weren't you going to visit Jeannie today? She's pretty worried about you. She says you called her the other day and acted like you were in a lot of trouble. She wanted me to see if I could help or something," Ethan said.

"I think you should stay out of this! Neither of you know anything about my life!" Alex yelled.

"I know a hell of lot more than you think I do. I know about Vuillard. I was even up there to visit him the other day, but he wasn't around," Ethan retorted.

Alex looked panicked.

"I even had a nice long talk with that asshole Giacometti's girlfriend the other day and now I know a whole lot more about *him*. I'm no fool, Alex. I've worked for the government long enough to recognize what's going on. I'm not going to sit back and watch you trash the Post name and our family's reputation when they carry you off to some federal prison."

"Well, so that's all you really care about, isn't it? The glorious *Post* name," Alex grabbed Ethan's sweaty shirt, pulling him around. His fingers cut into Ethan's skin as he pushed him back against the counter. Ethan reeled from the unexpected force.

"*No*, that isn't the only thing I care about. I told you I cared about you, too, but you don't believe that. Sure I care about the family. Jeeses, dad didn't raise us to be *criminals*. He was a career naval officer, for god's sake."

"I hated the son of a bitch!" Alex hissed into Ethan's face, then cringed as Ethan's fist crashed into his mouth. He reeled backwards against the counter clutching his jaw, and braced himself for another blow. Ethan stopped mid-motion, startled by his own violence and his brother's sudden frailty.

"What the fuck am I doing?" Ethan yelled, aghast at his brother's frightened expression. Drops of blood formed at the corner of Alex's mouth.

Ethan said, "I'm sorry. Let me get you something for that."

———

Behind the Post home and on the other side of the little woods, Bobby raised his head slowly from the kitchen table. Indentations from his watch had etched themselves into his left cheek while he dozed, his arm acting as a pillow. It was almost eight o'clock and the phone hadn't rung. He'd been waiting all night. They were supposed to call, and he was getting worried.

CHAPTER TWENTY-THREE

Alex turned his face into the cool water, letting the shower soothe his smarting face. Why the hell did Ethan have to hit me? He wondered. Hell, maybe he deserved it.

Jeannie's face materialized in the pooling water. A smiling face like when they were married and happy. Last night he'd been so certain what he should do. He envisioned himself running into Jeannie's arms, telling her the whole story and then calling that number from the blue pages to turn himself in.

But then *Papa* had ruined those plans with that stupid idea to meet him in North Carolina. Hell, I didn't think it was stupid last night, Alex thought. I nearly jumped for joy.

I can't go through with *this,* Alex realized and suddenly felt disoriented and frightened. That's why *Papa* wants me down there. He's going to *kill* me.

Struggling, Alex extinguished the shower stream and stumbled from the tub. His hands shook as he unzipped the leather toiletry kit, impatient at having to apply deodorant and brush his teeth. He nearly tripped over the cotton rug in his bedroom. The closet door moved too slowly along its track. With a burst of strength, he crushed himself against it, springing it from its track and heaving it to one side.

The tightly pressed pants and starched shirts hanging there affronted him now, like monuments to the petty vanities he'd allowed to control his life. He felt sick. From a hanger deep in the closet he found an old worn pair of blue jeans and put them on. They looked silly with his brown socks and fine leather shoes, but he didn't care.

His fingers moved nervously through his unkempt hair as he headed into the kitchen and retrieved his car keys. Ethan had vanished. Feeling his jaw, he realized it still hurt. He'd almost forgotten the pain, but now it only reminded him of what he had to do.

Papa's silver Grand Am was gone. Thank god, Alex thought as he climbed into his BMW. No more distractions. But where had he gone? And where was Julio? He glanced nervously up and down the street, but saw no cars.

He floored the Beemer's accelerator, backing violently from the drive-way. The tires spun as he shifted into drive and raced from the neighborhood. At the tall brick stanchions, he paused momentarily, searching his rearview mirrors for any sign of pursuit. The road was clear.

If they see me leave like this, they're going to know something's up, Alex thought. For a moment he thought he saw a shadow next to him in the trees, like a stalking figure. He envisioned Julio with his gun. He turned abruptly, and accelerated around the corner.

Do they know about Jeannie? Do they know where she lives? If they wanted him, would they go there? He racked his brain, trying to remember what he'd told them over the years.

Shit! Of course they knew about her. That would be the first place they'd look for him.

Maybe I should call her, he thought. Have her keep an eye out for suspicious cars.

You're losing your mind, he yelled to himself, cursing as a red light forced him to stop. He braked the car severely, the jolt throwing him forward against the steering wheel. They don't have any reason to distrust me. Hell, I fell for *Papa's* bullshit last night, hook, line and sinker. They think they've got me right where they want me.

He breathed hard, steadying himself, but he still checked the rear mirrors again. This time he thought he saw a silver sedan approaching slowly from behind. At the next intersection he turned east. It was nearly ten o'clock and traffic was beginning to build. He wove the BMW a quarter of a mile, then pulled it swiftly into a McDonald's parking lot. Quickly he circled the building and then stopped, studying the road in front of him.

There were too many cars, but he thought he saw the same silver sedan drive past. Perspiration began to form along his temples and drip down over his cheeks. He brushed it away violently with his hand and watched the silver sedan slow down in front of the restaurant, then speed up again until it disappeared down the road.

Was it all in his mind or *was* he being followed? Alex couldn't be sure. He parked the BMW, and entered McDonalds, suddenly hungry. Moments later he unwrapped an egg sandwich at a window booth, his eyes glued to the road outside. Ten silver cars must have gone by as he watched, confused, unable to distinguish them from the one he'd thought he'd seen.

Jeannie's little house seemed like a fortress in his mind. I'll make it there by afternoon, he thought. I'll just drive carefully for a while and make sure I'm not being followed; then I'll head south. I can hide out there. Sure. Even if Julio comes after me, I'll be safe.

His hands felt as slippery as the egg sandwich, as sweat trickled down his wrists and into his palms. His shirt ringed with perspiration as he shoveled the remaining bites into his mouth and stood up.

Walking nervously from the restaurant, he studied the parking lot, assuring himself Julio wasn't lurking nearby. His muscles tightened as he saw a short dark haired man in sunglasses approach from a parked car, but a little boy ran quickly to his side, and Alex relaxed.

He eased the BMW back into traffic and executed a quick U-turn from the left lane. From his mirror he saw the McDonalds behind him and what he was sure was the same silver sedan pull rapidly out of the lot. He concentrated on the vehicle in his rear mirror and watched as it lined up for the same U-turn. A honking horn brought him back to the road and he slammed on the brakes, the BMW barreling down on a car stopped at a red light in front of him. Jesus! The BMW stopped inches from the car's rear bumper and the driver stuck his head out the window, yelling something. Alex flipped him off and stared again into his mirror. The silver sedan was just making the U-turn.

When the traffic light changed, Alex gunned the engine and wove himself deeper into the traffic, away from the silver sedan. But what was that? Another car gunned its engine too, and was rapidly catching up to the BMW. This car was old and black and slowed about three car lengths behind.

Alex downshifted and turned violently at the next intersection. Sweat trickled into his eyes, blurring his vision. Without thinking, he pointed the car back toward his house.

He was shaking visibly as he ran into the house, searching for Dan. Julio won't try anything with Dan around, he figured. Dan has a gun, Alex knew. Together they'd go to Jeannie's, but he wouldn't tell Dan his plans. Fuck Dan, really. After today, Dan Giacometti would just be a small chapter in the story he'd tell the FBI.

Dan was just a loud, obnoxious asshole who'd never be as big a part of the De Yambi organization as he was, Alex thought. He'd only put up with him because of Vincent. Dan talked big, Alex thought now, but didn't seem to know much. Why the hell Vincent had ever done business with him, he couldn't figure out. Anyway, the feds would be happy to hear about Giacometti. And that blonde bitch of a girlfriend. Just what had she told Ethan, anyway?

Figuring he'd send Giacometti on to the airport alone after they made it to Jeannie's, Alex mounted the stairs and pounded on his door. He struggled to compose himself, knowing he looked nervous, sweaty and disheveled. He ran his hands back through his hair, and pounded again.

"Giacometti, let's go. We're outta here. Right *now*."

———

"He drives like a fuckin' maniac just to get a McMuffin? Come on, you're not tellin' me that's all he did?" Stuart's voice intimidated Steve Maxwell, despite the fact Maxwell was taller and out-weighed him by at least thirty pounds.

"I tell ya, we were with him from the time he left the house. I even went inside with him. Got a McMuffin myself," Maxwell said, trying not to sound defensive. Stuart looked like a cartoon character, in his dirty white shirt, blue jeans, loafers and frizzy hair. Lack of sleep didn't wear well on him, in his looks or his attitude.

"He was really nervous. Kept wiping sweat off his face and he sat by the window, just watching. I think maybe he thought he was being followed," Maxwell added the last statement reluctantly.

Stuart's look was a sneer. "Yeah, no *shit*."

"Boss, he's leaving again," Ralphy's voice called from the backyard. Stuart rushed outside, leaving Maxwell bewildered in the kitchen.

"Anguilo's with him. They're takin' the Beemer again. Maybe this is it. They loaded a big suitcase into the trunk. They must be headed to the airfield."

Stuart raced back into the kitchen and found Maxwell standing where he'd left him.

"Get back out onto the street and get the other cars with you. How many we got left?" Stuart asked.

"Bobby and another unit went with *Papa* early this morning and we haven't heard from them in over an hour. They were traveling south. We've got three vehicles left."

Stuart thought for a minute. If he sent them all, there'd be no one left at the house. They still didn't know where Ethan Post kept his plane but Anguilo was sure to lead them there. Damn Maxwell. He hadn't copied the airfield information from Post's personnel file after all. Rookie or not, he'd fucked up.

"I think we'll be covered. Just don't *lose* them, Maxwell. I don't want any more mistakes from you."

The words cut Maxwell like a knife, and he swallowed hard.

———

"What do you mean, you're riding with Alex? What about *me*?"

"Jeeses, Samantha. Just shut up and be flexible. This is a mild change in plan. I need to stay close to Alex. Be his buddy, remember? That's my job. Yours is to go along and make the best of it. It's just a three-hour trip to the airfield where Ethan Post keeps his plane. We'll meet you there. I've written directions on this paper. You'll drive the Mercedes. It'll be comfortable. Sorry. It's the best I can do," Dan added.

Samantha grimaced and grabbed the yellow lined page. Dan's attitude probably stemmed from her sleeping solo last night, rather than in the bed next to him.

"I've got to go now. Can you get these bags for us?" Dan asked, and rushed from the bedroom door before she could protest.

———

It was almost twelve thirty by the time Samantha turned into the small airfield, and drove past the aircraft tied to red anchors. She'd hoped by now she would see a surveillance vehicle following her, but she'd been alone coming up the road.

Ethan's Jaguar was parked by itself in front of the brown wooden shed marked *Office*. There were no other cars. Alex and Dan hadn't arrived yet.

The faded wood sign with the smiling airplane greeted her as she walked to the little office shack. Somehow she'd envisioned a private airfield as being more lavish and this was a disappointment. The aluminum steps creaked under her weight, and the flimsy screen door had no latch. The weathered wooden siding ached for new paint. She feared a strong wind could reduce the structure to kindling with just one gust.

Paint chips fell from the door's molding as she opened it and walked inside. A desk was the only piece of furniture in the bare room, except for a make shift shelf jutting from one wall, supporting an ancient Mr. Coffee machine and some cracked mugs. Despite the dank surroundings, the teenage girl at the desk was smiling and humming to herself. She looked up as Samantha entered.

"This isn't exactly the Ritz, is it?" she asked, noting Samantha's expression. "I told my dad we need a nice couch and maybe some plants to make it more homey but he says pilots don't really care about that stuff. Can I help you?"

Samantha slid her feet across the tattered linoleum, crossing the room to the girl at the desk. She was cute in a high school cheerleader sort of way. She looked to be about sixteen. Her brown curly hair was pulled up high in a silver plastic clip, and she wore a short clingy black top over blue jeans.

"I'm looking for Ethan Post. I'm supposed to be flying with him this afternoon," Samantha said.

Ethan's name seemed to evoke excitement and Samantha could feel herself being sized up, as if she were the competition.

"You're flying with Ethan? He told me some people were joining him, but I guess I thought they would be *guys*."

Samantha laughed.

"Yes, I guess I'm part of the group. Where can I find him?""He was in here just a few minutes ago, filing a flight plan. By the way, my name is Jennifer."

The girl stood up and extended a heavily bangled arm toward Samantha. She was barely five feet three. Samantha shifted her shoulder bag and clasped the outstretched hand.

"Hi, I'm Sammy. Do you work here alone?"

"Just on the weekends. My mom stops in sometimes and does the books. But I grew up in this place. I've been working the weekend shift since I was twelve."

She said it as if it had been centuries since she was twelve.

"You'll find Ethan outside by the big hanger over there."

Samantha checked her watch. It was late and Dan should be here any minute. Waiting for him inside the office was an option but there was no chair to sit on. The other option, meeting Ethan at the hanger, scared her.

Jennifer watched her closely. Samantha smiled and shrugged.

"I'm really new at this. I've never flown in a small airplane before. Have you?"

Jennifer laughed. "Oh, you've got nothing to worry about. I've known how to fly since I was eleven. I'm a pilot. My mom's a pilot and of course, my dad too. It's really cool. You'll love it."

"Are you kidding?" Samantha was truly impressed. Somehow she'd assumed Jennifer spent all her time reading teen magazines and chasing boys. Jennifer's little smile was friendly yet superior, knowing that at least in this respect she was better than her competition.

"So, tell me, what's a flight plan?" Samantha asked.

Jennifer walked around to the front of the desk like a teacher, and pushed herself up onto it, facing Samantha, her feet dangling.

"A flight plan is something a pilot files with the airport he's leaving from. It tells where he's going and any stops he has to make in between. Like for fuel and that kind of thing. They do that in case something happens and we have to go looking for them. We know the general course the pilot was going to take."

Now that's helpful, Samantha thought.

"Can I see the plan Ethan filed?"

Jennifer leaned backwards over the desk, and extracted a logbook from a drawer. She showed it to Samantha.

"It says you're going to Southport, North Carolina. See, it gives the latitude and longitude of the airport. There aren't any stops indicated along the way, because the Beech doesn't need to refuel. The trip is short enough to make it on one fill up."

"The Beech. Is that a kind of plane?" Samantha asked.

"Exactly! It's short for Beech craft. That's the kind of plane Ethan has. It used to be his dad's. It's got the long nose," she said, pointing again out the window.

"It's a great plane but I think Ethan's having some trouble selling it. There was a guy in here the other day. He went out to the hanger to look at it and everything. But then he left. I guess it's more plane than he could afford."

Samantha noticed a large paper map of the United States tacked to a wall. She walked over to it and searched for Southport. She found it at the southern end of North Carolina, right on the ocean. It looked rather remote.

"It's a really neat flight down there, if you fly along the ocean. I think that's what Ethan wants to do because he asked me to keep checking the weather. There's a storm system moving up the coast from Florida and he's worried some clouds or fog might roll in later this afternoon. But I don't think it'll be a problem if you leave pretty soon."

Maybe it will be a problem, Samantha thought, if Dan and Alex don't show up.

CHAPTER TWENTY-FOUR

"What's goin' on, Alex? You're driving like a crazy man."

Dan figured he'd better say *something*. Ever since getting into the car, Alex had been looking over his shoulder and into the rear mirrors and not paying attention to driving. And *now*, they'd almost hit a pedestrian. Besides, Dan was sure they'd passed that shopping mall twice and they were wasting precious time. They needed to be at the airfield in three hours and at this rate they wouldn't make it.

Alex was sweating profusely; his hands slipping over the steering wheel.

"We're being followed!"

Dan laughed uncomfortably. How the hell should I respond to that, he thought. Yeah, we're being followed by a bunch of inept surveillance guys who can't keep out of sight. Dan looked out the rear window and scanned traffic. The four-lane road teamed with weekend shoppers. They'd passed car dealerships, malls and row after row of fast food restaurants, stopping almost every three minutes for a traffic light.

Dan had to hand it to him, though. Alex was making a pretty good effort to ditch the surveillance; gunning the car at each light, running the ambers and early-reds when he could, weaving in and out of cars. It would have been funny if Alex didn't look on the verge of a stroke.

Since it wasn't in his best interest to point out surveillance, Dan tried calming him instead.

"Who do you think it is?" he asked, nonchalantly.

"It's Julio. He's back there. He's been following me all morning. I can't ditch him. I think he's got a few other guys working with him, in other cars. They're all over the place!"

Obviously terrified, Alex spun the BMW into a U-turn amidst a chorus of excited honks and squealing brakes. One car nearly broadsided the BMW, but Alex accelerated them out of danger, and down a mall service road. Dan gripped the dashboard, suddenly anxious at Alex's paranoia.

Alex's pupils dilated with fear. Did that black sedan just mirror his U-turn? Would it barrel down on them? Alex smashed the accelerator to the floor, widening the gap between the two cars. He didn't want to wait to find out.

Would they start shooting at him through the rear window, blowing his head apart into the windshield? He could just see Julio's ugly little eyes, and Arturo's sleepy sinister stare.

Dan braced himself against the dashboard and pulled his seatbelt tighter.

Alex gunned the engine around a tight turn, and looked back over his shoulder. Was that the same black sedan back there? Maybe it was navy blue. But it seemed to be racing down the same strip he'd just traveled. There it was in the shadow of the mall. Following him, *pursuing* him, *stalking* him. He was caged. He fired the BMW down an alleyway and burst into the open parking lot. Then he saw the silver sedan. Ahead of him at the end of the parking lot. Alex turned the car swiftly between the rows of parked vehicles, twisting his head side to side. The black car; now the silver car; now the black.

"*Alex, look out!*"

Dan's cry dissipated in the sudden explosion as the BMW careened at full speed into a semi-trailer truck.

———

Jennifer's desk held an old telephone. Samantha looked around for a more private phone, but found none in the room, or in the small alcove to its rear. There was a hallway off the alcove, but Samantha couldn't tell where it led. Not having her cell phone was distressing.

"Is there a phone I could use for a minute? I promised my father I'd call him and tell him where I was going."

No. The desk phone was the only one. Samantha looked through her shoulder bag for the small piece of paper she'd hidden inside the back compartment. It was a breach of security to have anything with her that would tie back to the task force, particularly the command post telephone number. But she was glad she'd kept it, just in case. She pulled it out.

"You don't know his number?" asked Jennifer.

"He's at the office," Samantha replied in explanation, wondering if she'd been as observant, or nosey, when she was Jennifer's age. The phone rang nearly ten times before a gruff voice answered.

"Command Post."

"Hi, this is Sammy Wilde," Samantha said, knowing that they'd think she dialed the wrong number.

"I think you have the wrong number," the voice responded.

"No, wait a minute. I *do* have the right number. I have a message for Bobby. Would you take it down, please?" her voice was insistent.

"Bobby who?" the man asked. Samantha laughed lightly, and winked at Jennifer.

"Yes, for *Bobby*," Samantha emphasized the name. "Please tell him Sammy called, and that Alex, Dan, Ethan and I are flying to Southport, North Carolina this afternoon. We're probably leaving within the hour from the Meade Valley Airport outside Annapolis."

"Outside Annapolis?" the voice asked, more attentive this time.

"That's right, the Meade Valley Airfield outside Annapolis. We don't plan to make any stops, and they tell me it's a two-hour flight to Southport. Have you got all that? I don't think Bobby knows these details and I want to make sure you'll give him the message."

Jennifer must think I'm talking to a child, Samantha thought.

"You're Sammy Wilde and you're flying to Southport, North Carolina this afternoon," the gruff voice barked back to her in confirmation. "Who is this Bobby who needs to get the message? *Lady*, you're going to have to give me more information."

Oh god, thought Samantha. This guy is so dense. Doesn't he realize I'm sitting here talking in front of someone and that I can't be more specific? Maybe he's just weekend help. Maybe he's not familiar with the operation. But he did seem to understand the significance of my being in Annapolis.

Samantha smiled at Jennifer again, and rolled her eyes in implied exasperation.

"Washington," she said into the receiver. It was handy his last name was the same as the city nearby.

"Oh, and if you can't get a hold of Bobby, just give Stuart the message. He'll make sure Bobby gets it. You do know Stuart, don't you?"

"Lady, I think so. At least I know *a* Stuart. If it's the right one."

"I'm sure it is. Now you make sure either Stuart or Bobby gets this message right away."

"I understand. I'll see what I can do."

Samantha replaced the telephone receiver thoughtfully, wondering if he understood at all. Jennifer studied her.

"Are you dating Ethan?"

Samantha laughed. "I have good news for you. We're not dating. In fact, Ethan doesn't think too highly of me right now. You might have a chance."

Jennifer smiled at her with new hope as Samantha rose from the desk and walked out of the office. The screen door bounced loudly against the frame.

———

With his head buried under the airplane's hood, Ethan didn't notice Samantha walking the nearly one hundred yards across the tarmac toward him. He was studying a dipstick that he'd just pulled from the engine case when he finally looked in her direction. The sun caught his eyes, and they flashed like bright blue beacons. She felt her legs grow wobbly. She stopped. He jammed the dipstick back into its slot in the airplane's engine, and wiped his hands on a rag, all the while watching her. She was afraid to go any closer.

"You're late. Where are the others?"

Ethan wore khaki shorts with a braided leather belt and a white ribbed shirt. His long, tanned legs were bare down to his leather topsiders. A faint humid breeze blew through his brown hair.

Samantha shrugged. It was futile explaining that she wasn't responsible for Dan and Alex's absence.

"I don't know where they are. Dan was supposed to be here with Alex by now. I suppose they're on their way."

Ethan walked around the airplane toward her. His jaw line tensed.

"We need to take off soon. There's fog down along the coast and we need to reach Southport before it rolls in."

"What does that mean?"

Ethan regarded her, his blue eyes piercing her light cotton blouse.

"If the fog rolls in, we can't land. We won't have enough fuel to get back here, so we'd have to land somewhere else. It's too risky. We have to take off really soon," he said emphatically, as if Samantha had the power to make Dan and Alex appear.

"I'm sorry. I don't know where they are."

"Did you bring any bags?"

Samantha nodded.

"They're in my car."

"We might as well get them into the plane. That way we can leave immediately when they arrive."

Ethan began to walk back toward the office, ignoring her. Samantha jogged to keep up.

"We don't *have* to go. Maybe this isn't a good idea after all," Samantha ventured, breathing a little harder.

"It's a *great* idea. The best idea I've ever had," Ethan retorted, not looking at her.

"I think you just want to know what Alex is up to. You don't really want to become involved," she said.

Ethan stopped and spun on her.

"I don't *get* you. You're just Giacometti's girlfriend. Why the *hell* do you care?"

"You could screw up your career. Sometimes it's good being the white sheep," Samantha replied, wishing she could explain everything to him, particularly the fact that she *wasn't* Dan's girlfriend. She felt sorry for him that he didn't have all the pieces to this puzzle and sorry that she couldn't be the one to enlighten him. But she was particularly sorry she had to keep lying to him.

Ethan lifted his bag easily from the Jaguar's back seat, and locked the car. Without looking at Samantha, he placed the bag on the ground between the cars and bounded up the steps to the office.

Jennifer backed away from the window quickly as he came through the door.

"When are you guys going to take off? I just got another weather report. The fog is rolling in pretty quick," she said.

Ethan frowned. "What's the ceiling?"

"Four thousand feet from here to Norfolk and thirty five hundred along the North Carolina Coast. You'll be *VFR* all the way down the coast if you leave right away," she said, indicating the height of the clouds they'd have to fly through.

"Yeah, that's the problem," Ethan replied.

"Hmm. Do you think you'd leave without them?" Jennifer asked, and hoisted her young body upon the desk.

The thought had occurred to him. It could be his only chance to meet *Papa* on his home turf and perhaps discover the secret details to his operation. Without this trip, he'd be back to square one, with a suitcase full of suspicions and no facts to back them up. What a waste to blow this chance. The thought of living another week, or maybe longer not knowing was unbearable.

"Won't they be mad if you left them?" Jennifer asked.

"Mad doesn't even come *close*," Ethan said, and laughed as he envisioned his brother pacing back and forth along the tarmac, running his hands through his hair and cursing; incredulous that Ethan would have left.

"We'll give them another fifteen minutes," Ethan said, walking toward the door.

"I'll call the weather service back in ten, okay?"

"Great," said Ethan.

Outside he retrieved his bag and followed Samantha who was now half way to the airplane laden with her own suitcase and Dan's duffle bag. He caught up and grabbed Dan's duffle from her grasp.

"Jeeses, this thing is heavy. What's he got in here, machine guns?"

Samantha wanted to say she'd been thinking the same thing. Ethan stopped beside the plane.

"I think I put a map on the front seat. Climb in and make sure, will you?" Ethan directed.

Samantha leapt onto a narrow grated rubber pad on the wing's surface that seemed the only route to the airplane's front seat. She walked two steps up the padding to unlatch the door. It felt too flimsy in her grasp. She'd expected it to be a heavier metal.

The front seats looked like the driving compartment of a minivan. She stretched her leg into the plane and slid inside.

Ethan watched her until she was out of sight. Moving quickly, he opened Dan's duffle bag, pushing the rough metal zipper along its track. He felt through the contents to the bottom of the bag. No guns. Just some underwear, t-shirts, a pair of pants and shoes. He ran his hand along the edges of the bag, feeling nothing foreign.

Samantha found the map right away and waved it out the window.

Ethan re-zipped the bag quickly and stuffed it roughly into the cargo compartment. It caught onto something. Ethan pushed harder, forcing the bag toward the back. It still caught. Impatient, he lifted the bag slightly, allowing it to finally slide over the obstruction. He loaded his own bag next, and Samantha's overnight bag last. With both hands hidden inside the compartment, he felt through her bag and then swung the cargo door shut.

He climbed upon the wing; then stopped. He appeared absorbed in thought.

"Get out," he said finally. Gruffly.

"We're not going?"

"I changed my mind. *You're* not going. I have to take off in the next ten minutes, or I won't make it before the fog. No one else is here yet. My choice is to wait for the others and risk the fog, or leave now. I'm going to leave now, and you're not coming."

Samantha didn't move.

"You'd leave without Alex and Dan? That makes no sense." Ethan reached out and wrapped his hand around her bare arm. As she pulled her arm away, his hand slid down onto hers. She made no move to pull it away.

"Ethan, I'm going with you. You shouldn't go alone. You know that. You don't know those people."

"And you do?"

"Maybe. We should go together. It's better that way."

Reluctantly he allowed his eyes to meet hers.

"This is bullshit," he said, but withdrew his hand and closed the passenger door, locking her inside. He walked around the front of the plane, past the two barrel-shaped engines, and entered the plane from the other wing. He pumped the fuel mixture switch three times, and opened his window.

"Clear!" he yelled out the window. Slowly, the propeller began to turn until it blurred into a gray circle.

A low, steady roar engulfed the planes' cabin, vibrating Samantha's insides. Using a combination of movements between the foot pedals, the throttle and the steering column, Ethan turned the plane around on the tarmac and taxied toward the runway.

The airfield was bordered by trees, and looked like it had once been a farm until concrete replaced the corn.

Samantha saw only blue sky over the end of the plane's long nose. To see the roadway, she had to look out the side window, and even then the wing obscured her view. She craned her neck forward, stretching against the seatbelt to see more of the airfield ahead of her. Seated next to her with a control panel and throttle between them, Ethan watched her contortions.

"Don't worry. When we get in the air you'll be able to see everything. You've never been in a small aircraft before?" he shouted to be heard above the engine's noise. She shook her head.

Ethan made his final preflight instrument adjustments then slowly and deliberately forced the large black throttle lever forward. The propeller whirled into high speed. The engine noise was deafening. The plane bounced forward, gathering speed at a geometric rate. Trees rushed past, their green leafy heads a blur.

She watched Ethan's feet push forcibly against the floor pedals, steadying the plane to keep it straight. With one hand still on the throttle, he pulled back against the steering column with his other hand, and with a gentle leap, the plane was in the air.

It climbed gently into the afternoon sky. Samantha watched the small airfield office below become tiny. Ethan climbed the plane steadily into the air, banking a right hand turn. Holding tightly to the bottom of the seat, Samantha peered out over the countryside; still fearful she might fall through the flimsy door. She could see the entire stretch of road from the interstate to the airfield. It was deserted. Alex's BMW was nowhere to be seen.

CHAPTER TWENTY-FIVE

Dan braced both hands against the dashboard and whispered a prayer as the BMW barreled full speed into the solid mass of the parked semi-trailer truck. He wished he'd worn his bulletproof vest instead of packing it away. He knew he wouldn't walk away from this crash.

————

Steve Maxwell couldn't believe his eyes. He sat stunned, bile rising in his throat. Braking his silver Chevrolet to a stop, he threw it into park and bounded from the automobile just as flames exploded in front of him.

"Outpost! Come in Outpost!" Karen Alexander's panicked voice jolted the air.

"Outpost! This is Karen! We need emergency equipment immediately. Ambulances and fire equipment. *Right away*!"

Maxwell ran toward the wreckage despite the intense heat. From out of nowhere, Karen appeared at his side. She signaled toward the car door and together they grabbed the handle and pulled hard against it, willing it to open.

————

Ethan leveled the aircraft and began a slow gentle ascent toward Chesapeake Bay. The windshield that had limited Samantha's view earlier was suddenly a panorama revealing water, land and roadway below. Releasing her death grip on the seat, she wiped sweaty palms against her shorts. Through his aviator sunglasses, Ethan watched her and laughed.

"You get used to it after a while," he said, his voice no longer a shout.

"I doubt it. I've never done this before."

"No shit," Ethan replied.

"Oh well. It's just one more reason for you to hate me," she said.

"What makes you think I hate you?"

"God, Ethan, just about everything. I know you don't trust me. I guess I'm not asking for your trust. I just want you to know I'm not your enemy."

She glanced at him sideways. They sat in silence for a few minutes, the engines dull throb filling the vacuum.

"Why were you at Vuillard's the other day?" he asked, finally.

"Vuillard is a friend of Dan's. More like an acquaintance, really. Dan had a set of keys for the apartment, so I just wandered up there to make some telephone calls. That's when you arrived."

Ethan considered her response.

"Okay. I think that's *bullshit*, but I'll believe you for now."

"Is it my turn? I want to ask you the same question. Why were *you* at Vuillard's that day?"

"It's like I told you before. I'd stopped by Alex's but he wasn't there," he began.

"Now, that *is* bullshit," Samantha interrupted.

"How would you know?"

"Alex was at his office."

"How do you know this?" Ethan asked, regarding her coolly.

Because he's under investigation by the FBI and the task force has him under surveillance, Samantha wanted to say. She sat in silence instead.

Ethan continued. "How about this. Vuillard and Alex are close associates. I didn't want to find Alex, I wanted to talk to Vuillard."

"I think that might be closer to the truth. You wanted to talk to him about getting into his organization. Like what you told me in the lounge?"

"Yeah, about getting into his organization," Ethan replied slowly.

"And *Papa*? Do you hope to talk to him about getting into *his* organization? So you can make lots of money, and buy a new sports car and a yacht? And that's the reason you left Alex behind, because you figured you could get *Papa* alone and make a pitch to him?" Samantha asked and watched Ethan nod unconvincingly.

"Well, it makes perfect sense to me. A fine upstanding American who's spent fifteen years in military service. A respected naval officer. Yes, if I were a businessman like *Papa* you're certainly the first person I'd pick to join my corrupt organization."

Samantha's sarcasm hung in the cabin air. Ethan studied the horizon.

"So why did you insist on coming with me this afternoon?" he asked. "That doesn't make much sense either. You left your boyfriend behind to go off flying with another guy. Don't you think he'll be upset?"

Samantha whistled softly. *Upset* wasn't the word for how Dan would react. Or Stuart. And her actions probably would push Bobby's loyalty to the breaking point. She could tell them she did it for the case, believing that the government needed information about *Papa* immediately. That this would probably be a chance of a lifetime, what with Ethan so intent upon going, and the probability he'd screw up the case for them if *Papa* got wise to his private investigation. *Papa* would undoubtedly see through Ethan like glass. So Samantha had to go, regardless of the consequences.

They'd close her *Confidential Informant* file at the police department for good, sealing it with black tape, a skull and crossbones on the cover. Under no circumstances should this woman ever be allowed to work with the government again, the caveat to the file would read. The most exciting experience of her life would end in shame.

"Yes, Dan will be upset. But I didn't want you to go alone," she said simply.

He looked over at her, her face turned toward his, and read sincerity in her eyes. Reaching out with one hand, he patted her knee.

"Thanks."

The houses below became dense. Samantha could see some light aircraft off in the distance at different elevations. She pointed them out. They flew along in silence.

"We're almost to Norfolk," Ethan said eventually. He reached for the radio microphone and adjusted the frequency monitor to Norfolk air traffic control, and radioed his position.

"Tower, this is November 8847N."

"Roger, November 8847N. Ascend to three thousand on heading one-five-five. Re-contact when you have reached thirty seven degrees north latitude."

"Roger," Ethan replied, and directed the aircraft toward the southeast. Gently he pulled back on the control bar, and raised the plane toward three thousand feet. The clouds were thicker at the higher altitude. Samantha could see them above the plane now, almost kissing the wings.

The air was bumpier now, and the plane bounced frequently. Each movement jolted her stomach, but eventually she became used to it, and started regarding the movements as a free carnival ride.

Ethan allowed the plane to roll over the waves of air, gently bouncing the plane, its occupants, and their bags in the rear cargo area.

Samantha's overnight bag shifted from side to side in the half filled rear compartment, colliding occasionally with Ethan's lighter duffle. Dan's bag shifted the least, caught as it was on top of a small metal box. The edges of the box were rough, and the weight of Dan's bag on top of it had allowed the box to cut into the duffel's canvas trim, holding it firmly in place against the subtle movements of the plane.

At three thousand feet, Ethan leveled the plane and inched the nose downward until it flew even with the horizon. The five hundred foot difference in altitude had no impact on Ethan or Samantha, although the air was somewhat thinner. But within the small metal box inside the cargo compartment, the insignificant change in air pressure had a decidedly different effect.

A tiny pressure gauge taped to the small metal box's inner wall detected the three thousand foot level. As the little pressure needle bounced against a wire soldered into the number *three* on the little dial, it jolted a cushioned vial riding next to it. With each jolt, a drop of acid splashed out, dripping onto the adhesive tape below and eating away at the sticky fabric attached to the crude, homemade bomb inside the metal box. The adhesive held a strong wire spring open, like a mousetrap. When the acid ate through the tape, the spring would snap shut, completing the electrical circuit and igniting Julio's kitchen sink creation.

CHAPTER TWENTY-SIX

Where the hell is this guy going? Bobby wondered as he eyed his fuel gauge fearfully. The little metal pointer was anxiously jumping up and down over the *E*, and he knew he couldn't hang on much longer. Besides, he had to take a piss, *really* bad. *Papa* and Julio had driven south for almost a hundred eighty miles.

"What do you think, Green Six? Is this guy ever gonna stop?" Bobby radioed.

Green Six had the point position now. They'd been jockeying back and forth for the past three hours, giving the Silver Grand Am enough room on the interstate so they wouldn't blow the surveillance.

"Beats the hell out of me. How's your fuel situation?" Green six asked.

"Not good. I'm gonna have to pull off at the next exit. Can you cover him alone? I'll probably need a half hour to catch up with you," Bobby replied.

"No problem. Take all the time you need," Green Six laughed, knowing that was the last thing Bobby was going to do. A large sign signaled the approaching exit and a smaller blue one assured him there'd be a gas station somewhere close by. Bobby edged his gray Caprice into the left lane, when Green Six called from point.

"Looks like they're getting off, too. You can breathe a little easier. I'll hang with them until you make your stop. Maybe they'll get something to eat."

———

The ground below disappeared and was replaced with water as the plane headed south from Norfolk and along the Atlantic Ocean. Samantha looked out her side, noticing they straddled a thin strip of deserted land. On her lap rested an open topographical map and Samantha charted their progress over the Currituck Sound toward Kitty Hawk.

The dense, moist clouds directly above the airplane cast the cockpit into shadow. Ethan radioed the Norfolk air control and advised they were leaving controlled airspace. He pointed to the map, indicating he planned to turn to the southwest, and cut across the Albemarle Sound and over a series of lakes on a direct line to Southport.

Samantha studied the map, trying to find the various visual landmarks that pilots used to pinpoint their location over land. She was searching for a particularly large lake when Ethan reached across and released her controls from their locked position.

Carefully he extended the co-pilot steering column to within her reach and adjusted the lever under her seat to move her even closer. Samantha watched his motions with a mixture of excitement and concern.

"It's time for a flying lesson. I can't have anyone flying with me whose terrified of this aircraft," he announced, and began pointing out the various controls along the flight panel. He pointed to a dial with a little airplane in the middle and a black line cutting the dial in half.

"That's your horizon. When the airplane's wings are above that line, you're climbing. When they're below the line, you're descending."

When the little wings dipped to the right, it indicated the plane was turning toward the right, and vice versa.

"That's a real handy gauge because sometimes you think you're flying straight and level, when the airplane is really veering off course," he said. Samantha smiled nervously.

"This gauge is the altitude indicator. It tells you how high you're flying," he continued. The indicator read three thousand feet.

In the middle of the panel was an airplane set against a numbered compass, with north being zero, or three hundred sixty degrees. This was the heading indicator. Right now the airplane was pointing to two hundred ten.

"Due south is one hundred eighty. So now we're flying thirty degrees west from due south."

This was pretty cool, she thought. It all makes sense.

Ethan sat back away from the controls and pointed to her steering column. Samantha looked at him in panic. He can't possibly want me to fly the plane, she thought. But he just sat there, daring her to place her hands on the flight controls. Hesitantly she clasped one side of the curved column, and then the other. The steering mechanism looked like the control bars for a video game. She held it gingerly, fearful to move it, afraid that she might somehow plunge the plane into a death spiral.

After a few minutes, she looked up at Ethan.

"How am I doing?" she asked, then nervously turned her face back to the front. He pointed to the little airplane in the horizon indicator. Its wings were above the black line.

"I'm climbing?" Samantha asked in disbelief. It hadn't felt like the plane was climbing.

"Just a little. I want you to push gently against the control column and see if you can bring the little airplane back down to the horizon."

This was the touchy part. She pressed forward too delicately at first and the little airplane remained above the horizon line. Then she pressed too hard, and it dipped below the line. Looking up, she could see the nose of the plane had dipped downward also, and was now pointing toward the ground. She had to pull back on the controls to bring the nose up. She pushed and pulled for a few minutes on her own, feeling her palms grow sweaty. Finally she had the little airplane level with the horizon. She looked up at Ethan triumphantly.

"But now your heading is off," he said, and pointed to the other gauge, its airplane pointing toward one hundred ninety. In her concentration, she'd flown the plane twenty degrees to the east. Carefully she steered the control column subtly to the right.

"Watch your horizon," Ethan called to her. That damn little plane's wings were starting to dip below the black line again.

He let her struggle with the controls for a few minutes more before bringing the lesson to a close. She rubbed her sweaty hands against the seat and flexed the muscles stiffened by the death grip she'd had on the plastic bar.

"You did great. You've got a natural sense for positioning the plane."

"Yeah. *Sure*," Samantha replied skeptically.

"It just takes practice, Sammy. You've got a good head. You seem intelligent. With a little practice, you'll be ready to solo."

"How many women have you taught to fly?"

"Dozens from start to finish. But they were mostly naval officers who spend their whole day in a plane. You might be my first female civilian."

He smiled and then leaned across the center throttle panel and reached his right arm across her shoulders, drawing her toward his grinning face.

"That was fun," he said. He lowered his face toward hers and kissed her gently on the mouth.

Ethan's lips were warm and wet and soft and they slid easily over hers. Samantha felt again the sharp electrical arrows piercing her body as she kissed him back. He released her, heaving a great sigh.

"See, I *can* be a gentleman when I try," he said, returning to the flight controls. Samantha melted back against the passenger seat.

Without warning, the plane suddenly heaved forward, the nose pointing upwards to the sky, then violently downward toward the ground. A loud thud reverberated from the rear of the plane, through the passenger compartment and into the cockpit, shaking the fuselage's metal skin and sending rippling aftershocks vibrating along the metal panels.

Samantha heard her door vibrate against its hinges, and she instinctively grabbed for the bottom of the seat to keep from being shaken from the plane. The plane swung sideways and Samantha watched in awe as the ground twisted in slow motion beneath her window. Her vision blurred momentarily as adrenaline pumped furiously into her system, dulling her reflexes and slowing her realization processes. A panicked scream rose in her subconscious but the plane's movements mesmerized her conscious and she sat silently instead.

Samantha turned to Ethan, and watched as his feet pumped furiously against the floor pedals to stop the plane's violent yawing. His face was set in grim determination, as his hands struggled against the control column, pulling the plane back to level flight. The nose wanted to point downward, and stopping that inclination was his immediate mission.

The nose dropped again and Samantha felt sudden vertigo, as the wing outside her window seemed to flip sideways, and then pass right above her head. She watched it cut a wide arc through the sky, then roll the plane over and cut the same arc across the ground. She looked across out Ethan's window, and saw his wing turning around too, led by her wing into the slow, graceful spiral. Looking back toward her window, she saw the wing again circle through the sky.

Samantha gazed in wonder at Ethan's strong hands gripping the control column. His arm muscles, from his wrists to his shoulders, were flexed to exhaustion as he pulled the controls backward and into his chest, and held them there. Despite his efforts, the plane kept turning around and around, its nose pointed to the ground. As his strength ebbed, he wrapped one arm around the control panel and flexed it between his forearm and biceps, transferring the strain to his stronger muscles, pulling the controls back, back, as far as they would go and struggling to hold them there. The muscles along his jaw pulsed with the exertion.

Suddenly the spinning ground disappeared and Samantha saw only blue sky as the spiral released and the plane began to climb. Ethan pushed the control bar carefully forward, trying to gain as much altitude as possible without losing the airflow over the wings. As if watching a carousel come to a slow stop, Samantha watched the propeller cease motion.

Deep red ridges cut Samantha's palms where she'd gripped the metal seat supports.

Heavy beads of sweat formed along Ethan's hairline, and dripped down onto his collar. He ripped his sunglasses off and threw them onto the back seat. Samantha saw his blue eyes flash in grim concentration.

He took a deep breath and forced it slowly out through his teeth. Then he lifted the radio microphone to his mouth.

"Mayday! Mayday! This is November 8847N. I have total engine failure, repeat, total engine failure with probable structural damage. I'm making a forced landing on a heading of two ten about one hundred twenty miles southwest of Norfolk."

His voice was remarkably calm. He released the talk button for a moment and turned to Samantha.

"We're going to have to make an emergency landing. I need you to get out the map, and determine exactly where we are. You'll have to use visual landmarks. You'll find them on the map. I want you to start looking for a place to land, an open field, or a deserted road, or something away from trees and houses and anything that we might hit going down. I'll be looking too, but I have to raise someone on the radio first."

Her hands shook when she tried unfolding the map, nearly ripping it with one impatient jerk, but Samantha's mind was remarkably clear. She looked out the window over the wing and saw a small lake off to her right. She followed their flight path down the map, measuring about a hundred and twenty miles southwest of Norfolk. A series of three lakes appeared on the map in the general area where Ethan said they should be. If he was right, then a larger lake should be visible over her right shoulder.

Samantha turned around in her seat and looked out through the rear passenger window. Little sparkles of sunlight reflected up from the ground from a distance behind the plane.

"Ethan, at about ten o'clock you should see a pretty large lake out your window. Is it there?"

Her voice was too loud and too demanding, but he stopped adjusting the radio frequency for a moment to follow her instructions.

"I see it. Show me where we are."

Samantha took a blue pen from the glove box and circled the area of the three lakes, then pushed the map toward him.

"The little lake is right off my wing now," she said.

Ethan radioed again, this time giving his coordinates. No response. He checked his altimeter. It read eighteen hundred feet, but it was dropping quickly. He'd lost almost a thousand feet of altitude in the spiral. That wasn't good, but it was preferable to spinning into the ground like a corkscrew. The rear section of the plane felt like it was dragging, and he'd lost a lot of rudder control they'd need for a safe landing. Whatever had happened in the rear of the plane had broken the fuel cables to the engines, and probably damaged the landing gear. He wouldn't know for sure until he tried to put the wheels down, and he wasn't going to do that until the last possible moment. He needed to glide as long as possible until they found an adequate place to land.

He looked backwards out his window, toward the tail section. He frowned.

"Sammy, look out your window. Tell me if you see anything along the bottom of the plane, like a rip or something."

Samantha turned around in her seat, and looked. Her eyes traced the aircraft's skin back towards the cargo compartment. A sheet of charred metal curled out from under the plane directly below the cargo compartment. It's blackened, ragged edge looked like a burned piece of paper.

Ethan's *Mayday* message echoed in her ears. *Total engine failure.* Probable structural damage. She remembered the heavy thud that pitched the plane forward initially, then the rippling aftershocks. She felt the skin on her arms go cold and clammy. Taking deep breaths was difficult but she forced air into her lungs and turned back toward Ethan. Her head ached and little black spots appeared before her eyes. She slumped into the seat. Ethan reached across and grabbed her neck, forcing her head down toward her legs. Gently he massaged her back, pushing blood up her spine and into her head.

"Come on, baby, I can't lose my co-pilot just yet. Take nice, slow deep breaths. What did you see back there that scared you so much?"

His voice was calm and joking because he already knew what she'd seen.

Samantha wrapped her arms around her knees and rested her head against them, her face turned toward him. His warm hand continued to massage her back, under her shirt now, his skin against her skin.

She said, "There must have been an explosion. The bottom of the plane has been blown apart. It looks like it came from the cargo compartment. Is there anything back there that could cause an explosion? Any machinery? *Anything?*"

Her voice trailed off. Ethan shook his head grimly.

"There shouldn't be," he said, thinking about the bags he'd searched. There *shouldn't* be.

"When you're ready to sit up, I'll show you where we're going to land. I've picked a soft place because I don't think our landing gear is going to be much help."

Slowly she raised her head, and peered out her window. The ground was now startlingly close. Directly below her was the small lake she'd seen earlier, but it looked much bigger now, and was surrounded by a relatively wide swath of beach. But beyond the beach was a brief field of grass, bordered by endless stands of trees.

"We're going to land on that grass down there. It'll be a little tricky because of all the trees, but if you'll notice, there are trees everywhere else. We haven't much choice. I'm going to fly down here a little bit further, turn around and see if the landing gear is working. Then it's *show time.*"

He smiled at her reassuringly. His fingers reached out toward her. When he found her hand, he gave it a tight squeeze. Then he winked and dropped her hand, knowing that he could no longer delay the inevitable task. Gently he banked the plane into a gliding turn, rounding the southern end of the lake. Holding his breath, he pushed the landing gear lever. Nothing happened. The altimeter now read three hundred feet. There was no turning back.

"Thirty seconds until impact. Put your head down between your legs and wrap your arms around your neck!" Ethan's voice was stern but not panicked.

Samantha looked out the window and saw them glide effortlessly over the trees. Then she looked down. The ground was rising steadily to meet the plane.

"One hundred feet! Fifty feet! *Thirty feet!*"

Samantha had her arms wrapped around her neck, but she was too mesmerized by the approaching ground to do anything more than crouch. They were so close to the ground, she could jump. They *had* to be safe. Couldn't the plane just skid to a stop?

They were suspended at twenty feet for an eternity, the cockpit totally quiet.

The fuselage scraped the ground first, screeching across the sand like the Harlem Boys Choir ripping fingernails along a giant blackboard. Then the sound became muffled, almost quiet as Samantha realized the plane had bounced into the air, turning a massive somersault on its long nose. Holding her breath, she waited for the inevitable crash against her back. When it came, it knocked the wind out of her, forcing the hard material of the dashboard down against her arms and driving her chest into her knees.

The airplane turned violently upside down, crushing the cockpit windshield, the momentum catapulting it upward yet again to skid along on its left wing. The wing broke apart wildly on impact, its jagged stump caught against the beach's grassy edge, absorbing the plane's waning forward momentum to drag it finally to a stop.

CHAPTER TWENTY-SEVEN

"What the hells' wrong with that bird? Why won't it stop that incessant *chirping*? It's making my head pound. I could fall asleep if it would just *shut up*," Samantha thought.

Swatting it seemed a logical idea. It seemed so close. Samantha's hand reached out but there was no room to move. She tried to look up but something pinned her down. In a wave of panic, she wondered if her back was broken. Then she remembered she'd clasped her hands behind her neck. Concentrating, she willed her fingers to move. Tears of relief flooded her eyes as she felt the fingers twitch. Slowly she edged them along her neck and head, feeling for what was above that pinned her into this position and praying that it was something she could move.

The dashboard crushed against her head, but her back was free. Carefully she pulled her arms down from behind her neck, hoping that they weren't broken. They responded stiffly to her brain's command, but they *did* respond. Samantha brought them down by her side.

She had room to turn her head now but she couldn't contort her body inward enough to clear the dashboard and sit up. She studied the area at her feet. Her best option was to slip down off the seat and onto the floor under the crushed dashboard, then pivot around, and slither through the open space between her seat and the center throttle controls.

It was a tight squeeze.

When both knees were on the floor, her head was free to turn. She heard no sound from the seat next to her. Ethan's legs were pinned against the door by the collapsed steering column, his feet still resting on the floor pedals.

Samantha wiped a hand across her face, surprised that it was wet. Her breath caught in little gasps as she realized she was sobbing. Tears streamed down her cheeks as she reached for Ethan's leg, trying to move it closer to her.

His body lay limp against the seat, his head resting against the cushion. The seatbelt strapped across his chest held him securely but it was already starting to discolor with blood seeping through his shirt. The wound appeared to start at his left shoulder and cut across his chest, maybe caused by the collapsed door or the broken windshield.

She hoisted herself up from the floor, scraping her back against the ragged dashboard. A sharp pain shot down her spine, but it was her only pain so far. She straddled the throttle and reached across his body. Blood streamed from his forehead just above the eyes. Samantha pressed hard against his carotid artery feeling a faint pulse. She leaned into the collapsed door panel that crushed his left arm. It didn't move.

"God damn it, *open!*" she cried. She threw all her weight into one final effort.

The door scraped on its hinge and then flew open.

The throttle control cut deep into her left hip as she hoisted herself over and onto Ethan's lap, straddling him.

Her teeth ripped at his cotton shirt, tearing it open down to his stomach, exposing his finely muscled abdomen. She rubbed her hand along the smooth warm skin.

"I've had fantasies about this chest. They didn't do it justice," she said.

There was a deep gash on his left shoulder. She pulled her blouse off over her head, and bit into the thin cotton material. It tore easily into two pieces. Carefully she pressed one piece against the wound, applying direct pressure.

The cut above his eyes had already turned his face and his collar crimson. With the other half of her shirt, she pushed the blood away, and parted the cut with her fingertips. She felt herself grow queasy as blood gushed onto her hand, but she steadied herself. The wound was only a half-inch deep, and there was no bone showing through.

"*This* isn't going to kill you," she whispered, and pressed the blouse hard against the bleeding. With both hands, Samantha kept pressure against Ethan's body, feeling momentarily helpful.

His right arm looked fine, but his left wrist was starting to swell. Gingerly she laid it across his lap, beneath her legs. She picked up the good arm and began massaging it hard. She worked her way down to the fingers, waiting for movement or a muscle flex or *something* to indicate his neck wasn't broken. No response.

"Ethan, *wake up*. Ethan."

She patted his face gently; then *harder*. Blood saturated the blouse bandages. Pushing herself up from the seat, she swung her left leg around to the other side of his body, and climbed backwards out the door and onto the wing.

Her knees screamed in protest as she extended them for the first time since the crash, but they worked to lower her body to the ground. A wet, matted clump of hair fell forward, tinged with red. Running her fingers gingerly down the nape of her neck, she felt a sensitive and moist area. She studied her fingers, but couldn't distinguish Ethan's blood from her own.

The afternoon sun warmed her back. The infernal chirping bird sat in a tree overhead. A still crystal blue lake extended thirty yards in front of her. These were all incongruous images to the shattered and ravaged airplane in her midst. Somehow she'd thought that commotion immediately followed accidents like this. That soon people would run to her, offering help. She listened for any footsteps. Any voices. *Sirens.* There were none.

The grassy ground was soft beneath her feet. Walking around to the front of the plane, Samantha saw the crushed nose cone that had cartwheeled the plane end over end. She gasped, seeing the wreckage on her side of the plane, the window and door supports folded inward by the crash's force. She walked in a daze across the sandy beach to the lake, the clear water warm to her touch.

Quickly, she took off her Sketchers and socks to wade into the water, stopping as the water level reached just below her shorts. She splashed cool water on her arms and legs and neck, rinsing the blood away.

From her pocket she extracted her socks, soaking them in the lake water, then turned and walked back toward the wreckage. She could see a blackened trail of upended earth cut into the sand and grass. The plane's tail section had broken away completely upon impact and lay fifty yards down the beach. What was now the end of the plane looked like it had been ripped open by massive jaws, the bottom metal blackened as if by fire.

Climbing back onto the wing stump, Samantha leaned over Ethan and pressed the dripping socks against his forehead. She propped one there and gingerly washed the red smears from his face and neck with the other. The water felt cool against her skin. She hoped he might feel it too; enough to awaken him from his deep sleep.

The water loosened the bandage on his forehead, allowing her to remove it. She stood again, and trekked back to the lake, rinsing the blood soaked material that had once been her favorite blouse. She felt that somehow she had betrayed the gauzy peach colored garment, turning it into a bloody bandage.

A group of ducks swooped down from the sky, landing in the water and sending tiny wavelets rippling around her legs. Samantha squinted into the sun, its brilliance dulled by the encroaching cloud cover.

What will I do if he doesn't regain consciousness? Samantha wondered. There were no houses nearby that she could walk to and call for help, only a roadway somewhere through the trees that she'd spotted from the air. I've got to have a plan.

But her mind was empty and exhausted, void of any thoughts or ideas. As she wrung out the blouse and the socks, she noticed her hands start to shake. Her mind willed them to stop, but instead the jerking motion grew more intense, moving up her wrists to her arms and shoulders until her whole body was convulsing. She hugged her arms against her bare skin and sobbed.

———

Little bits of sunlight peeked through the accordion blinds, sending alternate stripes of shadow and light over *Papa* and Julio's seated figures. Bobby noticed with satisfaction that the booth behind them was empty. He slid onto the diner's vinyl seat and pressed his back against the rear cushion, listening intently. A waitress arrived and he ordered coffee. *Papa* and Julio held menus. He could hear them ordering hamburgers and French fries. Good. They were going to be here awhile. He signaled the waitress and requested French fries and a chocolate sundae, knowing his order would arrive before theirs, so he'd have a chance to eat.

Papa's voice was a quiet mumble, but Julio's tough New York accent carried better. He was laughing.

"Should be over by now, boss. Soon as they hit three thousand feet, Boom! I'm a fuckin' *genius*."

Bobby heard *Papa's* strained breathing.

"Are you sure it worked? How many tests did you run on it?"

"You'd question a *genius*? Fuck, boss, ya can't run too many tests on these things. Hell, my neighbors would complain. But it worked. I know it did. Arturo planted it perfectly. Ain't nothin' gonna save that plane."

"Are you sure he can be depended upon?"

"Hey, we've used him for a lot of stuff in the past. Fuck, he's my best triggerman. He doesn't screw up. All he had to do was put it in the cargo bay. Then, when the plane hits three thousand feet, it starts to work. Pretty soon, *KABOOM!*" Julio savored the explosive sound.

"And they'll all be on board? Are we sure of that?" *Papa's* voice sounded nervous.

"Hey, boss, sure. Everybody. Your problems are over."

"I regret the pilot. A fine man," *Papa* said.

"Yeah, hey, what can you do? But I think he was up to something, anyway. We needed 'em all taken out. Yeah, I guess I regret the blonde," Julio said and laughed.

Papa signaled to him as the waitress approached with their order.

"No more talk. Just eat now."

Bobby's knees felt weak, but they managed to raise him to a standing position. By the time he hit the diner's front door he was at a full run, racing around the building.

Agonizing moments elapsed before he heard his cell phone connect and the telephone ring at the Pollard house. Many hours had passed since they left.

Maybe Birkwell's there, Bobby thought, panicked, wondering whom to call next. The FAA? The State Police? He thought of Samantha's measured statements the night before. That there was no reason for *Papa* to plan this trip. *Unless.* Bobby swallowed hard at that thought.

Stuart finally answered.

"Where the fuck are you? All hell's broken loose here!" Stuart screamed into the phone.

"Jeeses, Stuart, what's happened?" Bobby held his breath. Did he already know?

Stuart paused.

"There's been a crash."

Bobby reeled backward, almost breaking the tiny phone against the brick wall.

"Jesus, Mary and Joseph," Bobby whispered.

"Alex's BMW hit a semi. It blew up. Anguilo might make it but Post ate it."

Bobby held the phone and waited, his mind failing to assimilate the information Stuart gave him with what he'd just overheard from *Papa*.

"What about the *airplane*?"

"What airplane? Aw, shit, Bobby. We've been tied up with the *crash*. Yeah, we did get a call from the command center over an hour ago. Apparently your blonde friend called to say they were going to, ah, to, now where the hell did she say? Oh, Southport, North Carolina. I don't even know if they're still waiting at the airfield for Anguilo and Post to show up."

Stuart started to laugh.

"God, I'm sorry Washington. I guess I just haven't had enough sleep these past two days. I know it isn't funny. Jesus, the target of our investigation is dead, and who knows, maybe Anguilo will die next. And we've got this blonde playing detective in some little airfield in another state. This is such a *fuck up*."

Stuart burped a few more giggles.

"There's a bomb on the plane!" Bobby said.

"*What?*"

"There's a *bomb* on the plane," Bobby repeated. Stuart's laugh sounded more like hiccups, and Bobby knew he had his attention.

"Last night when Samantha said *Papa* had to have another reason for them to fly to North Carolina? It was because there's a bomb on the plane. I just heard Julio talking about it. He built it. He wanted them all taken out. Alex Post, Anguilo, Samantha and probably Post's brother, too. He said it should be over by now."

"Where are you?" Stuart croaked.

"About fifty miles south of Norfolk, in a diner. Julio and *Papa* finally stopped for food. I just sat behind them, in the restaurant. They started to talk about the bomb."

"We've heard nothing. *Nothing.* Maybe they're full of shit. When Maxwell pulled Post from the wreck, hell the guy was barely alive. And you know *what*? He asked for *us*. Didn't want to go to the hospital. He wanted to go to the F.B.I. office. Maxwell didn't know what to say. Then the guy went all-limp and that was it. Died right there in their arms. Agents Maxwell and Alexander are on their way back here now. They're pretty shaken."

Bobby thought he recognized compassion in Stuart's voice, but then remembered he was very tired. Maybe it was just exhaustion.

"Boss, I'm gonna need Maxwell to find out if Ethan Post's plane is still at the airfield. If it is, he's going to have to search it. Carefully. I'm also gonna need your *okay* to bring the state police in on Julio and *Papa*. They can help us follow them, until we hear from you about the bomb. I don't want to take any chances of losing *Papa*, and if anybody's gonna do any arresting' in this part of the south, it ain't gonna be a black cop from New York City."

"Do you know where they're headed?" Stuart asked.

"Nope. Southport is my only guess."

"Okay, do it. Find a way to call me back in one hour."

Bobby nodded, closing the phone. *Papa*'s silver Grand Am was parked about forty feet down the parking lot. Cautiously, Bobby looked over his shoulder and walked determinedly to a point beyond the rear of the car. Looking away from the diner, and into the street, he raised his right leg, and swiftly kicked out the taillight. Little shards of red plastic scattered onto the concrete. Bobby corralled them with his foot and nudged them under the car and out of sight.

CHAPTER TWENTY-EIGHT

The trek from the lake to the airplane had grown monotonous, the ducks no longer flying away each time Samantha entered the water, accepting her now as part of their environment. An hour had passed since the crash, and Samantha felt her strength and her hope waning. If Ethan brought a cell phone, Samantha couldn't find it. She'd lost count of how many messages she'd broadcast and how many frequencies she'd tried on the plane's radio, but no one had responded. The radio itself dangled from the destroyed dashboard, so the lack of response wasn't any real surprise, but she continued to try anyway.

Earlier she'd wondered how long she should stay with the wreckage, and with Ethan, before giving up and trying to find a way through the trees to the road. She'd given him fifteen minutes to regain consciousness, timing it carefully with her watch. But he didn't wake up. She gave him five minutes more, then five minutes after that, then five *more* minutes in endless increments until she stopped the futile exercise, realizing she wouldn't leave him, no matter how long.

She'd remembered Jennifer's explanation of the flight plan, and Ethan's conversation with the Norfolk control tower. It may take a day or two, but someone, somewhere would start looking for them and find them.

With the cool, wet rags, she cleaned the blood from Ethan's hair, running her fingers through it as she did so, feeling the intimacy of his nearness, his warm breath against her bare arms.

She'd rolled the bloodied shirt back away from his chest and shoulders, and washed the tanned, smooth skin that she had once longed to touch. She'd pressed her head against his chest and listened for his reassuring heartbeat. She'd told him how she felt when she first saw him, and why she had to run away from him that afternoon at the Waldorf, because she couldn't trust herself to be with him one minute more.

She'd found an eight-inch strip of wood among the trees, and washed it in the lake. Taking the laces from her canvas shoes, she'd splinted the wood to his left forearm and laid it carefully against his lap.

Her hair had dried over the past hour, and her back had stiffened. The gashes along her neck and shoulders were closing and each time she reached into the airplane to hoist herself across his body, she felt them stretch and tear.

Walking back to the plane, she noticed the heavier moisture in the air and watched as thin veils of fog began to form between the low clouds and the lake's surface. Within an hour they'd be blanketed by it, and invisible.

She sighed as she stretched her body into the plane, cringing as the skin at the back of her shoulder separated again. Her knees now sought their familiar position along Ethan's sides, and she rested her bottom against his legs. Slowly she ran the cool rag along his chest, watching the water bead into little droplets on his skin.

With her fingertips, she rubbed the water across his breast and over the nipple, tracing with her finger the circle of delicate dark skin, watching the water bead and feeling the surface harden at her touch. She moved her face close to her fingertip and licked the water away gently with her tongue.

Samantha laid her head against his face and traced the sensitive, perfect surface of his lips with her fingers. They felt warm and alive. She remembered how they'd felt against hers when he'd kissed her today. She reached down with her mouth, and gently licked the water drops from his lips. Unconsciously, she pressed her lips gently against his. His mouth was warm and smooth to kiss.

Slowly his lips began to part against her own and stretch to cover hers. She was sure she felt his tongue against her lips, sliding warmly over them, tracing their lines.

His right hand lifted to her back, the fingers running upward along her spine, pulling her body toward his, feeling his arm against her bare back, her chest against his. His hand moved over her shoulder blades until it wrapped itself around her neck, pulling her closer and closer.

When he finally let her go, Samantha collapsed against his body with uncontrolled relief.

She lifted her face from his, realizing this hadn't been her imagination. His blue eyes gazed into hers. His smile was gentle as he pushed the hair back from her face and massaged away a tear.

"I guess I scared you pretty badly," he whispered.

She shook her head.

"That was some way to wake up, 'though."

"I'd tried everything else. That was the last thing I could think of that might work," Samantha said.

"How long have I been out?"

Samantha sat back unsteadily against his legs and checked her watch.

"Almost an hour and a half."

"God. I don't believe we both made it out alive. Are you all right?" he asked, his eyes moving over her body, coming to rest on the thin lace bra. His hand moved to the little garment, his fingers tracing the lacy cups against her chest.

"Did I miss something?"

"Look at your shoulder."

Ethan looked down at the remnants of her gauzy peach blouse, now a stained bandage pressed against his skin. Gingerly he rolled it downward, exposing the jagged gash cutting from his armpit to his chest. The blood had clotted long ago, and Samantha had wiped the wound clean. It was already starting to close. He looked at her again, his expression appreciative.

"I seem to have found myself a co-pilot *and* a nurse. Do I have any other injuries?"

"I think the door frame hit you in the forehead. You have a nasty cut up there. And the other half of my shirt."

Ethan fingered the dressing, reluctant to remove it and discover the damage underneath.

"Anything else?"

Samantha pointed downward to his lap and Ethan saw his splinted left arm.

"I thought you were sitting on it," he said, and started to laugh.

———

When the Carolina state trooper pulled in front of his car, it hadn't occurred to him he was trying to stop him, but that was what was happening, and Bobby followed him to the shoulder of the road, braking carefully over the uneven pavement.

The trooper exited his cruiser, dangling the radio microphone in one hand, signaling Bobby with the other.

"It's for you."

Papa was probably a quarter of a mile ahead of them now, so Bobby felt safe exiting the vehicle, knowing Green Six and the other trooper were keeping the silver Grand Am company in his absence.

He grabbed the microphone quickly.

"This is Detective Bobby Washington, NYPD. D 'ya have a message for me?"

"Yeah, ah, Detective Washington? We have a message for you from U.S. Attorney Mr. Stuart Birkwell. Mr. Birkwell advises that Mr. Ethan Post and Miss Sammy Wilde took off from the Meade Valley Airport around one this afternoon. Now, I'm gonna skip the details because I want you boys to come into the barracks as soon as possible, but the Norfolk air tower has reports of a *mayday* message shortly after Mr. Post's plane would have flown through their airspace. Now, we got a search underway for them, but that area is pretty remote and boggy. I understand you're followin' the two men that say they put an explosive device aboard the plane? Is that right?"

Bobby's mouth felt dry and acidic and his arms too heavy to hold the microphone.

"Yeah, that's what I overheard, at a restaurant about an hour ago," he said.

"Okay. I'm gonna need you boys to pick up those two characters in the silver Grand Am, and bring 'em in with you. Mr. Birkwell confirms the probable cause for arrest. Now, I know they're armed and probably pretty dangerous, so you folks make it look as casual as possible when you stop them, ya' hear?"

"Yes, sir." The trooper replaced the microphone.

"I'm gonna make a traffic stop," he told Bobby. "Any suggestions?"

"They got a broken taillight. I think that'll give you all the excuse you need," Bobby answered.

————

The small lake was cloaked now in haze as Ethan began his review of the crash scene. His legs felt like stiff wooden boards and his movements were laborious, but he welcomed the dull pain with each step, knowing it signaled only superficial trauma, the kind that wouldn't last more than a week or two. Samantha helped him rig an arm sling from his torn shirt to minimize his wrist pain.

Ethan hobbled around the plane.

"See that charred metal curling out from the bottom of the cargo compartment? It indicates there was a downward blast. Something directed the explosion downward instead of outward and into the cabin. That would have killed us immediately. What was it?"

Ethan fingered the burned and damaged metal skeleton above the compartment. It was mysteriously intact. A small copper coil embedded itself in the charred metal, burned into it by the blast's force.

Ethan paused. A small swatch of nylon mesh material was stuck to the intact metal skeleton. He tore it free to study it more closely. The mesh was extremely tight, the fibers dense. He looked up toward what had been the ceiling of the cargo compartment. Remnants of the meshed material were fused into the metal.

Ethan stood up slowly, fingering the material. He passed it Samantha.

"Does this look familiar to you?" he asked, his eyes still studying the plane's remains.

"No. What do you think it could be?"

"Whatever it was, it saved our lives. From what I can determine by looking at the plane and the pattern of damage and burns, there was some kind of explosive device on this plane. This little copper coil here is a spring, usually found in a timer."

"You mean a *bomb?*"

Ethan nodded.

"It looks like this material was on top of the device, and directed the blast downward. We lost a lot of airplane function, but we didn't blow up," he explained.

"So somebody put a bomb on the plane, but wrapped it in this material, so it wouldn't completely destroy us? I don't understand that. I thought the purpose of a bomb was complete destruction."

Ethan smiled. "We were damned lucky. Look at this closer, Sammy. Does it look familiar to you?"

Samantha fingered the material, wondering what could be built strongly enough to diffuse an explosion. It looked remotely familiar, the tight mesh she recalled had fascinated her once before. But the memory was from too long ago, she couldn't place it. Ethan noted her concentration.

"Would your buddy Dan have had something made of this material?"

Samantha fingered the material. She looked at Ethan.

"You *know* what this is. Tell me."

"I think its *Kevlar*. They make bullet proof vests from it."

"Yes, that's *it*. Dan has one of those. That's why his bag was so *heavy*. Why you thought he had guns in it, or something, back at the airfield. He always has his vest with him. I've tried it on before. It weighs a *ton*. He must have hid it in the duffle bag."

"And I had a little trouble getting his bag into the compartment. I must have wedged it on top of the bomb. God, I'm glad I did," Ethan said.

They stood side by side on the grassy beach, quietly staring at the wreckage. A group of ducks flew over their heads and landed on the lake, the splashing the only sounds in the late afternoon air.

Quietly he moved toward her, his hand reaching for hers. She entwined her fingers with his, feeling their warmth.

She turned to him and buried her head against his chest, feeling his heartbeat, this time so strong against her own. She moved her chest against his relishing the feel and sound of the life they had both almost lost.

His hand traced the muscles up her arm, and then gently across her back, over its wounded surface and then, more forcefully down her spine. She raised her arms around his neck, her fingers massaging the back of his head to the rhythm of their increased heartbeats.

Grasping her hair, he pulled her head backward. Samantha could feel his mouth against her neck, and his body flex as he kissed her, more urgently, pressing his mouth almost violently against her skin. She felt his tongue lick the furrows of her collarbone, and glide in burning softness over her shoulders.

She sensed his fingers tug against her bra's thin white lace, then felt the warmth of his hand as it surrounded her breast, his mouth moving downward until his lips encircled her nipple, his tongue tracing it, his teeth framing it, hardening it and sending violent spasms through her body.

With both hands she clung to his shoulders as he lowered her to the grass, his body disregarding pain, consumed with the touch and feel of her breasts and her abdomen and her bare legs as they wrapped around him.

Samantha watched as he rose above her, his right hand releasing his leather braided belt, sliding his clothing off, his beautiful naked body silhouetted against the gray charred hulk of the dead aircraft. She watched breathlessly as he slid his hand over her breasts and down her stomach, pulling away her shorts and tossing them aside.

Samantha held her breath. Ethan's stomach muscles tightened as he lowered himself toward her; smooth mounds framing his powerful core. They contracted toward his groin. Her eyes followed the line downward toward the curling brown hairs forming the soft background to his amazing life muscle. She gasped and writhed with passion as he pushed his life into her.

———

Julio's body tensed, and his hand reached instinctively to the cleft of his back, feeling the gun, gripping it securely as he pushed himself flat against the seat cushion.

Papa shot him a threatening glance and mashed his cigar into the dashboard, burning a dark hole into the vinyl and forcing a spray of hot red-hot ash onto the carpet.

"They use no sirens. That is wrong. If I was speeding, there should be sirens," he hissed.

His right foot poised over the accelerator, ready to crash down upon it and lunge the car into full speed. But he was no fool. The Grand Am was no power match for the two Highway Patrol cruisers, and such action would irrevocably secure his fate behind bars.

"Go for it, old man. Make 'em fuckin' work for it!" Julio hissed.

But *Papa* shook his Panama hat and slowed the Grand Am onto the shoulder.

"We do not know what they want. We will see what they want."

"Yeah, the fuck we will!" Julio spat at him, the muscles of his pock marked face pulsing, his body coiling like an animal ready to spring.

Clouds of fog billowed across the highway as the North Carolina State Troopers angled their cruisers behind the Grand Am, the gray mist dulling their vision, reducing the driver and his passenger to shadows.

Bobby slid his gray Caprice in quietly behind the cruisers, and listened as the loud speaker directed the driver and passenger to slowly exit the vehicle. The shadows became like statues inside the car, the trooper's orders dissipating into the moist, saturated air.

Lying on his side, Bobby carefully reached for the passenger door, quietly releasing its handle, pushing it open. With measured movements, he crawled from the car and inched his way along the roadway, shielded by the police cruisers.

The trooper issued his order again, but the figures inside the Grand Am remained frozen.

High grass grew for a foot out from the shoulder; then descended into a gully that Bobby now lowered himself into. Crouching among the grass, he eased forward until he was even with the silver vehicle, his hand now firmly gripping his Sig Sauer .38 automatic. He steadied himself against the soggy earth.

Suddenly he saw Julio's shadowy form dive from its upright position. Aiming instinctively at the base of the car door, he watched it fly open and Julio roll furiously from within. Two gunshots exploded from Julio's gun into the police cruiser, then a third shot rang out and Julio was dead; the top of his head spattered against the Grand Am's silver paint.

Papa lunged his hulking frame sideways across the front seat, his white Panama hat bouncing behind Julio onto the gravel. He looked up now into the double barrel of a shotgun.

"We only ask twice," the state trooper drawled, staring down into *Papa's* steeled eyes.

———

Ethan's head rested on Samantha's chest. Slowly he raised it and studied the plane one more time.

"This was meant for Alex. He knew it was coming. He was acting crazy with worry this morning. We got into a fight. Maybe your boyfriend was a target, too. *Papa* could have eliminated them both. And I didn't even see it coming. I was so stupid!"

Ethan rolled himself away from her, covering his head in disgust.

"I almost flew four people to their deaths just because no one would tell me what was going on. And I almost killed you."

Pain in his eyes was deeper than the brilliant passion they'd just shared. Her fingers searched for his hand.

"You didn't almost kill me. You saved my life. Our lives. You only wanted to protect Alex. That was your goal. I understand that."

Samantha dreaded the conversation that would come next. She lay motionless, unwilling to disrupt the moment.

Ethan sighed heavily, and shook his head.

"You couldn't really understand what I was trying to do. Hell, what I planned would probably have hurt you, too. See, I don't even know how much you're mixed up in all this. After I met with *Papa* this weekend, I planned to go to the FBI and tell them all I knew about *Papa*, his operation, your boyfriend, and Alex. Tell them everything, before they found out. *Before* it was too late to help Alex."

"They already know," Samantha whispered.

"What?"

"They already *know*."

"But how? How could they? And how would *you* know if they did?"

Ethan looked at her as if for the first time. Samantha felt chilled by his gaze.

"Who are you?"

"My name is Samantha. Not Sammy. Samantha Wilde."

"And that asshole, Giacometti, is he your boyfriend?"

"No."

"Yeah, so that's why you didn't sleep with him last night. That's why I found you alone in the guest room. What is he, some kind of undercover cop?" Ethan's words were almost biting.

"His name is Dan Anguilo, and he's an undercover detective with the New York City police."

"And *you*?"

"I'm no one. I teach middle school. Dan and I are friends. He asked me to help out last weekend, to be his date for Alex's yacht party."

"And *Papa*?" Ethan continued his interrogation.

"*Papa* is a target of the investigation, as is Alex. He apparently is connected with a drug cartel."

"And Alex was laundering the money. I knew it! That's exactly what I thought was going on, but I couldn't be sure. And *you* wouldn't tell me," Ethan said.

Samantha laughed wistfully, remembering his determination at the Waldorf.

"I *wanted* to, but I couldn't. It would have blown the undercover operation. You've got to be able to understand that much. I really would have told you, if I could."

CHAPTER TWENTY-NINE

The first car that approached slowed down, the occupants eying them and their bloodied clothes, and then sped up down the road. This didn't surprise Samantha. They looked a mess. In place of her destroyed peach blouse, she had tucked the bottom half of Ethan's shirt into her bra straps. The top and her shorts looked like a tie-dyed ensemble until anyone got close enough to correctly identify the gory crimson color.

Off in the distance Samantha saw another vehicle approach. Ethan walked to the center of the highway, determined that this would be their vehicle of rescue. To his relief, it was a police cruiser.

The state trooper slowed to a stop, studying Ethan's bare bandaged torso and Samantha's bloody outfit through the windshield. Before they had a chance to explain, Samantha could hear the police radio squawk.

"We're lookin' for a white male, brown hair, blue eyes, thirty four years of age, six-feet three inches tall. And a white female. Blonde hair. Green eyes. Five-feet-eight. Let us know if you see 'em."

The trooper studied them carefully, then smiled, and picked up his microphone.

"This is Charlie 15, headquarters. I think I'm lookin' at 'em right now."

"So, tell us, Charlie 15. Are you lookin' at two corpses, or are they alive?"

"Looks as if they've been through a war, but they're alive," the trooper replied happily.

"Roger. Pick 'em up. Proceed to the county hospital. We'll send some people to meet up with you there."

"Roger that."

The trooper replaced the radio transmitter and exited the cruiser.

"So, how did you find us? It's pretty deserted out here," Samantha asked.

"A fellow called you in. I guess he drove past you or somethin' a few minutes ago. We've been lookin' for a crashed airplane and a couple a bodies all afternoon. I'm right pleased that ain't what we found."

"Yeah, us too. How did anybody know we'd crashed? Did they hear our mayday broadcasts?" Ethan asked.

"I don't know all the details. I think someone will explain it better when we get to the hospital. Looks like ya both don't need any more distress. But I guess they was followin' a couple a guys just north of here a few hours ago. They probably had somethin' to do with your crash. One of 'em was killed. Got the other at the barracks up near Williamston. That ain't too far from here."

"You mean the people who planted the bomb on our plane?" Samantha asked anxiously.

"Oh, ya 'all know about the bomb? I didn't want to tell ya too much, in case it might upset ya and all. I don' know the names of the men, but an FBI agent from up north, an' a

Detective from New York City helped us out on the arrest. I think they're gonna charge the alive one with murder, or attempted murder now, because they're the ones responsible for the bomb. But they'll have more information for y'all at the hospital. We'll be there in just a few minutes."

The trooper assisted Ethan into the cruiser's back seat. Samantha crawled in the other side and sat back against the seat. He must be talking about *Papa* and Julio, she thought. Which one was dead?

Ethan draped his good arm across Samantha's shoulder and held her. They didn't speak at all enroute to the hospital. Once there, emergency room attendants laid them both on stretchers and quickly pushed them inside, and into separate rooms.

A nurse offered her water and aspirin, and Samantha accepted them gratefully. She was then probed, x-rayed, and bandaged. They placed a thin cotton blanket across her lap, and she felt clean, safe and secure. The nurse finally wheeled her into a curtained cubicle and fluffed a soft pillow behind her head.

"You're gonna be mighty stiff for the next few days, sweetie. And pretty weak. Your muscles have been through an awful trauma, but they made it out just fine. No broken bones and no internal injuries. You'll just need to rest."

The nurse was in her mid-fifties, and wore scrubs decorated with cartoon characters. Samantha touched her arm lightly as the woman turned to leave.

"The man who came in with me, Ethan Post, how is he doing?" she asked.

"The doctor is setting his broken wrist. We had to give him quite a few stitches in his head and chest, so he's a little groggy from medication. But the doctor couldn't find any internal injuries or any other broken bones, so he'll be back to his old self real soon."

"Thank God," Samantha sighed.

"I think you were both very *lucky*," the nurse said, patting her arm. She drew the cotton curtain aside. "There's someone here to see you."

Bobby stood with his hands stuffed in his pockets, a relieved smile on his face.

"I want you to know I tried to convince Stuart not to let you go today. I thought the trip to North Carolina was a set up. Once again, you were right. We followed *Papa* and Julio. I overheard them talking about the bomb. That's how we knew to start looking for you. Then we were going to arrest 'em."

Samantha watched him closely as his voice trailed off. She sat forward in the bed.

"You shot one of them, didn't you? Which one?" Samantha asked.

"Julio. I knew he was going to try something. I didn't know if you were okay. I thought you were dead. I thought he had killed you." Bobby looked like he was about to cry.

Samantha sighed and reached for his hand. He took hers silently.

"Bobby, I told Ethan everything about the undercover operation. And that Dan's a detective targeting Alex as a money launderer. We were almost blown apart today and he saved my life. I had to tell him. I owed it to him. And you were right. He was planning all along to go to the FBI with the information he developed."

She paused for a moment. "Sorry. These meds make me woozy. You should have seen that plane, Bobby. I don't know how Ethan managed to land it safely. And it looks like Dan's bulletproof vest was really what saved our lives. It was in his duffle bag. Ethan must have shoved it on top of the bomb when he loaded it in the cargo compartment. It kept us from blowing up."

Bobby winced.

He said, "So you should be in a body bag right now instead of draped like an angel in a white hospital sheet? Is that what you're telling me, princess?"

Samantha smiled. "That's right. We were *damned* lucky. But where were Dan and Alex? Why were they late? We couldn't figure that part out." Samantha noticed Bobby's expression turn grim.

"I'll get to that. Tell me why you took off without them first," he said.

"There was fog rolling in and if we didn't take off when we did, we wouldn't have been able to go. Ethan was determined to get close to *Papa*. He figured this was his only chance. I couldn't talk him out of going and then I couldn't let him go alone."

"I know *you* couldn't, baby. I'm glad you wanted to help him. Might have turned out worse for him if you hadn't been there," Bobby said.

"I know. Alex's shady activity really upset him. I told him you would work out a way Alex could turn himself in."

Bobby dropped his eyes, and looked down at the floor. He studied his shoes for a moment.

"Baby, I don't think we have to worry about Alex anymore. He and Dan didn't make it to the airfield on time because they got themselves in a bad wreck. Alex is dead."

A picture of the balding accountant with his expensive clothes flashed in her mind. It was a picture of a man she'd never liked but whom Ethan had loved despite his faults, and whose future he was willing to fight for.

Bobby continued. "The whole crash was pretty tragic. Seems Alex was goin' to turn himself in. To *us*. But he got scared when he thought Julio was followin' him this morning. Turned out it was really us. That's when he plowed into a truck."

"And Dan?" she asked, holding her breath.

"Dan's in pretty bad shape, but he'll live. He has some internal injuries and broke both his legs, but nothing they can't patch up. They'll probably put him out on disability now, or maybe give him a desk job. Don't think he'll like that very much."

It's the end of his undercover career, Samantha thought sadly, wanting to turn back the clock twelve hours.

"He wants to teach," she whispered.

"What, baby?"

"Dan told me that if he couldn't do undercover work, he wanted to teach at the police academy. Maybe he'll get his chance after all."

Carefully she pulled herself up to a seated position and swung her legs over the side of the hospital bed.

"What! You ain't leavin' before I tell you the only good news I've got!"

Bobby revived some of his enthusiasm, and held her by the shoulders.

"I need to find Ethan," Samantha insisted, pushing his arms away.

"Come on, baby, this'll only take a minute." She looked up into his smiling face, and stopped.

"Okay, Washington. Tell me the *good* part."

"Right now, Assistant U.S. Attorney Stuart Birkwell, aka your bastard, is planning a ticker tape parade for *you* and *me* down the streets of New York City."

"I don't believe you!"

"Aw, baby. You disappoint me. You used to believe everything I said. Well, some of that's true. Seems you and me were responsible for his best day of arrests *ever* in his career. And thanks to us, he's taken down almost the entire upper echelon of the De Yambi drug cartel, including their chief accountant and money launderer, Vincent Vuillard, aka the *Baron!*"

Samantha gasped. "They found the *Baron*? How?"

"They just followed your investigative trail. Your whole theory was right. He'd shot himself, then saved the bullet so he could create a crime scene on the yacht. Robbed the cartel of eight million dollars and then holed up in Hong Kong until the money and his precious grandfather clock could be delivered to him there. He was already booked on an early flight to Switzerland. A couple of Hong Kong policemen posed as deliverymen this morning and carted Mr. Vuillard back into the protective clutches of the U.S. Government. Found him at a swank hotel in Kowloon, sipping cognac and hobbling around on a fancy cane. Ha! Pretty cool, eh *partner*?"

Bobby held her by the shoulders, and pulled her carefully to him, as she wrapped her arms around his waist.

"Yeah, *partner*, that's pretty cool," Samantha breathed. She pulled away and looked up at him. "Does this mean it's over? The investigation? You and me?"

The thought suddenly saddened her. Bobby leaned over and kissed her forehead.

"You never know. Maybe you'll want to join the police force or the FBI after this. You're really damned good at this detective shit. You've made me excited to be a detective again. Maybe when I retire, I'll look you up, and we can form our own detective agency. We'll call it *Salt and Pepper, Inc.*, or *Bobby and the Bimbo* or somethin' like that. That'd be fun, right?"

"We'd have to work on the name," Samantha said.

Bobby's cell phone rang.

"Yes, she's here. It's for you," Bobby said, extending the tiny phone. It was Stuart Birkwell.

"We're all happy you're alive," Stuart's voice rang stiffly through the receiver.

"Thanks."

Silence.

"Was there more you wanted to say?" Samantha asked.

Stuart cleared his throat. "I figured you wrong. You're a bright young woman, and you performed like a professional. As good, or even *better* than an FBI agent or detective could do in the same circumstances. You should give this line of work some thought."

"Are you *recruiting* me?" Samantha laughed.

"Sure. Maybe. Give me a call next week and we'll talk about it further." Stuart hung up.

Bobby whistled.

"You should keep it in mind. The education department's loss could be the red, white and blue's gain. It's not bad work. You showed me that. We have our bad eggs. That detective in the cheap suits, Lenihan? They suspect he's the mole to *Papa's* organization. His kids have been privately schooled for years and he didn't do that on my salary. He told Julio we suspected Vuillard and that we were looking for the eight million dollars siphoned off. Probably pissed Papa off and led him to plant the bomb on your plane," Bobby said.

"Does Ethan know about his brother yet?" Samantha asked.

Bobby nodded.

"Take care of your stud, baby. I'll be in touch." Bobby winked at her, then turned and walked out into the corridor.

Samantha found Ethan in the room next to hers, sitting on the end of the hospital bed, his left wrist encased in a plastic cast and large swaths of white bandages wrapped around his chest. A narrow white band covered the stitches in his forehead. He didn't notice her at first as she stood at the door, studying him, watching the wide, rounded shoulders heave with a deep sigh. Strands of brown hair rested against his temples.

She crossed to the bedside and stood before him, her fingers pushed the hair away from his face. Feeling her touch, Ethan raised his head. The blue eyes were clouded and sad as he reached out his uninjured arm and drew her to him, burying his face in her hair. Gently, she laid her head against his chest and allowed her arms to hold him.

Eventually he spoke. "So how are you doing?"

"They want me to be a FBI agent. Can you imagine that?" she heard herself say.

"Do that later. I think I'd like you to stay with me for a while," Ethan said.

"I can stay with you forever," Samantha whispered.

"I just might need you that long," he answered.

The End

J.G. Matheny draws from real life to infuse her mysteries with intrigue, realism and humor. A former F.B.I. Special Agent, she is no stranger to the world of bombs, task forces and murder. Now a nationally recognized financial crimes expert, she brings personal experience, knowledge and style to Samantha Wilde's story.

Wilde at the Waldorf, and the second in the Samantha Wilde series, *Wilde at the Amherst,* draw from her experiences as an F.B.I Agent assigned to the New York Office and reflect the neighborhoods and night life of New York City during the 1990's.

J.G. Matheny now lives with her family in the mountains west of Denver, Colorado. She is an avid skier and outdoor enthusiast. She holds a Bachelor of Science from the University of Wyoming and a Master of Arts in Journalism from New York University.